THE GIRL WITH THE DRAGONFRUIT TATTOO

CARRIE DOYLE

Poisoned Pen
PRESS

Published by Poisoned Pen Press, an imprint of Sourcebooks
P.O. Box 4410, Naperville, Illinois 60567-4410
(630) 961-3900
sourcebooks.com

Printed and bound in the United States of America.
KP 10 9 8 7 6 5 4 3 2 1

To Nadia and all the Caribbean fun we've had.

CHAPTER

1

The Caribbean island of Paraiso is known for its lush scenery, uncrowded white-sand beaches, excellent snorkeling, delicious local food, and charming people. Las Frutas, the island's premier luxury resort, has been a favorite destination for discerning travelers for over fifty years. Boasting two world-class golf courses, twelve clay tennis courts, a shooting range, polo fields, a marina where you can dock your yacht, and several outstanding restaurants, Las Frutas will fulfill all your wildest dreams.

Plum Lockhart's fingers paused above her computer's keyboard. The description felt generic and trite. Not to mention totally fabricated. If someone were to put her on a witness stand, she would not be able to honestly swear under oath that she had met one person who had all their wildest dreams fulfilled at Las Frutas. They may have had a great vacation, yes. Or more recently, they may have ended up murdered, which was unfortunate and quite tragic. But she couldn't write that.

> Set on the edge of the sparkling Caribbean Sea, the four-thousand-acre resort is situated on a former sugar plantation...

Okay, she had to stop there as well. Now that the world was finally acknowledging the traumatic history of plantations, it was not exactly a selling point or something to brag about. The Rijo family, who owned the resort and all the sugarcane fields on the island, were both revered and reviled.

> Boasting a vibrant nightlife and a slower pace of life, Las Frutas Resort...

Again, Plum hesitated. Wasn't that an oxymoron? Peaceful and frenetic? She sounded confused. Plum sighed deeply and snapped her laptop closed with frustration. Her colleague Lucia glanced up from her desk and stared at her through her thick glasses, her wise eyes scrutinizing Plum.

"What's wrong?" asked Lucia with concern.

The sixty-four-year-old stocky grandmother was a reassuring presence at Plum Lockhart Luxury Retreats. Lucia was calm, practical, rarely ruffled, and fortunately one of the most competent and sharp Paraisons Plum had met.

"It's so unlike me, but I'm having a difficult time updating our website and marketing materials," Plum responded tartly.

"Why do we need to update it?" asked Lucia. "It's perfect."

Plum gave her a patient and, yes, patronizing, look. Lucia might be savvy, but Plum prided herself on being an expert at marketing and promotion—she would own up to self-promotion as well. She had the esteemed career to prove her expertise. Her tenacity had helped her ascend her from a lowly intern at a beauty magazine to the editor in chief of *Travel and Respite Magazine* in only a decade. When the world of publishing went belly-up and her magazine job imploded earlier this year, Plum left New York City and moved to Paraiso, diving into a new profession as a villa broker leasing beautiful mansions to vacationers. She was proud that she had been nimble and able to reinvent herself without missing a beat.

True, there were a few bumps along the way. Plum had initially gone to work for Jonathan Mayhew Caribbean Escapes (she would claim he wooed her; he would claim she begged him), but it had ended badly, and after only a couple of months, she had set out on her own and established her eponymous firm. There were also the pesky abovementioned murders on the island, which Plum somehow found herself embroiled in through no fault of her own. She swore she would run for the hills next time she suspected anything close to homicide in her path.

Despite the setbacks, there was good news as well. Her agency was gaining traction: she had several villas she now represented, and clients were reaching out to secure houses for their vacations. Plum's romantic life, which had been nonexistent until recently, showed a glimmer of promise.

"Lucia, it's important to remain current," explained Plum

in a tone she thought was instructive but was in reality slightly condescending. "That's why I am constantly tweaking."

"Tweaking, twerking—your silly stuff isn't necessary," said Lucia, waving a dismissive hand in the air.

Plum sighed. "Oh, really?"

"Oh, really, yes," agreed Lucia emphatically. "Everyone knows Paraiso is the best island in the world. That's all you need to say."

Plum smiled. "I love your patriotism."

Lucia shrugged. "You can call it patriotism; I call it fact. And no matter how many fancy words you use like *breathtaking, exotic, tropical*, it all means the same thing. I wouldn't waste any more time on your descriptions of 'twinkling' seas."

Plum shook her head and stood, her five-foot-ten-inch figure looming over her tiny gray-haired colleague. "A misused adjective can decimate a business. You have to trust me. It's why I was an instant success as soon as I stepped foot in Paraiso."

Fortunately, Plum was already striding toward the kitchenette and did not see Lucia roll her eyes. But Plum knew her colleague well enough to call her out on it.

"Don't roll your eyes at me." Plum sniffed, swinging open the refrigerator door and leaning down to scan the contents. "Power is perception."

"Says who?" mumbled Lucia from the other room.

"Says about a zillion online business and marketing courses I took," chirped Plum, who was always proud of her efforts to better herself and advance her career.

Plum could hear Lucia retort in Spanish, but as she

was still not completely fluent in the language ("Not even close," Lucia would say), she couldn't understand what her colleague had said. Plum didn't see anything worth eating in the fridge (despite it being fully stocked) and slammed the door shut with gusto. Her eyes flitted around the kitchen and zeroed in on the platter of Lucia's homemade cheese and guava tarts on the counter. In her past life, she hadn't cared about food, but Paraiso had unleashed her taste buds, and she couldn't get enough of the local fare.

After grabbing a large glass of hibiscus iced tea, Plum wandered back into her work area, which also doubled as her living room. Much to her dismay, Plum was still residing and working in a modest town house in the northernmost part of the resort. It was meant to be temporary, but there was little inventory available now that it was high season. Plum would just have to wait to secure a more appropriate accommodation and a workplace that befit the stature she felt she deserved.

"Your power is not helping you at all," mumbled Lucia. "Dead bodies are piling up."

Before Plum could answer Lucia, her cell phone rang, and she returned to her desk to answer it.

"Hi," said the deep voice on the other end of the phone. "It's Juan Kevin."

"Hi!" boomed Plum enthusiastically as she dropped into her chair.

Lucia's expression broke into a smirk. Plum, riled that she still couldn't afford separate offices and the decorum of discretion, swiveled her chair around so her back was to her colleague. Now Lucia would be unable to witness the goofy unedited grin that had taken over her face.

"How are you today?" Juan Kevin asked.

Plum had recently had a very cozy lunch date with the tall, dark, and handsome director of security at Las Frutas, known as Juan Kevin Muñoz, and she felt like a teenager in the throes of a major crush.

"I'm well. Finishing some marketing copy before I head off to the big event," cooed Plum, in a voice that surprised even her. Was she flirting?

"Yes, that's right," he said. "It's Carmen Rijo's ladies' luncheon."

"Yes," agreed Plum. "My social calendar is completely empty, and then both Carmen Rijo and Alexandra Rijo decide to have a lunch and dinner on the same day. Seems like an odd choice of scheduling for two women who hate each other and were married to the same man."

"Oh, but it's not," Juan Kevin corrected. "It's actually extremely calculated. Alexandra Rijo, wife number one, always had her Las Frutas Charity dinner on the first Friday in April. But when Carmen, wife number two, came along…"

"You mean when Emilio *left her* for Carmen," interjected Plum.

"Yes," conceded Juan Kevin. "Well, Carmen was obviously excluded from that dinner and decided she would have an annual lunch on the same day."

"I'm surprised she didn't have a dinner the same night," remarked Plum. She stared out the window at a lizard crawling up the palm tree. "She's certainly competitive."

"True. But Carmen is also shrewd and understands that people would attend Alexandra's dinner over hers, and why risk the embarrassment of hosting a dinner when all the luminaries are at your rival's?" explained Juan Kevin.

"But a lunch?"

Juan Kevin cleared his throat. "I prefer not to engage in gossip…"

"Please be a gossip," insisted Plum.

She could hear him sigh on the other end of the phone before he spoke. "Some less charitable people say that she likes to overserve the ladies at her lunch so they don't end up making it to Alexandra's dinner."

Plum laughed. She appreciated Carmen's cunning. "I suppose I should be careful," conceded Plum. "Because I definitely want to attend both."

"That's what I want to ask you. Would you like me to pick you up on the way to dinner?"

"That would be lovely," she said.

Plum averted her eyes and purposely did not look at Lucia when she hung up the phone. Fortunately, Lucia was discreet enough to refrain from commenting on the burgeoning love affair. After reopening her computer and making a few more attempts at amending the website, Plum clicked off. She decided to casually change the subject.

"So, what's going on in the world according to *Chisme*?" asked Plum.

Chisme was the Spanish word for *gossip*. It was also the name of a magazine that circulated through the whole network of resort workers at Las Frutas. It detailed all the squabbles, fights, marriages, divorces, and affairs of the villa owners and vacationers. No one knew who wrote it, but every story always turned out to be true.

Lucia shrugged and flipped closed her copy. "The owners of Casa el Kiwi are getting a divorce because the wife was having an affair with a professional golfer."

"Really?" asked Plum. "Not sure I know them. But perhaps they'll want to rent or sell their villa with the impending divorce. Their misfortune could be our little gold mine."

She wrote down the villa's name and made a note to do some due diligence. "What other gossip items are there?"

Lucia scanned her magazine and began clucking before glancing up. "You know the Norwegian zillionaire Arne Larsen?"

Plum shook her head. "I don't think so."

"He owns Casa el Caqui?" asked Lucia, who continued speaking when Plum gave her a blank look. "He has recently bought a house on the ocean in East Hampton, Long Island, and paid sixty-eight million dollars for it. *Dios mío!* Who has that money to spend?" muttered Lucia.

"Sometimes it feels like there is more than one percent out there." Plum sighed.

"*Sí,*" agreed Lucia. "And it says the house in East Hampton is a turn down!"

"A turn down?" asked Plum, confused. Then she smiled. "A teardown, you mean."

"They are going to wreck it. It says here it is next to a hotshot named David Gifford. He is head of Universal

Telecoms. And he bought his house for ninety million dollars and tore it down!"

A surge of competitiveness seized Plum. "Well, it would be nice if they would all forgo East Hampton and buy a house through me here in Paraiso."

"That would be nice," agreed Lucia. "But not tear it down. Too much."

"Agreed."

Development at Las Frutas had exploded due to high demand, which was both good and bad. It was great for Plum's business that there were always people looking to rent or buy villas, but the construction everywhere could be annoying.

"Isn't it time you go to your fancy lunch?" asked Lucia, glancing up at the clock on the wall.

Plum nodded. "Yes, I should get ready."

"Make sure you wear a necklace made of garlic to ward off the evil spirits," Lucia muttered. She was not a huge fan of the Rijo family in general but particularly disliked Carmen, whom she regarded as a dangerous home-wrecker.

"I'll see what I can find in my jewelry box." Plum laughed. Her colleague might be full of superstitions, but Plum actually knew Lucia was incredibly astute and her radical suppositions usually ended up being prophetic.

Plum went upstairs to her bedroom to freshen up. She changed out of her casual work outfit and applied a thick layer of sunblock (her chalk-white skin burned to a crisp without it), then stood in front of the meek air-conditioning unit until it dried. She longed for the day she could move and have central air. Once the gummy SPF cream had been absorbed, she donned a short-sleeved navy shirtdress with crisp white buttons and slid dangly earrings through her lobes.

Then it was on to the bathroom to apply her makeup. As she smoothed gloss on her lips, she eyed her case of false eyelashes and debated. She hadn't been wearing them lately and had enjoyed the more natural look. Not to mention that they often peeled off because of the mugginess. But the events today were important for networking and her career, and she had to look like a professional success. Therefore, she took the painstaking time to paste on the lashes over her blue eyes, blinking and tearing up as she did so. She was definitely out of practice!

Plum carefully brushed out her long strawberry-blond Botticelli curls. As usual, the humidity instantly rendered that useless, and her hair immediately returned to its Little Orphan Annie origins. Frustrated, she tied it up in a chignon and stomped out of the bathroom. She felt cursed by her curly hair. Plum had been compared to Nicole Kidman in looks, both favorably (Kidman circa 2010) and negatively (Kidman circa 1990). She preferred to think of herself as looking like the 2010 version, when Nicole had clearly hired a stylist and full-time hairdresser, but she supposed being compared to her in any capacity was flattering.

After putting on a pair of open-toe navy leather espadrille wedges, she stood in front of the mirror and assessed herself. Her mind immediately went to Juan Kevin, and she wondered if he would approve. There had been one long kiss so far, and her heart quickened thinking of the future. It had been a daytime smooch, when she was leaving his house after a delicious lunch he had prepared for her. He had taken her in his arms and kissed her gently as his arm slid down her back before he released her. At the time she had wanted more, but now she was excited that they were taking it slowly. Or at least had been taking it slowly. She had other plans for tonight.

CHAPTER

2

LEMON VERBENA, COCONUT, AND SEA mist scented the languid April day. The sun was blazing down as Plum steered her golf cart toward Carmen Rijo's cliffside mansion. Although Plum had recently purchased a used car she revered and doted on, she had opted to leave it at the condo and drive the golf cart to the party. She had learned that the small vehicle could be squeezed into tight spots, which afforded her an immense advantage when she attended large gatherings with a clotted parking lot. While her fellow revelers angled for the valets' attention, she could quickly abscond.

There was zero breeze and a cloudless sky, and Plum could already feel her body temperature rise. This would be her first spring living in the Caribbean, and she would have to remember to stay hydrated and SPF protected to survive. A sun hat was simply not an option; it made her feel old-ladyish and dated, like one of those extras on an eighties soap opera with big shoulder pads.

Plum turned down a road that hugged the coastline and

headed toward the Mediterranean behemoth where Emilio Rijo had spent his last years with his trophy wife, Carmen, before his death. It was situated on a peninsula with its own private beach at the westernmost end of the resort. Plum harbored wild fantasies about representing all these villas one day and renting them out for top dollar. It was part of her grand professional scheme.

After giving her name to the guards at the gate, she circumvented the valets clamoring to park her golf cart and pulled under a shaded palm tree at the end of the driveway, ignoring the valets' dirty looks. She gazed up at the capacious mega mansion with its barrel-tiled roof and large picture windows and put on her party face. Even though she had navigated all levels of society on her own, she often experienced waves of insecurity when she remembered her humble beginnings as a lower-class girl from the middle of nowhere. Quickly taking a deep breath and brushing all other thoughts away, Plum followed the stream of women entering the house. She walked through the double-height reception hall with a winding floating staircase and lavishly embellished decor to reach the lush garden.

"I'm so happy you could come," purred Carmen Rijo when Plum reached the front of the long receiving line. Carmen double kissed Plum and clasped her hands with her own heavily bejeweled ones, which Plum noted were cold.

"Thank you so much for having me," Plum replied.

"I invite the most important and successful women on Paraiso to my exclusive lunch. You, my new friend, are one of them," she announced in what Plum considered a rehearsed manner.

"I'm flattered," said Plum.

"And may I say your hair looks so interesting today," added Carmen. "I know you are up on all the fashion trends, so this new natural look with frizz must be in all the fashion magazines."

Plum's hand flew to her hair, and she realized some of her curls had escaped her chignon and were hanging freely and haphazardly in twisted side ringlets. She wanted to scream.

Alternatively, Carmen, a bombshell in every sense of the word, was completely done to perfection. Her long glossy black hair cascaded down the back of her sexy red cocktail dress in an effortless manner. Her makeup was immaculate, with her plump lips painted a bright red and her heavily lashed dark eyes lined a deep charcoal.

"My hair has a mind of its own," said Plum with faux casualness.

"Now, you must have one of my signature cocktails," Carmen insisted. She snapped her fingers at a waiter holding a silver tray full of frothy drinks and summoned him over.

"These are the Carmenitos," she said when the waiter arrived.

Plum demurred. "I'm not a big day drinker. I'll just have seltzer," she said to the waiter.

Carmen waved her red lacquered fingernails in the air. "Don't worry, I have virgin Carmenitos also. They have the pink umbrellas in them."

"Oh, okay," Plum said with hesitation. She retrieved one

from the waiter and took a sip. It was actually quite good. "Delicious."

As Plum was still a relatively recent arrival to the island and had mostly kept herself busy with her work or by inadvertently solving murders, she had very few acquaintances. Nearly all the guests seemed to know each other and broke off into small klatches to gossip and catch up. Plum tried not to allow the exclusion to faze her. She strolled around the sprawling grounds, clutching her mocktail and giving the impression that she was intensely interested in the pink and yellow hibiscuses, white and magenta bougainvilleas, and flaming-orange pride of Barbados that edged the property.

"Plum? How are you, sugar?" drawled Leslie Abernathy in her Texan accent.

"Leslie!" said Plum with an enthusiasm that surprised her. "Good to see you."

Leslie Abernathy was an extremely fit and tan blond in her sixties who passed as a much younger woman from a distance. The error could be jarring to people who approached her assuming she was a teenager only to come face-to-face with someone who had submitted herself to every surgical treatment and dermatological advancement possible. She also favored outfits one would find on a pop star, and today was no different. She had on a lavender romper with a plunging neckline.

"You too, doll," said Leslie, grabbing a cocktail with a blue umbrella from the waiter. She pressed her puffed-up lips onto the straw and drained a large swig. "Aren't these divine?"

Plum nodded. "Very delicious."

"I am so happy to be here today. You cannot believe the week I've had! There were some troubling circumstances happening on my ranch in Waco, so I had to pop up to settle some scores and get some heads rolling! Let's just say you won't be seeing my former stepson around for a long, long time." She chuckled.

"Oh dear," said Plum, who recalled that Leslie had hinted at a dark and dangerous past full of sketchy ex-husbands.

Leslie smiled (as much as possible with her frozen face muscles). "Now, don't get your panties in a bunch, doll. He's still on the face of this earth, just won't be storming around the property that his daddy rightfully left to me."

"I guess that's...good," said Plum.

"It sure as heck is. And that's what I tell Carmen she needs to do with that nasty stepson of hers. Martin is a damn menace, and he makes her life a living, breathing hell! It's time she took matters into her own hands and taught him a lesson he won't forget," said Leslie firmly, taking a large sip of her drink.

"Martin is a very frightening individual," Plum agreed, recalling her own harrowing interactions with him. Her eyes flitted around the property to make sure he was nowhere to be seen. The last party she had attended at Carmen's, he had crashed and made a scene.

"I think you're giving him too much credit," said Leslie. "He's a bully, and you know what you have to do with bullies?"

She peered closer to Plum and gave her an expectant look.

"Teach them a lesson?" offered Plum.

"No! You need to hit them in the cojones!" Leslie roared before draining her glass and waving for the waiter to come over. She turned back to Plum. "Drink up! We are going to have a fun time."

"Okay," said Plum, taking a large sip. "After all it's only a virgin."

She thought Leslie winked at her but again couldn't be sure because of the Botox that had paralyzed Leslie's facial muscles. "Yes, a virgin, that's what I told all my husbands I was on my wedding night."

Before Plum could respond, Leslie distributed them each new glasses then linked her arms with Plum and began strolling toward the dining area. Ten pink-skirted tables with eight place settings each had been set under a wooden pergola wrapped in flowering bougainvilleas. There were giant floral arrangements in the center of each table, and there was a bottle of perfume at each guest's place—a generous gift from the hostess.

"I wonder when we'll sit down to eat," said Plum, who was feeling a little bit woozy and overheated. She needed some protein to counteract all the sugar in the drinks.

"Carmen always draws out the cocktail hour. But let's get a good seat facing the water," said Leslie. "If it's our lucky day, we'll spy some of the hunks Jet Skiing in the water. All these women around make me itchy. I could use a large dose of masculine eye candy."

"On the lookout for a new beau?" asked Plum.

"I'm not that formal. A lover for sure and hopefully a young stud with tight abs and a lot of energy. But I'll also settle for husband number four." Leslie giggled. "Or is it five?"

With that, she threw her head back and roared with laughter.

CHAPTER

3

DESPITE THE SHADE FROM THE blossoming flowers, by the end of the lunch, Plum found herself hot and steamy, not to mention somewhat dizzy. Maybe she had imbibed too many mocktails, but whatever it was, her head was starting to throb. Leslie had been a lively and entertaining lunch partner and had all the ladies at the table slack-jawed as she recounted her "rolls in the hay" with various men. She had been so garrulous that few other people spoke, which was perfectly fine with Plum. She had long harbored the snobby belief that women who lunch have little to say.

The large floral arrangement had blocked Plum's view of the other side of the table, and it wasn't until she rose to visit the bathroom between the main course and dessert that she got a glimpse of the very attractive dark-haired woman sitting directly across from her. Something about her was vaguely familiar, but Plum couldn't pinpoint why. The woman locked eyes with her as she passed, and Plum felt an instant wave of unease. How did she know her?

Before she thought twice about it, a voice shouted her name behind her.

"Plum! I don't believe it!"

Plum turned around and quickly found herself being embraced by Ellen Katz.

"I am *so* glad to see a friend," said Ellen, her smile as bright as the large diamond studs in her ears. "I don't know anyone here."

In the early days of her journalism career, Plum had worked at a beauty magazine with Ellen Katz, who was then known as Ellen Rosenberg. They had been instant friends in the trenches, despite being different on every level both in character and physically. Whereas Plum was tall and with a wild strawberry-blond mane, Ellen was tiny, whippet thin, and wore her dark hair stick straight. Back then, Plum had been singularly focused on climbing the corporate ladder (little had changed), while Ellen was singularly focused on finding a husband. A rich husband. After a brief tenure in magazines, she married (or landed, in her words) Hollywood producer Joel Katz and moved to Beverly Hills. Ellen and Plum had kept in sporadic touch since.

"Ellen, what are you doing here?" exclaimed Plum, pulling away and clasping her friend's hands. "I'm so happy to see you!"

"I finally got Joel to take a vacation—well, it's more of a working vacation, but it involves sunning and swimming. At least I got him out of Los Angeles! We left the kids at home, and we're staying on Robert Campbell's yacht."

She said her host's name as if Plum should know it.

"Who's Robert Campbell?"

"You know, the former rapper?" pressed Ellen.

Plum looked at her blankly. "Not ringing a bell."

Ellen smiled. "I *love* that you don't know. He's a *huge* talent manager. He no longer raps but is a wildly successful manager who represents all the *big* names. He also has a clothing company and is branching into film producing. That's how Joel knows him."

Plum nodded. "Not really my world."

"Not mine either," agreed Ellen quickly. "But Robert is an *incredible* guy. You'd actually like him."

"That's great," mumbled Plum, not sure what she would have in common with a rapper turned music impresario.

"We docked here for the night so Joel and Robert could play golf," explained Ellen. "Somehow Robert knows Carmen Rijo—he knows *everyone*—and Carmen invited all the women on board to the lunch. No one else was interested, but you know I can't turn down a party!"

Ellen glanced around at the crowd as if enamored with the entire atmosphere. It reminded Plum of how fun it had been to hit the town with Ellen in their early journalism days. Ellen always had a wide-eyed appreciation for everything she deemed stylish and exclusive. It filled Plum with a rush of nostalgia.

"I'm so glad you're here, Ellen. It's great to see you," said Plum.

"You too! Hey, you know what? You should come to dinner on the yacht tonight!" said Ellen brightly. "Joel would love to see you."

"I wish I could, but I already have something," said Plum. A goofy grin inadvertently appeared on her face, and Ellen gave her a quizzical look.

"Is it a date?" Ellen asked, her big blue eyes growing wider.

Plum blushed. "Yes, kind of."

Ellen rubbed her hands together with excitement. "It's about time you landed a man!"

"I'll see how it goes tonight, which is sort of our first real date."

"Well, I hope it goes well, not like that horrible date you had at Club Zasmo back in the day. Do you remember that?"

Plum laughed. She did remember that. How could she not? "That was the worst date of my life. The guy ended up leaving with the coat check girl. I thought we were a match made in heaven, and next thing I know he's taken off with that hot ticket."

"You dodged a bullet. Remember that guy ended up in some scandal? We read about it in the *New York Post* months later."

"That's right." Plum nodded. The memory was coming back to her. The guy, Elliot Niederhover, owned a trendy hotel in Cabo San Lucas, Mexico, that advertised in their magazine. Plum had met him through work, they went on that ill-fated date, and she never heard from him or about him again. Until there was a *New York Post* story about how he had been found tied up in his bedroom, near death. "He claimed he had some sexual interaction gone bad, but it was all very fishy."

"Yeah, something sordid," said Ellen. "Listen, in case your

date flames out, which I hope it doesn't, Robert's tender is docked at the marina, so come by any time tonight and we'll have you zipped out to the yacht."

Ellen scribbled down the name of the boat as well as her cell phone number on the back of one of Plum's business cards.

"Anytime?" mused Plum.

"We keep very late hours on the yacht," said Ellen. "Some nights go until morning. Lots of dancing and partying. Very festive."

"And Robert…"

"Robert Campbell," interjected Ellen.

"Yes, Robert Campbell," repeated Plum. "He doesn't mind random people coming on his boat?"

"He's very generous," said Ellen.

"Okay," said Plum, tucking the business card into her bag. As much as she would like to see more of her friend, she hoped her evening with Juan Kevin would be perfect.

They said their goodbyes as the other guests dispersed. Plum made her way to her golf cart and found she was having trouble walking. She stopped in the driveway to hold on to the trunk of a palm tree and stabilize herself.

"You okay, hon?" asked Leslie as she handed the valet her ticket.

Plum glanced around and realized her vision was swirling. "I feel almost…drunk."

Leslie put her hand on her hip and jutted out her waist. "Well, you were guzzling those cocktails like desert grass guzzles water."

"Mocktails," corrected Plum. She fanned herself with her clutch.

Leslie gave her a sassy look. "Those weren't mocktails, dollface. They were the real thing."

Plum's eyes widened. "But Carmen said…"

Leslie shook her head. "Carmen tells everyone that because she wants us all drunk as skunks. That way everyone passes out and can't make it to Alexandra's party. That broad cornered the market on tricks up her sleeve."

"Oh no," said Plum, sinking against the tree.

Leslie gave her a sympathetic look. "I suggest you get out of this sunshine, jaunt home, and take a long nap. Freshen up for round two because Alexandra's parties are always a lot of hoo-ha. Come on, doll, I'll give you a ride and send my valet to bring your cart for you later."

Plum slept through her alarm and awoke to a buzzing she had incorporated into her dream where she was a contestant on a game show. She woke disoriented, confused by the sunlight still streaming through her window and the fact she was in bed. She was a person who simply never napped.

She jolted up and looked at her phone. It was six o'clock. There was another buzz, and she realized it was the doorbell. When she arrived downstairs—rumpled, her hair askew, the indent of her phone on her face—she saw through the window that Juan Kevin, looking dashing as ever in a coat and tie, was standing on the threshold, to her horror.

"Just give me a few minutes, I'm sorry," she said quickly as she opened the door to him and fled up the stairs. "Make yourself at home. I'll be right back," she shouted over her shoulder.

She didn't even give Juan Kevin a chance to respond. After quickly splashing her face with water, smearing on makeup, knotting her hair in a bun, throwing on the slinky blue dress she had saved for this occasion, and thrusting earrings through her lobes, she squirted herself with perfume and returned downstairs.

"I'm sorry for the delay," she said in a relaxed tone she wasn't feeling.

Juan Kevin raised his eyebrows. "That was fast."

"Yes. Just had to get organized."

"You look beautiful."

"Thank you," she said quickly. "I'm ready." She was not deft at responding to compliments.

His eyes gazed at her appraisingly. "That was quite a quick transformation. I thought I might have caught you sleeping."

"Sleeping? No, of course not," she protested. "I was wrapping up a business call."

He smiled and stared at her appraisingly. She wondered if she had something in her teeth. Or maybe she still had pillow marks making indentions in her cheek.

"Something wrong?" she asked, grabbing her clutch from the hall table.

"Hold one a moment," said Juan Kevin from behind her.

"What?" asked Plum impatiently, thinking she did not want to be late. She snapped off the hall light and turned around hurriedly.

Without warning, Juan Kevin pulled Plum toward him, clasping her in an embrace. He placed his hands on her back gently but firmly. Before Plum knew what was happening, Juan Kevin had pressed his lips on hers and was kissing her and kissing her, their lips softening each time. After some moments, they finally pulled apart.

"That was...unexpected," Plum whispered.

"I didn't want to wait all night to kiss you," said Juan Kevin. "I wanted it to be a whole night of kissing you. A whole night of being with you."

Plum didn't know what to say. She felt breathless and giddy and thrilled to eliminate the mental foreplay of *will they or won't they*. This time, she leaned forward and kissed him. A fluttery feeling from the tips of her toes pulsed through her entire body, and she felt as if her heart was about to pop out of her chest. Now more than ever, she was looking forward to this evening.

CHAPTER

4

AFTER A THOROUGHLY ENJOYABLE EVENING, Plum accepted Juan Kevin's offer to return to his house for a nightcap. His house was in Estrella, the neighboring town, and although she only lived a stone's throw away from Alexandria's place, she didn't want to have a drink at her town house in case the evening ended with a sleepover. It would mortify her to have Lucia arrive for work the next day and find Juan Kevin flipping pancakes in the kitchenette.

However, Plum did insist that Juan Kevin drop her at home so she could pick up her own car. One thing life had taught her was no matter what, she needed to be able to make a fast escape. And since the Uber and taxi drivers on Paraiso were few and far between, it was best to have your own wheels. After Plum followed him to his house, they both exited their vehicles at the same time. The night air was supple and persuasive, and she could hear the whisper of nocturnal creatures in the trees above.

"What a gorgeous sky," said Plum, glancing up at the sky. "The stars are dazzling."

"I'm sure you appreciate that Paraiso does not have smog, unlike New York," Juan Kevin remarked. He had made it clear he was not a city person.

"In New York we don't call it *smog*, we call it *pollution*. Smog is in Los Angeles," she corrected.

"What's the difference?"

"I'm not sure," she said with a laugh. "It's just a thing."

"Fortunately, it is not a thing here in Paraiso."

"You Paraisons are all so passionate about your homeland," she said.

Plum's heart was thumping, and she was bursting with anticipation. The kiss before dinner had been a teaser, an amuse-bouche, if you will. She was ready for the main course. Plum glanced at Juan Kevin. He smiled slyly then, with one smooth move, pulled Plum into a tight embrace.

This is what falling in love feels like… Plum thought. She could kiss Juan Kevin forever. *Juan Kevin.* His name was ringing in her head.

"Juan Kevin?"

Plum and Juan Kevin broke apart, dazed and somewhat confused. Plum blinked as if she were a newborn. They turned toward the entrance of his house, where a woman was sitting on his front porch, shrouded in darkness. She stood, repeated his name, and walked toward them out of the shadows.

All at once Plum realized who she was. It was the woman she had sat across from at Carmen's lunch. And with a wave of dismay, Plum remembered why she recognized the attractive brunette: she had seen her having dinner with Juan Kevin at a restaurant a month prior.

"Victoria," said Juan Kevin in a tone of mixed surprise and confusion. "What are you doing here?"

Yes, "Victoria," Plum wanted to add. *What are you doing here?* But the woman didn't deign a glance in Plum's direction and instead stared at Juan Kevin with intensity.

"We need to talk," she said in a husky voice.

"No," he said sternly.

"It's important."

Even from this distance, Plum could see the fire in her eyes.

"It's not a good time," began Juan Kevin, looking at Plum's puzzled face and then back at Victoria.

"There will not be a good time to discuss what I have to tell you," Victoria said solemnly.

The moment was ripe with tension.

Ten minutes later Plum, as if in a trance, found herself driving home, angry and embarrassed. She hadn't waited for Juan Kevin to respond to Victoria's insistence for a private meeting and instead babbled some excuses and took off in her car. Why had she done that? Maybe deep down she'd felt he would choose Victoria over her, and she'd wanted to be the one to make the decision. And even deeper down, the thought had scared her. She was so grateful that she'd had the foresight to drive herself; it would have been humiliating if she couldn't make a hasty exit.

Who was Victoria anyway? Was she Juan Kevin's ex-wife?

Plum still wasn't sure. What she was sure of was that this Victoria was a horrible, evil witch, who undoubtedly wanted Juan Kevin for herself. She had destroyed Plum's romantic evening and was most likely scheming on how to get him to bed. Plum gripped the steering wheel tightly and cursed Victoria. How frustrating to end the night like this. And why hadn't Juan Kevin told the woman to take a hike? That was kind of annoying. He could have protested a bit more when Plum had said she was leaving.

But it didn't have to end this way, did it? She straightened in her seat. Ellen Katz had said there was a vessel waiting in the marina and she could just call and be swept out to the yacht. Why shouldn't Plum take her up on her offer? If Plum went home now, she would be spinning her wheels imagining every scenario that Juan Kevin and Victoria were engaged in. Instead, she had the chance to attend a fancy gathering on a famous former rapper's boat, one full of dancing and fun.

Plum knew very little about the boating community, but she could tell the aluminum three-decked super-yacht she had gingerly boarded was on the higher end of higher end. If yacht owners were the 1 percent, the owner of this boat was the 0.05 percent. The name emblazoned on the side of the boat was *Jackpot*, and it certainly felt to Plum that whoever owned this boat had definitely hit the jackpot.

Plum was fussed over by a crew clad in white uniforms who assisted her on board, swapped her wedges for chic terry slip-ons, and led her through the cream-colored interiors upstairs to a spacious sun deck where a group of revelers were having cocktails.

Ellen's eyes widened when she saw Plum, and she rushed over.

"I'm so glad you came! I honestly didn't think you would," said Ellen, air-kissing her as if she hadn't just seen her a few hours prior. Ellen's tone dropped. "But does this mean the date didn't go well? I'm sorry to hear that."

Plum shrugged. "Jury still out," she said. "Too complicated to explain, but not worth talking about."

Fortunately, before Plum had to unload her sad tale of rejection, a uniformed waitress offered her a glass of champagne, and Ellen's husband, Joel Katz, came over to greet Plum.

Even though Joel was a short, tubby, and balding man, he carried himself with the swagger and confidence of Brad Pitt. Plum could handle his brusque manner and forgave his aggressively socially ambitious modus for Ellen's sake, but she wasn't sure what her friend saw in him besides dollar signs. Or maybe that was enough for her.

"Plum Lockhart, fancy meeting you here," said Joel, his eyes sliding up her body unctuously. "You look fantastic."

"Thank you, Joel."

He embraced her, holding on a second too long as to make Plum feel slightly uncomfortable. He also pressed his entire body against hers, which made her quickly disentangle herself.

"You have taken really good care of yourself," he

remarked, still gliding his eyes around her body, appraising her as one would appraise a cow at a cattle auction.

"I try," shrugged Plum.

Joel jerked a finger at his wife. "This one works out like a maniac and has no more meat on her bones."

Ellen rolled her eyes. "I like to keep fit. You know that, Joel."

"What the hell happened that you ended up on a god-forsaken island?" asked Joel, ignoring his wife's response. "I thought for sure you'd be running some major publishing conglomerate by now."

"So did I," confessed Plum. "But the publishing industry is dead. No one buys magazines anymore."

"Yeah, that's probably true," said Joel.

"Good thing I got out of it when I did," interjected Ellen.

Joel snorted. "Elle, let's face it, you were never really in it. Maybe for a nanosecond, until you landed me and never lifted a finger again."

There was a frisson of tension between them that made Plum feel awkward. She immediately changed the subject.

"Love the chain, Joel," said Plum, remarking on the thick gold necklace with a diamond lavalier hovering over his hairy chest, visible because his shirt was unbuttoned practically down to his navel.

"Leo gave it to me," he said, his small eyes twinkling. He lifted his hand to fondle the lavalier. "I produced his last film. I said if he got a nomination, he better get me the most expensive thing in the front case at Van Cleef & Arpels. Obviously, he did. Love that guy."

"Oh Joel, you like anyone famous," said a voice behind him. It belonged to an attractive Black man in his early forties. He was tall and muscular, in an understated outfit, except for the large Rolex that gleamed on his wrist.

Joel turned and glanced at the speaker and then shrugged. "What can I say, Robert? Some people value kindness, some value charity, I value fame. That's why I'm friends with you, am I right or am I right?"

"Oh, Joel," admonished Ellen half-heartedly, although Plum was certain she had heard him say that many times.

"What?" boomed Joel. "At least I own it. All those idiots pretend they don't care about celebs, and yet they're only too willing to kiss ass when the time comes. I make no bones about famous people. They're my bread and butter."

The man rolled his eyes and turned to Plum. "I'm Robert Campbell."

His handshake was firm, and he looked intently into her eyes, something Plum appreciated. She had often found men of importance never took the time to greet unknown entities with any sort of enthusiasm or even general cordiality.

"Plum Lockhart."

"Ellen has told me you're old friends from your former working days," Robert said.

"*Her* former working days. I am still working," said Plum.

"What do you do?" he asked.

Plum filled him in on her new agency, while Ellen stood listening and Joel wandered away to talk to a gorgeous young blond in a shimmery jumpsuit who was draped on one of the sofas chatting with a Malaysian man. The luminescent young woman's flaxen hair shone a godly color in the moonlight, and she had that blush of youth, which made her irresistible. Joel squeezed in next to her so his knees were touching hers. Plum arched an eyebrow and wondered if Ellen had noticed just how close her husband was to the beauty. When Plum glanced at her friend, she saw Ellen had stiffened and her eyes narrowed into a look of contempt. Ellen appeared as if she were about to say something but then turned and motioned for the waitress.

"Another glass of white wine," Ellen requested.

Instead of going to fetch it, the waitress gave Ellen a disapproving gaze.

"Are you sure, ma'am?" asked the waitress in an accented voice that sounded Northern European.

"Of course, I am," Ellen snapped.

The waitress undoubtedly had noticed that Ellen had already had quite a lot of wine, but instead of protesting, she poured her another glass. She looked to be in her early twenties, with piercing blue eyes and dark eyebrows. Her hair was streaked in various shades of blond, brown, and blue and was tied back in a short ponytail. Despite her uniform, she exuded a rocker-chick vibe, and Plum thought her quite striking.

"Has it been a difficult transition, being at the height of the publishing industry in New York and then moving to an island?" asked Robert. "I'd think you would miss all the activity and commotion of the big city."

"Well, actually, there's been a lot of drama since I've been in Paraiso," said Plum. "Quite a few murders."

Ellen returned her attention to Plum, and a look of surprise appeared on her face.

"Murders?" Robert and Ellen repeated in unison.

"Yes, people dropping like flies," said Plum, swatting a mosquito away as she spoke.

"Anyone you knew?" asked Robert.

"Unfortunately, yes," admitted Plum. "And I had to ultimately solve the cases."

"*You* had to solve murders?" repeated Ellen.

"Yes," said Plum haughtily. There was something about this group and their successful lives that made Plum a twinge insecure and eager to brag.

"Are you a detective?" asked Robert.

"Not technically, or formally, or even by training," said Plum. "But I have a knack for sniffing out killers. I suppose murder is my thing these days."

"Did someone say 'murder'?" asked a beautiful Eurasian woman in her late thirties who strolled up to their group. She was clad in a flowy maxi-patterned caftan that looked exquisite on her slim figure but would look like a tent on someone larger. She wore dangling ruby earrings with a matching necklace. Her long hair was streaked with gold highlights and pinned back with a diamond broach. Plum thought she exuded effortless style.

"Do you know Suki Von Steefel?" asked Robert by way of introduction.

"You look familiar," said Plum, extending her hand. Sort of, she thought. But maybe Suki was just that type of jet-setting society woman she used to come across in her travels.

Suki gave her a limp handshake and shrugged as if used to being recognized. "Perhaps our paths have crossed somewhere," she said in a bored tone. "But I'm really more interested in what you were saying about tracking down killers. You work as a bounty hunter?"

"Absolutely not," Plum corrected. She immediately conjured the image of the heavily tattooed bounty hunters she had seen on a reality show. "I work in the luxury travel industry. Murder is more of a hobby."

Suki cocked her head to the side and arched an eyebrow. "Oh, how interesting," she said as if it were the least interesting thing she had ever heard.

"I'd like to know more about it," said Robert. He motioned for Plum to sit on one of the armchairs. "Tell us everything."

Soon Plum found herself holding court, regaling them with the stories of her past brushes with homicide—she did take a little liberty with her heroics, but the group was enthralled, and she told herself that as a guest on a multimillion-dollar yacht, she was required to be somewhat amusing. Besides her host, Robert, her friends Ellen and Joel, and Suki, the rest of the assembled guests also joined in to listen to her harrowing anecdotes. Even the waitstaff stood at attention eavesdropping yet pretending not to, as would be expected of them.

"This is out of a movie!" gushed the stunning young blond Joel had gravitated toward. It was revealed that she was an up-and-coming actress named India Collins. She had perfectly unblemished skin, piercing green eyes, and the wide-eyed innocence of someone thrown into an atmosphere they couldn't get a grasp on.

"Weren't you scared for your life?" asked India.

"Not really," said Plum. "I did spend a decade in New York City. The crime rate there is staggering under our latest mayor."

India looked both bewildered and impressed. "I'm playing a homicide detective in my next movie. Maybe you can give me some tips," she said excitedly.

Although Plum couldn't imagine this paper-thin childish waif being believable in the role of someone in law enforcement, she acquiesced. "Of course," said Plum. "I'd be happy to…"

The Malaysian man was Harris Low, and he had a jovial round face and laughed at everything anyone said, no matter how grim. He appeared to be steeped in money, judging by his wardrobe and the references he made to a suggestively fancy life. "Of course, I know Johnny Wisebrook from our days on the Riviera," he announced when Plum mentioned the rock star. He added, "The Rijos stayed at my island in Bali." But while seemingly social-climbing missives fell like waterfalls out of his mouth, his easygoing manner made it less irritating.

A bell tinkled, and they all looked in the direction of the entryway, where a tall uniformed chef stood, his large white toque almost grazing the top of the threshold. He was slight, midforties, with small dark eyes and dark hair peeking out under the iconic hat.

"Dinner is served," he said with a French accent.

"Thank you, Vadim," said Robert. He motioned toward the door. "Shall we go in?"

Plum, disconcerted that she had been interrupted during her storytelling, turned to Ellen. "Dinner? It's ten o'clock. I ate hours ago."

"Welcome to yacht world," said Ellen with a shrug. "It has its own wonky schedule. Being a good guest means you just go with the flow so you get invited back. I'd advise you to do the same."

CHAPTER

5

BEFORE TAKING HER SEAT IN the dining room, Plum asked the alternative-looking waitress, Lysette, where the restroom was.

"Follow me," she said.

Plum walked behind her down lushly carpeted stairs to a narrow hallway. The craftsmanship on the yacht was top-notch, as evidenced by intricate molding and pristine high-gloss paint. Lysette motioned toward a door, and Plum entered.

The glamorous powder room had gleaming black walls enhanced with silver picture-frame wainscoting. There was a black toilet and a vessel sink that sat atop a waterfall slab of marble flanked by two large towel holders. If the bathroom was that fancy, Plum could only imagine what the other rooms on the yacht looked like.

After washing her hands and refreshing her lipstick, she left the powder room and was surprised to see Lysette standing where she had left her.

"You didn't have to wait for me. I could have found my way back," said Plum apologetically.

"I heard you say you solved murders," Lysette said furtively. "You are the police?"

Something in her tone made Plum refrain from embellishing her career in crime. "No, I'm not the police," she protested.

"But you said you arrested the killers," Lysette insisted.

Plum hesitated. "I helped bring them to justice, but I sort of stumbled into it. I'm more of an amateur sleuth. Like a freelancer. Out of necessity, really. The Paraison police force needs all the help they can get."

Lysette remained undeterred. "But you have done it, right? You have worked with the police."

"Yes," admitted Plum cautiously. "I have."

Lysette moved nearer with a sense of urgency. Plum was uncomfortable. The girl had an unnerving intensity.

"If someone told you about a crime, you could prove who the killer was, correct? You could bring someone to justice who has escaped it thus far."

She was so close that Plum could feel her breath. There was a wild look in Lysette's eyes, and she was wringing her hands. Plum glanced down, desperate not to stare into her face anymore, and could make out the edge of a tattoo on her wrist. It was spiky and speckled, but she wasn't sure what it depicted.

"You can, right?" Lysette repeated.

Plum glanced up at her. "Maybe..."

"There you are!"

They both turned and glanced up at the staircase. Robert Campbell was standing mid-step, staring at them, a stern look on his face.

"Everything okay here?" he asked, glancing between Plum and Lysette.

Plum was relieved at the interruption. She smiled and moved toward him. "Wonderful. Lysette was just showing me the bathroom."

He gazed at Lysette but said nothing and instead turned toward Plum and said in a friendlier voice, "I have you seated next to me. I want to hear more about your rental agency. Perhaps we can do some business."

"I would love that," trilled Plum. Dollar signs flashed in her eyes. She instantly thought she would have to finagle some swanky villas with fancy powder rooms in order to please a man with such champagne tastes as Robert Campbell.

They returned to the mirrored dining room followed by a silent Lysette. Robert held out a plush black leather chair for Plum, and she slid in next to him. She glanced down at her place and saw the appetizer was blini and caviar, something she hadn't had in a long time. She was instantly transported back to New York at one of the fabulous soirees she attended, and truthfully, it felt wonderful. To hell with Juan Kevin and his beloved Victoria—this was where she belonged.

Just as Robert raised his glass of champagne and was about to make a toast, a stunning figure appeared in the doorway. It was none other than Nachelle Brown, the R & B pop singer who currently had three top-ten songs dominating the charts. Nachelle was dazzling in a white halter top—a vibrant compliment to her dark-brown skin—and she had on a long beaded skirt, channeling her inner belly dancer, complete with the belly button piercing and navel necklace.

"You weren't going to start without me, were you, Robert?" Nachelle said in a mock-wounded voice. She held her hand to her chest so her long fingernails decorated with colorful rhinestones reflected the light of the crystal chandelier.

"Of course not, babe, but maybe you could try and be on time once in a while," he said playfully, although Plum noticed a flash of anger in his eyes.

"I like to make an entrance," Nachelle insisted without irony.

Nachelle strode over to Robert and nibbled on his earlobe, after which he noticeably loosened up. She plopped herself into the empty chair next to him.

"We're so glad you made it, Nachelle," said Ellen in an ingratiating tone. "Dinner is no fun without you."

"That's what I've been telling Robert, but he refuses to listen," said Nachelle, who then picked up her blini and smeared the caviar and crème fraîche off by rubbing it on the edge of her plate before popping the naked mini pancake in her mouth. Plum had to restrain herself from dropping her jaw and licking up the discarded caviar.

Plum could tell at once that the energy in the room had shifted. Whereas before Robert had commanded everyone's attention, now it was Nachelle, and it was obvious to Plum that she was both capricious and vain, although definitely charismatic. Nachelle was completely disinterested in Plum, whom Robert introduced her to, and instead of returning Plum's greeting, Nachelle rudely summoned Lysette to order an Aperol Spritz. Joel, who was seated on the other side of Plum, boorishly leaned over her to talk to Nachelle—gush, was more like it—about how fantastic her latest song was. Nachelle looked bored but was clearly pleased by the attention.

The second course was linguine with freshly grated white truffles that fell like snowflakes onto the plate. Even if Plum had been absolutely stuffed, she would never refuse the opportunity to devour white truffles. They were the utmost delicacy.

"How did you get truffles this time of year?" asked Plum after hitting the pause button from eating so she could pace herself. "Aren't they usually only available in the fall?"

Robert smiled. "My motto is the rules don't apply to me. I'm used to going after what I want and getting it when I want."

Nachelle, who was tearing a roll in half and smearing it with a large clump of butter, rolled her eyes. "Robert doesn't take no for an answer."

"I love a man who doesn't take no for an answer," said Suki, who was giving Robert a provocative look. Plum glanced at Nachelle to see if she noticed this woman making overtures at her man, but if she did, she didn't do anything. Suki licked her lips before adding, "And these truffles are divine. The things that are hardest to attain are worth the most."

"As long as it's delicious," said Harris jovially.

Suki gave him a withering glance. "Nothing wrong with going after what you want."

Plum noticed that when Lysette went to shave the truffles

on Joel's pasta, he cupped her buttocks. Lysette froze. Plum glanced to see if Ellen had witnessed it, but she was talking to Harris.

"Joel, um, can you please pass me the butter," said Plum quickly.

Joel turned, dropped his hand from Lysette's butt, and handed Plum the butter. Lysette gave Plum a grateful look.

The pasta course was followed by filet mignon with white asparagus and rosemary fondant potatoes. Then there was a small silver dish of persimmon sorbet offered before a flaming Baked Alaska that drew oohs and aahs from the crowd. Despite having had dinner with Juan Kevin only a few hours prior, Plum ate with a relish that would indicate she had just completed a ten-week cleanse.

"This food is fantastic, Robert. You really outdid yourself," Harris said, complimenting his host as if he had cooked the meal himself.

"Thank you," said Robert.

Harris held up his fork and pointed it in the direction of Robert. "When you come to my weekend house in Phuket, I will have my chef make you something very similar but with an Asian twist."

"Are you planning a trip to Thailand without me, Robert?" asked Nachelle.

Before he could answer, Harris spoke for him. "You are, of course, invited, Nachelle—in fact, you are all invited!" he said to the group. "And Robert and I are cooking up a business scheme where we will be seeing a lot more of each other, so here's to many more nights like this!"

Harris raised his glass of wine, and everyone followed suit. Plum noticed Robert slowly raised his glass, as if he were reluctant.

"I'd love to go to Thailand," said India. "And ride an elephant. I love riding horses—"

"How fabulous," said Suki, addressing Robert. "When is this coming about?"

"I just need Robert to sign the papers!" replied Harris. He wore a smile on his face, but his tone was not lighthearted.

"India," said Robert, ignoring Harris. "Where did you ride horses?"

"I grew up on a farm in Virginia. And then I went to Foxcroft. It was one of the few boarding schools that allowed me to keep my ponies."

"Foxcroft?" mused Harris. "Posh."

India glanced down and put on a humble expression. "It was all I knew."

Plum had never heard of Foxcroft, but then she did not have a posh background, a fact that she resented but pretended not to bother about. She had grown up an only child in a ranch house in the middle of nowhere in upstate New York. Her parents worked blue-collar jobs and spent their paychecks at a local casino, and she could not be more working class. In fact, her real name was not even Plum—it was Vicki Lee. But she had chucked it as soon as she'd moved to Manhattan and reinvented herself.

"You can ride horses, ponies, camels, or unicorns at my house in Phuket," Harris told India. "I also have a race car track on my property."

"You have a race car track?" asked Joel, with interest. "You know I produced *Fast Car* parts one through seven, right? It's a passion of mine."

Ellen turned to Plum. "You can't believe how much time we had to spend at the racetracks while Joel did his 'research.'" She made air quotes with her fingers to show she was being sarcastic.

"Hey, you liked it as much as me," protested Joel. "Hanging around and racing with all the NASCAR guys. I got all the top drivers to give the entire cast and crew lessons."

Plum was impressed. "You raced also, Ellen?"

"A bit," she said. "I love driving fast and hard. I think I just have the constitution for it."

When dinner was over, they decamped to the deck. Plum was tired and ready to leave, although she wished she could magically transport herself home rather than take a boat to shore and then drive back to her town house. The thought of the journey exhausted her.

"Didn't you have so much fun?" asked Ellen as they filed through the doorway behind Harris and Suki. She linked her arm through Plum's. "This is really the way to live. You need to forget work, find yourself someone rich, and live happily—and luxuriously—ever after."

Plum gave her a tired smile. At one point that would have been her ultimate fantasy, and at first, she had to admit she felt like this evening was a homecoming. But after spending an evening with these people, she wasn't sure she belonged in this world anymore.

"I had a nice time..." began Plum.

"What the hell?" a loud voice bellowed behind them.

Everyone froze, and Plum turned around to see Nachelle standing in the entrance to the deck, yelling at Lysette. The pure white halter top that Nachelle had worn was now covered in red liquid, and a shocked Lysette stared down at her.

"I can't believe it," continued Nachelle, ranting at a frozen Lysette. "Can you not do your job?"

India, who was standing next to Lysette, grabbed some napkins off the table and began dabbing at Nachelle's top.

"Here, this will help," said India.

Nachelle grabbed the napkins out of India's hands. "You're making it worse."

"It was an accident, Nachelle," India replied.

"An *expensive* accident," sneered Nachelle.

India's voice filled with ice. "You shouldn't treat the staff that way."

Nachelle shook her head. She appeared to be about to protest, but then her entire demeanor changed. "It's fine. It's fine, not a big deal. It would be wonderful if people could properly do their job. But whatever. I'm going to change."

Robert watched her leave with a frown on his face.

Ellen gave Plum a saucer-eyed stare. "That was...unfortunate," said Ellen.

"I wouldn't want to be on the opposite end of that," said Plum. She watched as the other waitress steered a shocked Lysette out of the dining room. "She overreacted."

"Yes," said Ellen, before sighing. "Although it *was* a brand-new Gucci blouse."

Suki shook her head. "The crew must have some stain remover?"

"Oh, that is so useful. I should keep something like that in my purse," said Plum.

"I once salvaged a cashmere coat with that," said Suki. "I'll check my room to see if I brought any. It can work miracles."

The group was thinning, and everyone was a bit rattled. "I should go," Plum told Ellen.

"I'll get Robert to tell them to prepare the tender," said Ellen.

Plum said goodbye and thanked Robert for his hospitality. She was directed by him to follow an attendant toward the end of the boat. As they were walking down the corridor, she heard a sudden bang and turned around.

Suki had burst out of her cabin, slamming the door against the wall. She shook a vase of peonies overboard, sending all the beautiful flowers into the sea. Plum walked back toward her.

"Everything okay?" asked Plum.

Suki appeared disconcerted that Plum had witnessed her action. She wiped her hands off agitatedly. "Fine."

"Are you allergic to peonies?"

Suki shook her head. "No."

Plum stared at her and at the flowers, now being pulled away by the current. Suki followed her gaze before adding, "I despise them."

"I guess so," said Plum.

Then Suki turned on her heel and returned to her room.

CHAPTER

6

PLUM WAS DRAINED ON HER journey home, and it took all her effort not to fall asleep on the tender. She worried about Ellen, who seemed tense. Plum had agreed to meet her in the morning and accompany her to the stores in the marina for some retail therapy. Perhaps Ellen wanted to confide in her about the situation with Joel and his lecherous ways, and Plum told herself she would have to refrain from being judgmental and just provide a sounding board for her old friend.

She checked her phone on the tender and saw three missed calls from Juan Kevin as well as two voicemails but decided not to listen to them. What was the point? Plum was exhausted and didn't feel like engaging with him this late in the night. Better to push thoughts of him aside until the morning.

Plum woke up early, alert and full of energy. After showering and dressing in linen slacks and a pale blue top, she nibbled on some toast and had two cups of coffee. The entire time she breakfasted, she glanced at her phone before finally breaking down and listening to her voicemails from Juan Kevin.

"Plum, I'm sorry our evening was disrupted. There's no excuse, but I would love the chance to explain to you in person. Please call me back," said Juan Kevin in the first message.

"It's Juan Kevin again," he began in the second voicemail. "I want to make sure you're okay. I know, why wouldn't you be? But I was disappointed things ended like that between you and me, and I think you got the wrong impression. Can you meet me so I can fill you in on what happened?"

Plum held her finger over the delete button before deciding to let his messages sit in her inbox for the near future. Juan Kevin did sound contrite. And honestly, it wasn't as if he had planned for this hot tamale to show up and wreck her dramatic fantasies. But Plum never wanted to put herself at the mercy of a man, so she decided to refrain from calling him back before she had more clarity.

Lucia arrived, and there were business issues to discuss before Plum extricated herself to drive over to the marina and meet Ellen. Besides boasting comprehensive docking facilities that accommodated a wide range of vessels from opulent yachts to pleasure crafts and fishing boats, the marina had elegant squares and Mediterranean palazzi full of high-end restaurants as well as luxury boutiques. There was also a grocery store, which Plum tried to use as a last resort since it was geared toward tourists and vacationers and the prices were exorbitant.

Ellen was not outside their agreed meeting place (a store called *Finesse!*), so Plum found a patch of shade and dialed her cell.

"Sweetie, I'm inside with Suki and Harris. We simply could not wait one more second in the blazing heat," purred Ellen's voice on the other end of the phone. "I was positively melting."

"Yes, it's broiling," said Plum. She added with authority, "It takes some time to adjust."

Plum entered the store and found an attentive salesgirl carrying armloads of clothing to the dressing rooms. The curtains were closed, but Plum heard Ellen's familiar voice narrating from behind one.

"This is the cutest. What do you think, Plum?"

Ellen was clad in a frilly white eyelet dress. If Plum had to be honest, it was probably more appropriate for a girl celebrating her sweet sixteen than a thirty-five-year-old mother of three, although Ellen did genuinely look great in it.

"It fits you so well," said Plum.

The other dressing room curtain slid open, and Suki exited wearing a skintight leopard dress. She had a tall lanky figure, and the dress looked sensational on her, but Plum guessed she could wear a paper bag and still look chic.

"No, no," clucked Suki, moving toward Ellen and pulling at the fluffy sleeves on Ellen's gown. "This is too provincial. Honestly, not sure what the designer was thinking. It's like she was channeling 1982. This is not good for you, Ellen."

"But I like that it's youthful…" Ellen protested.

"Trying to be young is not going to help your situation. You want your husband to want you right?" Suki asked sternly.

Ellen's face reddened. "Of course," she said before fleeing to the dressing room.

Harris burst out from one of the other dressing rooms across the hall.

"Ladies, what do you think of this fabulous getup?" he asked, giggling. He spun around like a runway model, so they had time to examine his absurd outfit. He wore a pale-blue suede suit that was covered head to toe in the giant Gucci logo. The lining of the jacket was a lime-green shantung fabric, and the lapels were as big as airport hangars.

Suki put her hand to her mouth and laughed. "Harris, that is terrible."

"But so terrible, it's wonderful?" he asked eagerly.

Suki shook her head so hard that her dangling ruby earrings swung back and forth. "Completely gauche."

"Oh poo!" said Harris, waving her away.

While Suki and Harris rang up their purchases, Ellen quickly exited the boutique without purchasing anything. Plum followed her friend out.

"Do you want to go to Lazlo's?" asked Plum. She pointed across the cobblestone path at a store whose vitrine windows were filled with antique jewelry. "That's where all the rich islanders buy their diamonds and rubies."

"Absolutely not," said Ellen hastily. She steered Plum away.

"How about Jojo's?" asked Plum, pointing to a clothing store.

"Sure," said Ellen, who seemed more eager to find a garment than a bauble.

They immersed themselves in the racks of clothing. Ellen kept pulling out dresses, holding them up to her body, and then thrusting them back into the rack. Plum could tell Ellen was rattled.

"You know, Suki can be a bit of a bitch," said Ellen.

"I can see that," said Plum.

Suddenly there was a commotion at the front of the store. Plum and Ellen jerked their heads in the direction of the noise. There was shouting then a door slamming. And finally, a primal wail.

"UGH! I HATE the paparazzi," screamed Nachelle, flinging her shopping bags down on the floor. "Why can't they leave me alone?!"

Two large bodyguards followed behind her, closed the door, and pulled down the shades. The scampering throngs outside were silenced.

The eager shopgirl was instantly starstruck. "Oh, oh, oh, you're Nachelle Brown!" she shrieked.

"Yes," said Nachelle, who looked flustered. "Can you please get me some water? This chaos is making me trip."

Plum wondered if she would need to grab defibrillators to resuscitate the shell-shocked salesgirl, but she was able to pick her jaw off the floor and rush to fetch a cold bottle of water for the superstar. The girl's hand shook as she offered it to the singer.

Nachelle gazed around the room before her eyes narrowed on Ellen. "Where is everyone? I thought Harris was with you."

"He is, but he stopped to try on some Gucci."

Nachelle rolled her eyes. "I'm sure he'll just go for anything that has logos all over it so he can brag about his money!"

She spoke the truth, but the hypocrisy was not lost on Plum. Nachelle's handbag bore a Louis Vuitton monogram, and her belt had a giant *H* for Hermès. The double standard was evidently lost on Nachelle.

"Harris and Suki will be here soon," said Ellen, almost apologetically. Plum hated to see her friend suck up to celebrities.

"That's good. I want to check out all the stores," replied Nachelle, plopping herself in a soft armchair. "Is it me, or does anyone else find it so boring on the yacht? I would love to go dancing, go to clubs, but all Robert wants to do is have a stuffy dinner with all that fancy food. I can't take it anymore."

Before anyone could respond, there was a strong knock at the door. The bodyguard lifted the roller shade and then opened the door. Harris stood on the threshold.

"Honey, there are about four hundred million fans out there," Harris said in an exasperated tone directed at Nachelle. He had a sweaty sheen on his brow, and he was visibly distraught. "Time to get back to the boat ASAP."

"Oh, really?" Nachelle moaned.

"Silver lining," said Harris. "On the yacht, there are oysters and champagne screaming out our names!"

7

PLUM FELT AS IF SHE were watching the president of the United States in the throes of an assassination attempt, where Nachelle was playing the part of the president. As soon as Harris announced there were crowds outside the store clamoring to see the pop star, the two bodyguards went into full Secret Service mode and dragged Nachelle through the jostling fans toward the tender at the dock. Suki, Harris, Ellen, and Plum followed behind them, watching in amazement. The guards shielded the music star with their jackets and barked hostile threats to the onlookers. After shoving through the grasping fans desperate to touch or photograph Nachelle, the bodyguards flung her group into the vessel.

Plum was disoriented, but once they were by the tender, she glanced around and found her bearings. Ellen, Harris, and Suki were quickly helped onto the boat by the guards, one of whom held out his hand to assist Plum. She shook her head.

"Aren't you coming?" asked Ellen.

"I need to work," said Plum.

"We gotta go now," barked one of the guards.

"You sure?" asked Ellen. "If you change your mind, you know where to find us!"

"Yes, have a safe trip!"

The boat began to speed away, leaving the screaming and gawking throngs staring. Plum squinted as it left a frothy wake. The crowd started dispersing, but a woman rushed up to the edge of the dock, waving and yelling. It was Lysette.

"Wait! Wait!" Lysette yelled.

The boat didn't stop. Lysette looked deflated. Her arms were full of brown paper shopping bags.

"Do you need a hand?" asked Plum.

Lysette glanced up, gratified to see it was Plum.

"Oh, it's you, Miss Lockhart!" said Lysette brightening. "I wanted to talk to you."

Without warning, a large woman rushed toward them, her face frantic.

"Did I miss her? Did I miss my Queen Nachelle?" wailed the woman. "I am her number one fan!"

As the woman rushed to the edge of the dock, she inadvertently knocked over Lysette, causing all her shopping bags to fall over. Produce rolled out of one bag, and various baggies of pills fell out of another. They were all over the deck, in danger of the woman crushing them.

"Oh no!" gasped Lysette, who immediately fell to the ground, trying to collect everything. She clambered to pick up the baggies and swept them into her purse before Plum could see what they were.

Plum also hastily dropped and began helping her, as

the superfan continued howling, oblivious to the accident she'd caused.

Plum's phone buzzed and she glanced down. Lucia had written her that she needed to deal with the Mango house ASAP.

After gathering the produce and handing it back to Lysette, Plum rose.

"Thank you so much," said Lysette. "Do you have a minute? I wanted to ask you about murder—"

"Listen, I'm really sorry, but I have to go, I have a work emergency. Here's my card. Call me."

Plum rushed off before she could reply.

CHAPTER

8

"NOT THE BEST DAY TO go hobnobbing with celebrities," clucked Lucia when Plum finally returned to the town house.

"It wasn't intentional," said Plum defensively. She sighed and added, "It ended up going on much longer than I thought it would. What did I miss?"

"Where do I start?" said Lucia.

After a long, busy day, when Lucia at last agreed to go home in time for dinner with her husband, Plum finally texted Juan Kevin asking him if it was a good time to talk. He responded by saying that he would love to stop by on his way home from work at about seven o'clock if possible. Plum agreed. Better to be done in person. Easier to read nuances. She was still not adept at dating and felt her skills at communication were not best expressed by text or email.

She had enough time to shower and put on a light linen dress as well as refresh her makeup by the time the doorbell rang.

Damn, he smells good, Plum thought as soon as Juan

Kevin entered her house. He greeted her with an intimate smile, and his eyes shone brightly, but she sensed something hesitant in his manner.

"Can I offer you a glass of wine?" she asked, walking over to the kitchen and pulling out a bottle of Chablis.

"Thank you."

For some reason Plum averted her eyes and purposely didn't look at him while she pulled the wineglasses out of the cabinet. He followed her into the small space.

"Allow me to open it," he said, reaching to take the bottle from her hands.

"It's a twist-off," she said, easily removing the top and holding it up. "Makes for easier access."

He smiled.

There was an air of tension now that made the hair stand on Plum's neck. Was he going to dump her? They weren't even officially going out. If romance had a guidebook or road map, she would have nailed it by now, but left to her own instincts, she was at a loss. She poured a glass and handed it to Juan Kevin.

"Thank you."

"Out with it," Plum demanded.

"What?" he said, glancing up. His long dark eyelashes blinked twice.

Plum took a swig of her wine and steeled herself. "I can tell you have something unpleasant to say. I would rather know as soon as possible than pretend nothing is happening. I don't want to be the elephant in the room. So, okay, are you going to blow me off? What's the deal with that woman?"

Juan Kevin smiled. "No, no, Plum. Please, it's nothing like that."

"What is it, then?"

He sighed and placed his glass on the table. "Look, I should have explained everything to you before, but we were just getting to know each other. Victoria is my ex-wife." He paused before adding, "Clarification: I consider her my ex-wife, but we are still technically married."

"Oh boy," said Plum. This was messier than she had hoped. "Not sure I want to get in the middle of this."

Plum walked into the living room and plopped down on the sofa, the wine in her glass coming precariously close to the rim. Juan Kevin followed her.

"It's not like that," he implored, still standing. "The marriage is over. It ended acrimoniously, despite my best efforts…"

"Don't they all," murmured Plum, stuffing her nose in her wineglass.

"They don't have to," said Juan Kevin. "In fact, I pride myself on the way I behaved. If you must know, Victoria was unfaithful to me. She was the one who walked out on me for another man. I agreed to grant her a divorce, and when the other man broke up with her, she tried to get back with me, but I was done. She had broken my heart…"

He stopped, as if remembering. Plum felt a wave of sympathy then anger. How could that woman do that to this man?

"I'm sorry."

He shook his head as if shaking off his demons. "I'm

fine now, but Victoria is…relentless. She wants me back and won't sign off on the divorce. And really, it's not for any great love for me; it's for love of the unattainable. If I returned to her, she would drop me as soon as someone else came along."

"She sounds"—Plum knew she had to be diplomatic— "tricky."

He sat on the chair and rubbed his temples. "She wasn't always…at least I didn't think she was always…but she and her sister are competitive."

"Right," exclaimed Plum. "Carmen Rijo is her sister. And a master at cunning."

He nodded. "They come from humble beginnings and are determined to get everything they want. Unfortunately, I discovered too late that it's at any cost."

"Disgusting," said Plum. She had known a lot of people like that in New York City. And if she were honest with herself, she would confess she had been a tiny bit like that. Not in her romantic life but definitely in her work life.

"But enough about this. I wanted to explain then move on. It's not a proud moment to admit you were cuckolded, but I want to be transparent about my situation," he said. "For now, Victoria is trying to remain in my life, but I hope she'll agree to the divorce and I can move on. And I want to move on with you."

He said the last part with such intensity that Plum flushed. "Me too…" she sputtered.

He took her hand gently. "I'm serious, Plum. I can't get you out of my mind…"

He moved toward her and sat on the sofa. He softly lifted her chin and stared in her eyes. "I don't know what it is about you."

"I'm adorable and irresistible," she offered.

"*Adorable* would not be my word choice."

Plum pulled back and gave him a wounded expression. "What do you mean?"

"It's a compliment," he said. "Children are adorable. They are little and helpless and dependent. You are the opposite. You are feisty and self-sufficient and headstrong. That's what's irresistible about you."

Before she could respond, he moved his lips toward her and gave her a tender kiss. And then another one...

After several kisses and a long embrace, they eventually moved out to the balcony to stare at the sunset. The evening was still and sultry. The leaves on the canopy of palm trees below did not stir. The coquis, a breed of frogs that resided in the dense trees, began to make their music. Juan Kevin slid his arm around Plum's waist, and they stared into the distance, watching as the orange sun slid down to touch the horizon. They were engulfed in silence but full of everything that wasn't being said. Plum felt as if she could stay like this forever.

They were interrupted by her cell phone ringing. Plum had left it on the coffee table inside.

"Do you need to answer that?" asked Juan Kevin.

She could think of a hundred reasons why she needed to answer it, but she shook her head. "If it's a client complaining about the pressure in their shower, that can wait until the morning."

It stopped ringing but then immediately began ringing again. "Let me go turn it off."

She went inside and saw it was Ellen Katz, and there was already missed a call from her. Plum put her phone on silent. Ellen could wait.

After a few more romantic clinches, Plum took the lead and guided Juan Kevin up to her bedroom.

CHAPTER

9

IN THE EARLY MORNING HOURS, just as dawn was breaking, there was a loud knocking on the front door followed by a doorbell ringing, which roused Plum. She bolted upright in bed, only to see Juan Kevin had already risen and was putting on his pants.

"Are you expecting someone?" he asked, throwing on his polo shirt.

Plum shook her head, "No."

"I'll go see who it is," he said.

"Wait!" said Plum, pulling the sheets up to cover herself. "What if it's Lucia?"

"Lucia? Are you expecting her this early?"

Plum glanced out the windows and saw the sun had not even peeked out yet. "No. But maybe she arrived early for work and I bolted the door."

Juan Kevin gave her a quizzical look. "And what if it is Lucia? We should let her in."

"What will she think?" asked Plum.

"Do you care?" he asked.

"I think she would see it as unprofessional," Plum responded. The truth was Lucia was a maternal figure to her, and the thought of Lucia discovering Plum in bed with a man was disconcerting.

"I don't want to hide anything," insisted Juan Kevin. "What we have is good."

The knocking on the door became louder. Juan Kevin headed downstairs. Plum used the opportunity to quickly pull on the linen dress she had worn the night before and throw her hair into a ponytail. She had to smile as Juan Kevin's words echoed in her head. *What we have is good.* She descended the staircase.

A policeman was standing at the door, speaking to Juan Kevin in Spanish. Although Plum liked to believe she was fluent after a few online lessons, she didn't understand a word they were saying. They stopped talking when she approached.

"What's going on?" she asked.

"He has to bring you down to the marina," said Juan Kevin. "It seems they found a body floating in the water."

"*Sí*, you are to come with me at once," said the policeman. He had a baby face and looked not older than a teenager, a fact he seemed aware of and determined to conceal by adopting a stern demeanor.

"A body?" repeated Plum. "Who is it?"

"We have not identified the victim yet," the policeman said in an official tone. "But it is a woman."

"Lucia?" Plum gasped, fear seizing her by the throat.

"Lucia?" repeated the policeman, whipping out a notebook and writing down the name. "Why should you believe it is this Lucia?"

"Because that's the only woman I'm close to on this island," said Plum. "But I don't understand. How am I connected to this?" Plum asked, turning her attention back to the cop. "Why me?"

The policeman said something in Spanish to Juan Kevin, who turned to Plum and translated.

"He said Captain Diaz has forbidden him from revealing more," said Juan Kevin.

Juan Kevin drove Plum to the marina behind the police officer. She was a knot of nerves.

"You don't think it could be my friend Ellen?" asked Plum anxiously, suddenly remembering Ellen had called her twice the previous evening. "I should have picked up!"

"Don't jump to conclusions," advised Juan Kevin, who steadily maneuvered his car around a cluster of pink flamingos making their way across the street.

"But listen to this," she said. Plum played the voicemail Ellen had left on her phone.

"Plum," said Ellen in a breathy whisper. "I really need to talk to you. You're the only one I can trust on this. Something has happened. Call me."

"Did you try calling her back?" asked Juan Kevin.

"You don't think it's too early?" asked Plum.

"It may be too early, but if she's dead, she won't pick up," he replied.

"This is not a joking matter," said Plum, giving him a disapproving look.

"Call her," he commanded.

Plum dialed Ellen's number. "It went to voicemail. Now I'm really freaking out. What if it's her?"

"We'll find out soon enough."

When they arrived at the marina, the sun was pushing up above the bend of the coast, sending a glittering shaft of brightness across the sea. The heat was steaming off the water, and the humidity was rising. It was going to be a scorcher, thought Plum. She cursed herself for forgetting to apply sunblock on her way out.

It was still tranquil because of the early hour. The yachts were moored, bobbing gently in the small waves that slapped against their sides. There were a few fishing charters on the other side of the dock heading out with tourists, whose snatches of gaiety echoed through the marina as they embarked on their journey.

Several police cars surrounded an area that had been closed off with a tarp. An ambulance stood by, its engine idling. It was too early for gawkers; therefore, the small crowd was composed of people there in an official capacity— uniformed police officers as well as some personnel from the marina.

Plum exited the car. Juan Kevin took her by the hand and guided her along the cobblestone path toward the group. When they approached, the crowd parted. As if rising out of the ashes, a short, bald man with two dark eyebrows in the shape of upside-down Vs emerged. He jerked his head in their direction. A grimace instantly flashed across his face, and he straightened before waddling toward them.

"Senorita Lockhart. Once again, we meet over the most unfortunate circumstance," he barked at Plum.

"Nice to see you too, Captain Diaz," replied Plum, her voice dripping with sarcasm.

Captain Diaz grunted and turned to Juan Kevin. "I didn't know my officers had called you."

Instead of explaining that one of Captain Diaz's officers had interrupted him in bed with Plum, Juan Kevin replied, "You're aware that I know everything that goes on at Las Frutas."

Again, Captain Diaz grunted. "If that's the situation, I'd like you to identify the deceased."

He walked toward a gurney that held a body covered by a sheet. Plum took a deep breath and stayed back, uncertain that she wanted to find out who was underneath. Juan Kevin continued on with the captain and watched as he pulled up the sheet with a flourish. Plum braced herself. Her view of the victim's head was obscured by Juan Kevin for now, and she was grateful for that. He turned and glanced back at Plum and then down at the dead woman. Finally, he shook his head.

"I don't recognize her," he said.

Plum heaved an audible sigh of relief. It definitely wasn't Lucia, then. Hallelujah. But was it Ellen?

"You, young lady," Captain Diaz barked, while wagging a finger at Plum. "Come here and identify."

Plum walked slowly and reluctantly toward the gurney as if in a trance. Captain Diaz jerked the sheet up farther, tangling it and then untangling it, and as he did, Plum saw the victim's hand drop to the side. Plum knew at once who it was.

"It's Lysette," she gasped.

"Who?" asked Juan Kevin.

"She worked on the *Jackpot*. A yacht," said Plum, her eyes boring into the bluish arm that hung limply.

"How do you know? You haven't even seen her face." Captain Diaz demanded.

Plum pointed to Lysette's wrist. The spiky tattoo she had seen on it earlier was there.

"You recognize the dragonfruit tattoo?" asked Juan Kevin.

Plum nodded.

Captain Diaz arched his odd eyebrow. "Come over and look at her face."

Plum did as she was told. Lysette's eyes were closed, and her head appeared a bit bulged, but there was no doubt it was her. Plum slowly nodded confirmation.

"It's Lysette. I don't know her last name," explained Plum.

"A good friend of yours?" demanded Captain Diaz.

"No, I only met her the other day," said Plum, who found it hard to keep her eyes on Lysette. It was unsettling. "I was a guest on Robert Campbell's yacht, and she was his employee. I was invited there by my friend Ellen Katz. Actually..."

Plum abruptly stopped. She was about to tell Captain Diaz about Ellen's frantic calls, but she thought the better of it. What if Ellen was somehow involved? She didn't want to reveal anything to the Paraison police without consulting her old friend. Plum had little faith in their abilities.

Captain Diaz dropped the sheet back on top of the dead woman. "I will need a full statement from you."

"From me?" asked Plum, her voice rising. "Why me? I didn't even know her."

"A full statement," repeated Captain Diaz smugly, his serpentine face doing nothing to mask his pleasure at her discomfort.

"This is not necessary, Captain," interjected Juan Kevin. "Plum will give you the information about the yacht, and then we will leave. If anything else arises, you know where to find her."

Captain held up a plastic ziplock bag. Inside was a piece of paper. "We found Senorita Lockhart's business card inside this baggie found on the victim. We need to know why."

Plum was surprised, and Juan Kevin gave her a curious look. "My card?" she squeaked.

Captain Diaz nodded. "Your card."

"Well, I gave her my card the other day," said Plum, remembering. "When we were on the dock. She had wanted to ask me about murders…."

"Murders?" interrupted the captain.

Plum nodded. "When I was on the yacht, I told everyone about how I solved several murders in Paraiso."

The captain's eyebrows shot up. "*You* solved them?"

"You know I did," insisted Plum.

Before the captain and Plum could get into a heated debate, Juan Kevin interjected. "Let's not go at it," he chided.

"Okay," conceded Plum. "Lysette happened to overhear my conversation. She wanted to talk to me about the murder, and I was in a rush and handed her my card."

"Why did she want to talk to you about it?" asked the captain.

Plum shrugged. "I have no idea. Maybe she was a murder buff."

Captain Diaz gave her a skeptical look. "That's all?"

"Yes. I really didn't have time to talk to her. I'm sorry now that I didn't."

"I am not sure, based on your history, that you are telling me the truth," insisted the police chief.

"I am not the type of person who would lie," Plum spat out with indignation.

"Right, and you would never withhold information from the police?" he taunted.

Plum was about to dissent again when she stopped. Lysette had told her she wanted Plum to help her solve a crime and bring someone to justice. Was this at all connected to why she died?

"Of course, I would not withhold information," insisted Plum, standing straighter.

If she knew anything, Captain Diaz was the last person she would tell.

"I don't believe you," said the policeman. "You have done it before."

Plum wanted to protest, but she had to concede it was true. In the past, when she had worked on a case, she had not been very forthcoming.

Juan Kevin interjected. "It's early in the morning, and perhaps she needs more time to remember. Why don't I take her home now? If she refreshes her memory, we will call you."

Juan Kevin valiantly led Plum away, while Captain Diaz swore Plum had not seen the last of him and would have to answer more questions. As Juan Kevin drove her back, Plum tried Ellen two more times, but the call still went to voicemail. Plum was becoming more and more filled with dread. What had Ellen wanted? What happened to Lysette?

"I wonder if I should have taken the time to listen to Lysette when she wanted to tell me about bringing some-one to justice," said Plum, before filling Juan Kevin in on her interaction with the deceased.

"It looks like an accident. Don't think the worst," advised Juan Kevin when he dropped her in front of the town house.

"How can I not?" she asked.

"Let me give you something else to think about." Juan Kevin leaned toward her and gave her a lingering kiss. When they broke apart, he said, "I hope that took your mind off things."

"A little," she confessed, exiting the car.

"A little?" he repeated. "I'll do better next time. You won't even be able to think straight!"

"I'll hold you to that," retorted Plum.

He headed off to work and promised to be in touch later. Plum took a quick shower then attempted to attack her inbox.

CHAPTER

10

IT WAS ALMOST LUNCHTIME WHEN Ellen finally phoned her back. Plum was visiting Casa Tomate, one of her rentals, and had to extricate herself from a meeting with the landscaper in order to answer the call.

"I've been so worried! Are you okay?" asked Plum. She moved into a shaded area under a hibiscus tree.

"Yes," replied Ellen in a hushed tone. "It's been challenging. We've spent all morning talking to the police, who are still on the boat. They're not letting us set sail until the autopsy is complete."

"What exactly happened?" asked Plum.

"Lysette slipped and fell overboard. It's obviously an accident. I'm not sure why they're forcing us to stay here."

"Maybe they have some reason to suspect something more nefarious happened," ventured Plum. "Do you have any suspicions?"

"Not at all. I think the police are on a power trip," replied Ellen. "But they don't know who they're dealing with. With our connections, we can have them all fired at a moment's notice."

Plum decided to let that statement go. Ellen could be very snobby, but she was obviously under duress. "Is everything okay with you, though?" asked Plum.

"Yes, why wouldn't it be?"

"Because you left me that voicemail last night. I was worried…"

"Oh, that," said Ellen breezily. "It's nothing."

"Nothing? It didn't sound like that…"

Ellen laughed. "I was distraught because I couldn't find my diamond necklace. I thought it was in my jewelry box, and the staff and I looked everywhere. But then later Joel found it behind my tissue box. It must have slipped down. I'm sorry I bothered you about that. I was overreacting as usual. That's what Joel said."

The excuse sounded both fishy and rehearsed to Plum. "That sounds odd."

"I debated bringing such an expensive piece of jewelry on the yacht, I mean, I know there's security, but I've heard of staff with sticky fingers, and I decided it was that sort of crowd. But I must have mislaid it. Perhaps I had too much rosé. It's not a big deal."

"Okay," said Plum after hesitating. "But please let me know if you need anything."

"Of course! And listen, Robert adored you and wants to make sure I invite you to join us on the yacht. As soon as the police release us, we head to Jolly Island, followed by Mustique and then the rest of the Grenadines. Please consider joining us!"

The old Plum would have leapt at the chance. After years of working at a travel magazine, she had developed that insatiable need to explore everywhere possible. But it wasn't practical right now. "I would love nothing more, and please thank Robert, but I can't leave work now."

She also didn't want to leave Juan Kevin if she were being honest.

"I thought you might say that," Ellen replied, her voice full of disappointment. "You always had a good work ethic. Maybe too good. Never interested in fun."

"Work is fun for me," insisted Plum. "And besides, things are looking up with the guy I started seeing."

Ellen let out a little whoop. "Exciting! Okay, well, I hope everything goes well, but if you change your mind, let me know. I don't think we'll leave before tomorrow at this point. Come by tonight if you can, Robert will be screening Joel's new movie."

"I'm pretty exhausted," said Plum. "But thank you. And stay safe."

The afternoon was busy, and it wasn't until dinnertime that Plum had a chance to sit, have a glass of wine, and ponder Lysette's murder. Juan Kevin had a work event, which was fine for Plum as she was drained from the morning's incident.

She prepared a basic meal for herself and brought it on a tray to eat on her balcony. Plum's refrigerator was bursting with all the glorious produce she had purchased at the local supermarket, but she had prepared herself a meager meal of toast with cream cheese and guava jam. She told herself she was owed one day off from cooking, but the truth was she was not a chef and, despite her best intentions, never cooked at all. Every week she would dump the wilted vegetables and bruised fruit into the garbage and insist to herself that next week, when she wasn't so busy, she would return to the kitchen. That never happened.

Her cell phone rang.

"Hello?" asked Plum.

There was a long sigh on the other end of the phone. "You need to leave my husband alone," warned an accented feminine voice.

"You must have the wrong number," replied Plum, who was about to end the call.

"Plum Lockhart, do not hang up on me."

Plum shifted in her seat. Was it Victoria? Juan Kevin's ex. "What do you want?" said Plum truculently.

"I told you what I want. I want you to leave my husband alone."

"He's not your husband anymore." Plum sniffed. "At least not officially. Maybe technically, but not in his heart."

It sounded convoluted and she knew it. But she held firm. Victoria laughed a throaty, husky laugh. The kind villainesses emit on soap operas.

"He will always be my husband. And I am doing you a courtesy. Walk away from him now, and no harm will come to you. But if you do not do as I say, you will regret it."

Victoria disconnected just as Plum was scrambling to press the End button. Damn! She had wanted to hang up first. It would have been so satisfying. Plum couldn't decipher if she was more annoyed that she didn't win the first round or if she was generally mad about the call.

She was about to dial Juan Kevin's number to bitch and moan about his ex, and then paused. What would she say? She didn't want to ruin their blossoming relationship with complaints about Victoria. In fact, she didn't even want to mention Victoria to him. That would only give the woman power.

A sudden virulent downpour came pouring from the sky, and Plum rose to close the glass doors to the balcony. The weather in the Caribbean was so erratic—sunny and gorgeous, and then out of nowhere everything darkened, and a deluge of rain covered the island. Plum felt suddenly chilled by the meek air-conditioning coupled with the angry thunderstorm. She rose to put on a light sweater and make herself a cup of hot hibiscus tea.

Once she had prepared her tea and extracted a handful of the *coconetes* that were Paraiso's national cookie (according to Lucia), Plum planted herself on the sofa. She stared out at the cloudy sky and felt lazy. She would push all thoughts of Victoria and Lysette out of her mind.

Juan Kevin sent her a text that he was dealing with a work crisis but would she like a nightcap later, and she wrote him that she wanted to retire early. Plum was tired, but most of all she didn't want to appear too available. Let him chase her a little.

CHAPTER

11

PLUM SLEPT DEEPLY AND ROSE early to prepare for her appointment with a potential client, one whose mansion she was very eager to represent. Casa la Sandía (*watermelon house* in English) was an oceanfront villa in a premier location that would be a next level up from all the other residences Plum Lockhart Luxury Retreats currently represented. Plum's competitive juices were on fire as she drove into the driveway.

She parked her car and then pressed a buzzer at the teak gate. It swung open, and Plum entered then walked down a hardwood path flanked by rows of royal palms gently swaying in the breeze. She could see straight through the open floor plan all the way to the crystal clear sea in the distance.

Barbara Copeland, the owner, greeted her at the entrance to the spacious living room pavilion. She was a curvaceous woman in her fifties with expensively tinted blond hair, a prominent chin, and very large and very white teeth. Her face was completely made up, and a streak of cobalt eyeliner above and below each lid brought out the blue in her eyes.

"Call me *Barbie*," she insisted warmly after Plum introduced herself.

Plum entered the house, and as she did, so a small white toy poodle ran barking toward, her little nails clicking along the floor. As soon as she reached Plum, she took a giant bite out of her ankle. Plum yelped in both surprise and pain.

"Chloe, *no!*" said Barbie as she scooped up the dog. "I'm so sorry! You naughty, naughty girl."

"Don't worry," said Plum, she bent to rub her ankle. Although she could feel a sting where Chloe's teeth had punctured her skin, she put on a brave face and added, "Didn't hurt at all."

"You sure?"

"Yes. I love dogs. All animals, really."

"That's a relief," said Barbie. "Thanks for being understanding. Chloe is a good dog, really; she just gets nervous around strangers. Don't you, Chloe baby?"

Chloe, ensconced in her mistress's arms, continued to give Plum the evil eye and bark with a ferocity. But Plum gave the dog her biggest smile.

"I actually volunteer at the local animal shelter here," said Plum.

"That's wonderful," said Barbie.

"Yes, it's really great to help out," she said, although admittedly she had only been there a couple of times. It was on her to-do list daily, but it was hard to find the time. Plum made a note to try and visit this weekend.

"Let me show you around the place," said Barbie.

The house was a rhapsody of colors, muted blues paired with emerald greens and brilliant whites. The living areas had sumptuous sofas and comfortable sectionals. A chef's kitchen had top-of-the-line appliances. There were stunning Caribbean Sea views from every vantage point, and the gym and fitness room would rival the hotel's.

After the tour, Barbie led them past an open-air gazebo wrapped in magenta bougainvilleas to the poolside terrace. They sat at a table shaded by almond trees, and the warm tropical breezes carried the heady scent of lilies. Barbie offered Plum a glass of iced tea out of a pitcher with sprigs of mint and slices of lemon floating in it. Once they had engaged in brief small talk, Plum began her pitch.

"Barbie, your house is magnificent, and I really believe I'm the right person to represent it exclusively to my high-net-worth clients," began Plum.

Barbie stroked Chloe, who was still nestled in her arms, and kept her gaze on Plum. "I'm really not eager to rent it. That was the agreement when my husband Stan and I bought it, you know. No strangers in the house. That's why I spared no expense on fancy sheets and beautiful bedding."

"I understand," said Plum patiently.

Barbie rubbed Chloe's belly so rigorously that Plum could see the pink of her skin and the giant patches where she had lost her hair.

"But, well, you know, we're not here that much lately. My son got married, and my daughter had a baby. So it seems silly to just keep it empty."

"Absolutely. And I can assure you we are very discerning about who we rent to. Our clients are affluent, chic, and discreet," said Plum with confidence.

It was only a white lie. The fact was Plum rented to whoever had the money and secured the deal. It had proved troublesome only once in the past, when there was a murder, but that was old news.

"You screen them?" asked Barbie.

"Of course," said Plum. "We have only the most exclusive clientele."

"Except for the ones who commit murder," came a masculine voice behind Plum.

She didn't even have to turn around to see who had spoken. She had a visceral reaction where her skin instantly began to crawl. Plum could recognize that reptilian voice anywhere: it belonged to her nemesis and former business colleague, Damián Rodriguez. They had worked together briefly at Jonathan Mayhew Caribbean Escapes, and it had not gone well at all.

"Sorry to interrupt," said Damián. "But I believe I have come at the perfect time."

Plum watched as Barbie assessed Damián. Although a scoundrel, he was undeniably handsome with thick, wavy dark hair and movie-star looks. Women swooned over him, which irritated Plum to no end. Chloe resumed barking and wriggled out of Barbie's clutch, then scurried down to pounce on Damián. Plum turned around in time to see the poodle lock her fangs into his ankle. He inadvertently grimaced in pain, and Plum smiled with delight.

"Chloe, Chloe, come here, you naughty dog," commanded Barbie, snapping her plump bejeweled fingers with their dark-red lacquered nails.

Chloe ignored her mistress and continued to growl and yap around Damián's legs. He put on a frozen smile that Plum knew was insincere.

"It's really okay. She's a very good puppy, protecting her mommy like that," he cooed.

"She is a good puppy," agreed Barbie, rushing to collect her precious dog, whom she gathered in her arms. "Just scared of people."

"No worries, I love animals," said Damián. "I have two poodles myself."

Barbie's eyes lit up. "What a coincidence!"

"Or is it?" asked Damián, cocking his head to the side and putting on his most flirtatious expression. Plum had to hand it to him: he was very good at fluttering his thick eyelashes at any woman who could be useful to him.

"Damián, what are you doing here?" asked Plum.

He gave her a surprised look. "I have a meeting with this beautiful woman about renting out her villa."

Plum could see Barbie blush under her pancake makeup.

"Oh, Damián, I'm sorry, but our meeting is tomorrow," Barbie said apologetically.

"Tomorrow?" repeated Damián. "I had it down for today."

"No, it's tomorrow," said Barbie.

"I apologize. Of course, it would be my mistake, not yours. It must be subconscious—I was so very eager to make your acquaintance that I couldn't wait!"

That little liar, thought Plum.

Barbie turned to Plum. "I'm so embarrassed. You must understand I have to interview several rental agencies before we select the right one for our property."

"And undoubtedly you will select Jonathan Mayhew Caribbean Escapes. We have the most pristine reputation on the island. That's why we have been the number one villa broker agency for over twenty years," boasted Damián.

If Plum could have leapt out of her chair and strangled him, she would have.

"There is something to be said about that." Barbie nodded tentatively.

"Yes and no," said Plum quickly. "Often *old* agencies rest on their laurels and are no longer motivated to completely serve their clients. At my company, we are available day and night to make sure you're comfortable with our arrangement and not bothered with our renters. Your house will be returned to you in exactly the state it was left."

"Unless there is a dead person in your hot tub," added Damián, flashing his reptilian eyes at Plum.

"Yes, you just mentioned a dead person. What is all that about?" asked Barbie.

"It's not how it sounds," Plum insisted, even though it was. "When I worked at Jonathan Mayhew, a guest died on one of his properties."

"A property you were not supposed to rent out to him," snapped Damián.

"Damián, I don't like to blame the victim," said Plum in a patronizing tone. She didn't wait for him to respond and instead turned to Barbie. "And I don't want you to blame Jonathan Mayhew Caribbean Escapes for the fact a murder took place on one of their properties. I'm sure that won't happen again."

Barbie nodded then squirmed uncomfortably. "I'm not sure how to proceed, but I think it's best to meet with you separately, I don't want you to have to go head-to-head with your pitches to me."

"Of course not," agreed Damián. "Since I am already here today and am very eager to meet with you, perhaps I can wait inside until you are finished with Plum? I'm sure it won't be very long since she has had very little experience in real estate."

Plum shot him a vicious look.

"Sure, that's fine," said Barbie with slight hesitation. "I don't want you to have to come back. Let me just make sure my husband hasn't plopped himself in the den and you can sit there. I'll be right back."

Barbie put Chloe on the ground and walked inside, Chloe following her. Just after she disappeared, Chloe ran back and lunged toward Damián. He kicked the dog away.

"Damián! You can't do that," Plum reprimanded.

"I despise dogs. Filthy animals," he sneered.

"I thought you had two?" she asked.

"I will have whatever the client wants me to have. If that is a dog or a llama or a unicorn, I have no preference."

"You're shameless," she said. "And I am sure you were waiting outside all day to see if I was coming."

He threw his head back and laughed. "Plum, you must

understand you are no competition to me. Never have been and never will be. Please, do not flatter yourself."

"I never flatter myself regarding you," Plum retorted. "In fact, I don't even think of you at all."

Damián smiled and moved closer to her. She could smell the strong, overpowering scent of his aftershave. He slid his eyes greedily over her body from head to toe. "I think you do."

"That's absurd," she responded, in a voice less full of confidence than she would have preferred.

"Is it?" he asked, cocking his head to the side.

Barbie returned before Plum could respond. She fervently wished she had left him with some sassy and biting retort, but of course, her mind was a complete blank as to how to respond. She despised Damián now more than ever.

CHAPTER

12

"I WANT HIM DEAD!" PLUM roared, after slamming the front door to the town house. "If I could murder him with my own bare hands, I would."

Plum turned the corner from the foyer and saw Lucia was not alone, and in fact, sitting at Plum's desk, making himself all too comfortable, was Captain Diaz. Wonderful, she thought. Lucia gave her a shrug as if to say, *I didn't invite him here.*

"You're planning a murder, Senorita Lockhart?" he asked, his crocodile eyes gleaming. "I had hoped you would stay away from crime."

"Not literally," said Plum, frowning. "Although if something bad were to happen to Damián Rodriguez, I wouldn't shed a tear."

"What did that rattlesnake do now?" asked Lucia.

"Nothing I can't handle," insisted Plum. She noticed one of her folders was open on her desk, and Captain Diaz had evidently been perusing it. She walked over and snatched it away. "What can I do for you, Captain?"

He stretched back in Plum's office chair and gave her a wide smile. "I am pleased you phrased it that way because I do need you to do something for me."

"I'm sure you do," said Plum, walking over to the row of cabinets along the wall and shoving the file inside. "I know how incapable you are of doing your job."

"Very funny," he said. "I will let that pass. We both know I saved your life a few weeks ago…"

"Let's agree to disagree," said Plum.

"Captain, you cannot deny Plum has helped solve more than one murder in the short time she has lived on our island," chided Lucia.

"Maybe a bit," he admitted reluctantly before becoming serious. He leaned forward in the chair. "We were most fortunate Las Frutas is currently hosting a convention for the leading coroners around the world. They were more than happy to assist us and give a preliminary assessment of the cause of death for Lysette Nilsson."

"How fortuitous," said Plum.

"There are always so many conventions here," clucked Lucia. "Last week it was the NFL Equipment Managers convention. Next week, the Breast Implant Association of New Mexico."

"This time it was very useful," said the captain. "The coroners were more than happy to assist us. Normally an autopsy can take days or weeks. But they all set to work, and we were able to establish the parameters of Miss Nilsson's death."

"I thought it was fairly obvious that she drowned." Plum said.

"No. It is the case that she did not die from drowning," Captain Diaz remarked, shaking his head before giving a dramatic pause. His eyes slid from Lucia's horrified face to Plum's before he announced, "Lysette Nilsson had scratch marks on her arms as well as light bruising, as if someone grabbed her. Furthermore, she was hit on the back of the head with a blunt object—a fatal blow. She did not drown. There was no water in her lungs. She was dead before she hit the water."

"What does that mean?" asked Plum.

"We have every reason to believe she was murdered," he said solemnly.

"Murdered," repeated Lucia, who quickly made the sign of the cross. "*Díos mío.*"

"Yes," confirmed Captain Diaz. "Unfortunately, when we alerted her next of kin, they said she had told them that if anything were to happen to her, it was not an accident. She felt she was in danger."

Plum let his words hang in the air. Finally, she cleared her throat. "Did she tell her next of kin who she suspected?"

"She mentioned a name, but the connection was bad, so they didn't hear it."

"Terrible," murmured Lucia.

"What about now? Do you have a suspect?"

"We have many suspects, and they are all aboard the yacht known as *Jackpot*," he said.

Plum quickly thought of Ellen and her frantic phone call the night of the murder. Did she know something?

"Your expression is revealing," said Captain Diaz. "Do you have your suspicions about someone?"

"No," lied Plum hastily. "I don't."

He gave her a skeptical look. "As you can imagine, I will need you to start from the beginning and tell me everything you witnessed when you were aboard the *Jackpot*."

"I don't know how that will help," protested Plum.

"If I am to conduct a proper investigation, it is necessary for me to receive all the cooperation available to me," he said sternly.

"Fine," she said saucily. "Then please get out of my chair."

It was afternoon when Captain Diaz had finished questioning Plum. He had a flair for redundancy, therefore she had been forced to reiterate her observations more than once. She allowed Lucia to field all the work calls, but when Juan Kevin called, Plum insisted on pausing the interrogation to chat with him. They arranged to meet for dinner at Coconuts, the restaurant on the resort's beach, at 7:00 p.m.

After all the interrogation, Plum was tired.

"Can we be done, please?" she asked, exhaustion creeping in her voice. "I've told you everything I can remember down to the color of the powder room."

Captain Diaz slowly flipped his notebook closed. "We're finished for now. But prepare to receive more outreach from me. This case is only beginning."

"I know, I know, and you need my help to solve it."

He rose and shook his head. "We do not need your help to solve it. The Paraison police is the best force in the world. We would never ask for assistance from Plum Lockhart."

The following morning Captain Diaz had to eat his words.

For the second time that week, Plum was roused from her blissful sleep alongside Juan Kevin. The baby-faced officer yet again appeared at her door and demanded she accompany him. This time it was to the police headquarters, which was located equidistant between Las Frutas and Estrella, the neighboring town where Plum procured her groceries. Because she was in somewhat of a good mood from the previous evening, Plum agreed to follow him without much of a fuss but told him in no uncertain terms that she would only spare an hour and insisted on showering before she departed.

After she bathed and dressed, Juan Kevin handed her a cup of coffee in a to-go mug and placed a long, languid kiss on her lips when she walked out the door. That gave her a spring in her step and temporarily placated her. She was on a high if she were honest. The dinner at Coconuts could not have been more romantic. The temperature was balmy, the sunset was gorgeous, and the food was delicious. It was actually so perfect that it felt like the climax of a romantic comedy, where the couple finally gets together and has an evening to remember. She hoped she would not mess it up.

The police headquarters was a stucco building located on a dusty, unkempt lot with a burnt front lawn in dire need of irrigation. Listless stumpy trees dotted the property, and patches of bushes were scattered over the yard with no particular order. The interior was no great shakes either—it was stuffy, lacked air-conditioning, and was permeated with the stench of body odor.

"What's this all about?" Plum asked when she sat across from Captain Diaz. "I thought you had finished questioning me yesterday. I have had no further contact with anyone aboard the yacht and therefore have zero to add."

"Senorita Lockhart, I first want to thank you for coming," said Captain Diaz with a friendly smile that hung awkwardly on his face.

Plum was immediately suspicious. "Okay, what's going on?" She sat back in her uncomfortable wooden chair and folded her arms.

Captain Diaz's face instantly became serious. "It appears I do need your help after all."

"Oh?" She was looking forward to watching him grovel.

He shifted uncomfortably. "I do not like to involve civilians in police matters, but this time I have no choice. What do you know about turtles?"

"Turtles?" she repeated.

"Sí," he continued. "I am certain you most likely know nothing about turtles. You are a city woman, a New York City woman, and would not understand turtles. But in Paraiso—"

"In Paraiso you have over four species of turtles. The loggerhead, the green sea turtle, the hawksbill, and the leatherback. All endangered."

He stared at her with astonishment, his mouth agape. He

cleared his throat. "I was not aware you took an interest in our wildlife."

"Of course, I've always had an interest in wildlife, particularly turtles," she said smugly.

It was not true. Plum did theoretically love animals and volunteered at shelters, but it was Juan Kevin who alerted her about the importance of turtles on Paraiso and explained all about their history. Since then, any time an article on turtles popped up, she had read it and had become somewhat of an expert on the topic. Not to mention that she was now particularly careful at turtle crossings.

Captain Diaz shook his head with bewilderment before continuing. "Then I would like to show you something."

He snapped on his ancient computer and moved it to an angle where Plum could see the screen. It was an infrared view of a bearing wall. There were many on Paraiso, separating the Caribbean Sea from the land. The image was taken at night, and although it was shadowy and low light, the quality was good. The camera was positioned toward the water and depicted the waves slapping against the wall.

"If you will be patient, you will see what I am referring to," Captain Diaz said pedantically.

"I am patient," insisted Plum with impatience.

After a few moments, a small boat appeared. There were two figures inside, both wearing dark pants and shirts and baseball hats. Neither faced the camera, but they both pulled their boat along the wall and out of the frame.

"Am I supposed to know who they are and what they're doing?" asked Plum.

"Be patient," Captain Diaz reminded her. "*Tranquila.*"

Plum rolled her eyes. How many times had people told her to be *tranquila* since she'd arrived on Paraiso?

He pressed a button, and the screen shifted to another angle from a farther distance. The two figures had pulled the boat to shore and were now walking along the beach. They had their backs to the camera once again. Under the cover of darkness, they began bending down. Plum leaned closer and scrutinized. They were excavating turtle nests. Plum could see their hands removing clutches of eggs and placing them into slings they wore over their shoulders.

"They're poaching leatherback turtle eggs," Plum exclaimed with horror. "That's terrible."

Captain Diaz nodded. "Unethical, illegal, immoral."

The screen went dark.

"Do you know who they are?" asked Plum.

He shook his head. "No, but we do know something about them."

He pressed a button on the computer and returned to the first image of the boat. He zoomed in, and Plum noticed something she hadn't before. It said *Jackpot II*. She glanced up at him.

"Someone in the tender from Robert Campbell's yacht?" she asked.

He nodded. "Yes. We're not sure who."

"Can't you just get a warrant and go search?" she asked.

"We could. And perhaps we could find out who poached the turtle eggs. Or, once they see us coming, the criminal might dispose of any evidence before we can reach them. All they would have to do was throw the eggs overboard."

"Then what can you do?" asked Plum, irate. "They are decimating the turtle population. In twenty-five years when these turtles are supposed to hatch, there will be nothing."

"*Sí*. It is a crime," said Captain Diaz. "And we believe there's another crime that took place on the *Jackpot*, which is the murder of Lysette Nilsson."

She paused before asking, "Are they related?"

"It is still difficult to ascertain," he said. "That's why I need you to go undercover on the *Jackpot*. You said you were invited as a guest. Now you can do some good."

"Me?" exclaimed Plum, her voice squeaky. "Why can't you just seize the yacht? Shake them all down?"

"I would love nothing more," he said. "But there are international maritime rules."

"What are those?"

He leaned back in his chair. "If a crime had been committed in port, Paraiso would have jurisdiction. That is true with the poaching, but we cannot be certain it is true of the murder. It is unclear where the boat was docked, and with their money, they could argue it was out at sea. Therefore, if a crime transpires in international waters, the flag state, meaning the country where the vessel is registered, has jurisdiction."

"And where is Robert's boat registered?" asked Plum.

"Turkey," said the captain.

"Is that a problem?"

"It can be," said the captain. "Of late they have been providing a safe haven for billionaire yachts and protecting them against any sort of international sanctions and interventions.

It requires a serious amount of paperwork, and we do not have the capacity on our small island of Paraiso."

"That's why you want me to do it," said Plum.

"It is your duty as a Paraison," insisted Captain Diaz.

Plum was about to protest but stopped abruptly. She was flattered that he had referred to her as a local. She imagined that was difficult for him. To acknowledge she was now a tried-and-true Paraison. It had a nice ring to it. And the truth of the matter was that she was in the unique position to assist the police and prevent future crimes. She slowly nodded.

"Okay, I'll do it," she agreed.

He nodded his approval. "Very good."

"I hope I don't get killed," said Plum.

Captain Diaz's expression did not indicate that he cared either way. But he said, "You will need to be on guard. Now, I do know the captain of the *Jackpot*, and I have contacted him. He is a man named Dave Sanders. He used to live on Paraiso."

"Okay, so he's an ally?" asked Plum hopefully.

Captain Diaz emitted a deep breath. "I do not think he is a murderer."

"Oh great," she said sarcastically.

"I confess I am not certain of his moral character. When he lived on Paraiso, he was accused of stealing crabs from the nets of fishermen. Nothing was proven; however, he lived here under a cloud of suspicion. I would not exclude him from the list of potential turtle-egg thieves."

"But he may have escalated to murder," insisted Plum. "They say criminals start small and then move on to bigger things."

He shook his head. "I would doubt that in this case," said Captain Diaz. "He never displayed any violence. And again, nothing was ever proven against him about the crabs. Therefore, I advise you to be wary, but don't worry too much about him."

"Okay," she said glancing down at the scarred table in front of her. She wondered how many criminals had sat in her seat across from the police officer. "It's not really reassuring."

"I'll let him know you are working with me, just as an added layer of caution. But I will warn him not to tell the others."

"Is that really smart? What if he is the killer?" asked Plum.

Captain Diaz hesitated. "It is not ideal, but I need you to have him as an accomplice so you can move freely about the boat. And if he knows you are looking for a killer, then he will not suspect you of investigating his possible turtle-egg poaching. It's essentially providing you with a cover story."

"Okay," conceded Plum.

After they discussed their plan, Plum rose to leave. As she headed to the door, she turned back to the captain.

"I never understood. Why do they poach the leatherbacks' eggs?" she asked.

"Some people believe it is an aphrodisiac," he said with gravity. "But they will have to get their kicks elsewhere."

Plum was on her way home when her cell phone rang.

"You little brat! Were you planning on hiding this from me? Did you purposely wait until I left?"

It was Gerald Hand, Plum's former work colleague at

Travel and Respite Magazine as well as her frequent guest on the island. Gerald and Plum had a love-hate relationship full of extreme highs and extreme lows.

"What is it now?" asked Plum.

"You're hanging out with Nachelle Brown? You know she's my favorite recording artist. I cannot believe you didn't immediately call me to come down!"

"You would have really flown down here to see her?" asked Plum with skepticism.

"Of course!" shrilled Gerald. "Leonard and I flew to Argentina for *one* night just to see her perform."

"That seems like a colossal waste of time," said Plum.

She could hear him sighing deeply on the other end of the phone. "You don't understand art at all. In fact, aren't you toneless?"

"I'm not," protested Plum.

"Well, you're a terrible dancer. No rhythm whatsoever. That goes hand in hand with being toneless."

Plum could concede she was not the best dancer, but she was certain she could carry a tune. That said, she had no time to debate him. "It was very impromptu; my friend is staying on a yacht with Nachelle's boyfriend..."

"Big Bobby Park Avenue?" he interrupted.

"No, someone named Robert Campbell," she corrected.

"Yeah, duh, that's Big Bobby. He was the *biggest* rapper ever. Please tell me you heard of him."

She actually had heard of Big Bobby, but she was stunned to realize he was Robert. Big Bobby had gold teeth and wore Knicks jerseys back in the day. Robert wore khakis and button-downs. "I didn't make the connection," she conceded.

"Of course, you wouldn't," sneered Gerald. "Celebrities are lost on you. That's why I should have been there. I could literally break down in tears at this missed opportunity."

"It wasn't—"

"When are you seeing her again?"

"I don't think I am," lied Plum. She did not want to fill Gerald in on her new mission.

Gerald muttered some gasps and then curses. "Okay. Well, here are your marching orders: you have to swear on your life that if you are going to see Nachelle again, you will call me right away so I can hop on the next flight down."

"No."

"Pinkie swear."

"Absolutely not."

"Plum, I will not take no for an answer!!"

He hung up before she could respond.

When Plum went home, she decided to google the guests on the yacht. It was vital that she be prepared and glean any information she might need on the suspects. It made her shudder to think of them like that.

After pouring herself a glass of wine and plopping down on her sofa, she opened her laptop. Plum started with Robert Campbell, the owner himself. She couldn't reconcile the fact he had been a very famous rapper. He seemed so far removed from that world. But he had won several Grammys, first as a performer and later as a producer, and was a renowned businessman. Obviously, he was doing very well, judging by the yacht, Plum thought.

There were dozens of pictures and articles on Nachelle, but Plum only scanned them. They were tedious fluff pieces about Nachelle's music and style as well as a few gossip items about past boyfriends, who all appeared to be celebrities. Nothing stood out as a particular red flag.

Plum did discover lots of party pictures of Harris Low at various international galas, where he was among luminaries and other bigwigs. Lots of bigwigs. In fact, it appeared as if he knew every famous person. But Plum leaned in and scrutinized the images. In every picture Harris was squeezed between the celebrities. Almost as if he had interjected himself into the pictures and wasn't actually accompanying those people. Maybe she was overanalyzing.

Plum did uncover a long article in a British magazine about Suki. She was pictured with her husband, Gunther Von Steefel. It was about the castle they lived in outside of Munich. The pictures were of cavernous rooms full of ancestral antiques and walls clad with dark tapestries and coats of armor. The article detailed the family history, and there was a small picture of Gunther with Suki, who was resplendent in a long satin ball gown. Neither was smiling. Once again proving money did not buy happiness.

Plum found nothing on Lysette. She typed her name various ways, but it came up empty. Maybe there was some sort of filter that didn't reveal anything because she was European? Could that be it? What had she wanted to talk to Plum about? Plum wished she had stopped and listened. It was too late to save Lysette, but perhaps she could find justice for her.

CHAPTER

13

THE WIND WAS BLOWING IN Plum's hair, and mist from the crystal-clear turquoise water splashed her face as she approached the *Jackpot*. She was nervous this time, undoubtedly because her reason for being there was enveloped in deception. Plum had told Ellen that she would love to accompany them because things had not worked out with Juan Kevin and she needed a quick escape, but things couldn't be further from the truth.

When she had informed Juan Kevin she was leaving that morning, he was less than thrilled. He quickly headed over to her town house to try and dissuade her.

"This is too dangerous," he insisted. "I think it's unprofessional that Captain Diaz even asked you to go on the boat when there's a murderer on the loose."

Plum was buried in her closet. She then came out with several hangers full of gowns, which she put down on her bed next to her open suitcase. "I'll be fine," she said.

Juan Kevin scanned the pile of clothes on her bed. "How long are you planning on going for?"

"I have no idea…but it's a pretty fancy crew, and people seem to dress for every occasion from sitting on the deck to having tea," she said. "Which reminds me: I should bring a few hats."

Juan Kevin shook his head. He walked over to Plum and placed his hands on her shoulders. "I am anxious. I don't want anything to happen to you."

She looked deep in his eyes and saw his concern. "I'll be okay, don't worry. Captain Diaz said he's in touch with the yacht's captain, Dave Landers. Apparently, he used to dock here years ago, and they're friendly. He knows I'm undercover, and he'll look out for me."

Juan Kevin sighed deeply and dropped his hands. "I remember Dave Landers. He's not a bad guy…."

"See?" said Plum. She tossed a pair of shoes into her suitcase.

"But that doesn't mean he can keep you safe," insisted Juan Kevin. "You must promise me you won't do anything foolish or go out of your way to place yourself in danger. You do not owe it to anyone to solve this crime. I don't want you to be the next victim."

She glanced at him and saw his rueful smile. "I won't be."

She decided it was best to keep the information about Dave's possible crab theft from Juan Kevin. Maybe he knew anyway and had dismissed it. But before she could say anything else, Juan Kevin clasped her in his arms, leaned her back, and kissed her fiercely.

"You make it hard to leave," Plum said when they disentangled. Her heart was beating fast, and she felt weak in the knees. That was some kiss.

He gave her a piercing look. "I want you to know what you're missing so you come back to me quickly."

"I will," she promised.

"I would like you to take this with you on your trip."

He reached into his pocket. For one thrilling minute, Plum thought he might propose. Was he about to pull out a little velvet box with an engagement ring? Was this a whirlwind romance? But she was wrong.

"Those look like prescription pills," she said. Was it possible that she felt relief, disappointment, and confusion at the same time?

"It is," he said. "And I don't like giving you pills that aren't prescribed to you. In fact, it's illegal. But it's Valium."

"Oh, you want me to take one if I get stressed about all this investigating?" asked Plum, taking the bottle in her hand.

"Quite the opposite," said Juan Kevin. "I know you can handle anything. But in case you need to subdue someone—and I don't advocate drugging anyone—but if you discover—*when* you discover—who the murderer is, if you need to sedate them, you can use this."

"Thank you." She wondered if she should be as concerned as Juan Kevin appeared. Was she being totally reckless?

"Welcome back," said Robert Campbell when Plum entered the library with Ellen. He rose from the sofa where he was ensconced reading the newspaper and rose to give her a double kiss. "I am so pleased you decided to join us."

"Thank you for having me," said Plum.

"Yes, thanks so much Robert," added Ellen. "I'm so psyched to have Plum on board."

"Undoubtedly," said Robert before addressing Plum. "Have you been to Jolly Island before?"

Plum shook her head. "It's been on my bucket list since it opened to the public."

"It's the most exclusive boutique hotel in the world," purred Ellen. "I can't wait."

"It is beautiful," concurred Robert. "I was fortunate to have been a guest there several years ago, before Lord Rittinger opened his manor to the public. His daughter now runs it. It's one of the most magical properties in the tropics, and I don't say that lightly."

"Gorgeous," said Ellen.

"You've been there?" asked Plum.

"No," said Ellen. "But I've heard."

"We should be setting sail shortly, Plum," said Robert. "It's a fine day for it."

"I'm really looking forward to it. I haven't been yachting since Croatia a few years ago. I miss it," said Plum, before deciding to improvise. "Actually, I had been fascinated by the boating world. I was writing an article about yachting before my magazine folded, and it really piqued my interest. I wonder if at some point I could chat with your captain about it?"

Robert nodded. "Sure. I will make Captain Dave available to you."

"Thank you."

Ellen took Plum by the arm and led her away. They walked down the corridor toward a series of staterooms.

"Is everything okay?" asked Plum, her voice full of concern.

Ellen squeezed her arm and held it tightly. "I'm sorry things didn't work out with the man you went on a date with."

Plum swallowed. It didn't feel good to lie to one of her oldest friends, but she couldn't confide her true reasons for being on the boat without putting herself and Ellen in danger.

"It's fine." Plum shrugged. "There are so many fish in the sea."

"That's true," said Ellen without conviction. "But remember that newer, younger, and hotter fish are born every day, which makes it difficult for aging fish like us. You have to do everything you can to hold on to the man you love and your dignity."

Plum was astonished by the statement. Did Ellen really think that? How horrible to have such low self-esteem. If a man went for a hotter, younger version of Plum, then that woman could have him! Plum was about to respond when they stopped at an open door to a bedroom. There the staffer was situating Plum's suitcase on a stand.

"Hello, Miss Lockhart," said the stewardess with a slight curtsy when they entered. She had a pleasant face and a sweet Irish lilt. "My name is Saoirse." She pronounced it *sur-sha*.

"What a pretty name," Plum remarked.

"Thank you," Saoirse said. "This will be your bedroom. I was placing your things. Please let me know if there is anything else I can assist you with."

"Thank you, Saoirse," said Plum. She glanced around the elegant stateroom. The decor featured natural colors—taupe curtains, white and gray sheets on the queen-size bed, and beige wood. The forward bulkhead concealed a large TV, and there was a floor-to-ceiling picture window as well as mirrored doors that led to the bathroom. A plush pearl-colored wall-to-wall carpet covered the floor. "This is beautiful."

"Isn't it fabulous?" agreed Ellen. She plopped down in a linen chair. "It's all done by that famous French designer. I forget his name. Robert sources from only the best in the world. Everything is top-notch. We were actually in this room at one point. As were Suki and Gunther. We all did a bit of musical chairs. Joel prefers to be on the starboard side of the boat, so we switched. Then, when Gunther left, Suki insisted on moving down the hall for some reason. I think even Robert slept here one night when Nachelle accidentally locked him out of their cabin."

"Well, it's a beautiful room. I'm sure I'll be very happy here."

"Is there anything else?" asked Saoirse, who had finished fluffing the pillows.

"That's all, thanks, Saoirse," said Plum.

Saoirse took her leave, and Plum waited until the door was firmly closed before she turned to Ellen and spoke.

"What is going on?" asked Plum. "First you left me those

messages, and then Lysette died… What happened? And are you okay?"

Ellen took a deep breath as if about to say something and then stopped and released the air in her lungs. Then, once again, she appeared about to speak before stopping herself. Plum waited. It was an interrogation trick she had learned. Wait for people to speak, and don't offer platitudes or suggestions to direct the questioning. People want to talk; she just had to be patient.

"I'm worried about Joel…" Ellen said reluctantly.

Plum nodded but remained silent. She knew this was the only way Ellen would continue, and she was correct.

"I think…well, I think he's in trouble," said Ellen, her eyes darting all around the room and looking at everything except Plum.

"How so?"

"I think…he's a bit out of his league," said Ellen.

When they had descended into silence for a solid minute and it became evident Ellen would need some prompting, Plum finally spoke again.

"What kind of trouble?" asked Plum.

"I think it has something to do with a girl," said Ellen, who was nervously sliding her wedding band up and down her ring finger. "Look, Plum, you're not married, so you have no idea… It can be difficult. It's not like it is in the movies, not a complete happily ever after. Don't get me wrong: I love Joel, and I know he loves me. But you know, he has his needs. And some of them are pretty demanding, and I don't really have the time or want to fulfill them…"

She trailed off but glanced up at Plum as if imploring her to understand.

"I'm not following," said Plum bluntly.

"I mean, he's busy and I'm busy. I have the kids, I have Pilates, I have my committees and my tennis game and yoga. Not to mention that I need to look amazing all the time, so there is my daily blowout, consultation with my stylist and makeup artist, endless shopping, and I need to go out every night…"

"Okay," said Plum. It was a lifestyle she couldn't imagine. She, of course, had previously had a demanding job, but she smugly felt as if she could handle everything (she forgot she had zero personal life at the time).

"Anyway, I know Joel has his…friendships," said Ellen with a shrug. "When I first realized that was the case, I wanted to blow my brains out. I mean, remember all those times we discussed happily ever after? Marriage like a fairy tale?"

"I do," said Plum. She recalled one particular late night with Ellen when they stayed up and watched the sunrise over Central Park and talked about how they would be badass career women one day. Although, come to think of it, it was really more Plum rhapsodizing about how she would become a badass career woman. If memory served, Ellen wanted to become a corporate wife.

"Well, it's not really black-and-white," confessed Ellen, shifting in her seat. She smoothed down the zebra caftan she wore over her bathing suit. "You see, I can't be it all for Joel…and I don't want to be it all for him. It's too much. So he has his friends, and you know, they take care of his needs. And it's all unspoken and no harm done. Except on this trip...."

Her voice faded. Plum, who was sitting on the edge of the bed, leaned toward her. "What happened on this trip?"

"I think he developed more than just a passing fancy. I think he developed genuine affection for someone. And for the first time, I feel like my marriage is in jeopardy."

"Lysette?" Plum said with a knowing voice.

Ellen's face became confused. "What? Who?"

"The girl who died? Who worked here?" asked Plum.

Ellen's eyes shifted back and forth, and then she shook her head and said incredulously, "No. The maid? Please, Plum, who do you think Joel is? He's president of a major film studio. One of the biggest in the world. He's not going to fall for some low-level servant on a boat."

She said it so righteously that Plum half believed her. "I thought..." Plum stopped herself. She didn't want to say she had seen Joel grope Lysette. Or that she had any suspicions whatsoever.

"You thought what?" asked Ellen, her tone more aggressive than previously.

"No, nothing. My mistake. I suppose she's just on my mind..."

"Well, you thought wrong," said Ellen indignantly. "I was not referring to the hired help. I think Joel has something going on with India Collins. That slutty little starlet."

"Oh, that makes sense," said Plum, remembering how when she first arrived, Joel had been sitting close to the actress.

"Why does it make sense?" asked Ellen.

Plum quickly rebounded. "No, I mean, just because you said he's discriminating."

Ellen shrugged. "Yes. Joel has champagne tastes. And look, normally this wouldn't bother me. Joel has been a naughty boy, but I always forgive him. Because I know at the end of the day, he is mine, and his love and devotion to me are unwavering. But this time I feel a shift. I think India is more invested than his other girls. They just used him as stepping-stone. But I get a calculated vibe from her. I first met her at a premiere in LA, and she was very familiar with Joel. Next thing I knew, she had finagled an invitation on this trip. And...well, I have to confess something."

"What?"

"The other night when I thought my necklace was stolen? I swear I saw India wearing it. That's what set me off. But when I confronted her, both Joel and India said I was crazy. They said lots of people have diamond necklaces. But this one looked very similar to mine. Very. And how could India afford such a thing?"

"That's horrible."

"Yes, then they obviously saw how upset I was and later replaced it."

Ellen became very distraught. Plum rose from the bed and went over to awkwardly put an arm around her friend. She was not really the maternal touchy-feely type, so she clumsily patted Ellen's back. Ellen squished up her face in a way that Plum knew was her best effort not to cry.

"But why do you think Joel is in trouble?" asked Plum.

Ellen took another deep breath and then looked at her friend. "This girl has some sort of hold on him, and Joel is not someone who's toyed with. I think he's attracted to her for sure, but I get the sense that he's wary of her. When I try and bring it up, he tells me I'm paranoid and to shut up. But my concern is...well, that she has something on him. It has to be bad if he's giving her my jewelry. I woke up the other night and he was sitting on the window seat, staring out at the water. He looked tense and distracted. This is not the Joel I know. What's wrong? Why is he so stressed?"

Plum had no idea, but she wondered if Ellen was only partially correct. Perhaps Joel was distracted and tense because of Lysette and not India Collins. Did he have something to do with her death?

"Don't worry," consoled Plum. "It may just seem exacerbated because you're in close quarters."

"Possibly. But I need your help, Plum," urged Ellen. "I need you to keep an eye on Joel and India. Make sure they don't get too cozy. Do everything you can to keep them from each other."

It was a tall order. "I'll do my best," offered Plum.

"Thank you."

They were interrupted by a loud clanging, followed by a noise that sounded like a pack of elephants groaning. The boat rattled and vibrated.

"What's that?" asked Plum with concern.

"They're lifting the anchor," Ellen replied. "We're setting sail."

"Good grief, it's a hideous noise."

"Yes," agreed Ellen. "But at least we're leaving in the daytime. When they pull the anchor at night, I want to jump out of my skin."

"I don't blame you," said Plum, wondering what other horrors awaited her.

CHAPTER

14

AFTER ELLEN LEFT, SAOIRSE KNOCKED on Plum's door and told her Captain Dave was available and she would escort Plum to him. This gave her a quick chance to interrogate Saoirse about Lysette.

"I'm sorry for the loss of your colleague," said Plum as she walked behind Saoirse along the carpeted corridor.

Plum could see Saoirse's back slightly stiffen, but then the stewardess shrugged in a jerky, forced motion.

"Yes, it's quite sad," said Saoirse evenly.

"I would imagine you two were close," said Plum.

Saoirse quickly glanced back at Plum, then returned her gaze forward, jutting out her jaw in a determined manner. "We shared a bunk. I hadn't worked with her before. I only knew her for a few weeks."

"Oh," said Plum, somewhat disappointed. She had hoped they had been confidants and best friends. "Was she happy with her job?" asked Plum.

"Of course," said Saoirse quickly, in a rehearsed manner. "This is a wonderful place to work."

Plum knew Saoirse was giving her the party line, but she supposed it would not be good form for Saoirse to start criticizing her employment and the yacht. While Plum approved of the girl's discretion, she had to break it down.

"Saoirse," Plum said sternly and abruptly stopped walking. When Saoirse realized Plum was no longer keeping pace with her, she turned around and retraced her steps. "Yes?"

"What do you think happened to Lysette?" asked Plum.

"They said she fell off the boat—" began Saoirse.

"That's what they say, but you don't believe that, and I don't believe that."

Saoirse was very still. Then she sighed deeply. "No," she whispered.

"Then tell me what you know," demanded Plum.

Saoirse's eyes darted left and right, and she hesitated. Ultimately, she emitted another long sigh and spoke in a whisper.

"Everything was lovely in the beginning," she began. "The team was getting along quite well, really. I thought it would be a grand trip and Lysette and I would have a splendid time."

"And then?"

"And then the guests started arriving. At first it was all bonny. But it's tight quarters, and we're all thrust together servicing demanding clients. It can cause tension. I don't think Lysette was really cut out for this job."

"Why's that?" asked Plum.

"I think she had, I hate to speak ill of the dead, but

delusions of grandeur, as they say. I think she wanted to be rich and famous and had aspirations. Service didn't suit her."

Plum nodded. She knew only too well that the service industry was demanding. And she could only imagine how it was when you were stuck with entitled clients. "I can see how this crowd would be tough."

"Yes, but at first I think she thought it was an opportunity. Maybe she'd get discovered or something. It really didn't become a problem for Lysette until he arrived…"

"Who?" pressed Plum, leaning closer.

"Gunther Von Steefel," whispered Saoirse.

"He was here?" asked Plum.

"Yes," said Saoirse, her voice barely audible.

"How did Lysette know Gunther Von Steefel?" asked Plum.

Saoirse shrugged. "I'm not completely certain. I never could find out. But it was obvious they knew each other."

"How?"

"He and his wife had boarded the yacht and were chatting with Mr. Campbell and the others. I brought him a cocktail, and he had settled nicely. They were all sitting on the deck. He was telling a story the guests were finding amusing, and then he abruptly stopped. Frozen, as if transfixed. Everyone noticed it. He had gone completely white. And he was staring, his mouth agape. And we all looked in the direction he was staring at, and it was Lysette. And she also went quite white. As if she had seen a ghost. Likewise for him. It was so uncomfortable."

"And what did his wife do?"

"She didn't look happy either. She kept glancing between him and Lysette, and then Mrs. Von Steefel got an angry look on her face. You know, like she was quite put out. She barked at her husband to continue talking. So he finished up his story, but he was, you know, deflated. Not really enthusiastic anymore. Rushed the ending. Then they both quickly went to their room."

"And what happened after that?"

"I didn't see that they had much interaction. Lysette did her duties, and he avoided looking at her. I could sense some tension, but when I asked Lysette, she said I was imagining it."

"Did she say anything else about him?" asked Plum.

"Not so much about him, but she mentioned she was not very keen on Mrs. Von Steefel, although those are not the words she used," confided Saoirse.

"And you never figured out how she knew them?" asked Plum.

Saoirse's expression was strained. "Quite honestly, ma'am, I didn't really want to know. I like to do my job and get on with it. I don't want to hear grievances. I find it very distracting. I think perhaps if I had pressed, Lysette might have said why she didn't like them, but it wasn't my concern. We have too much to do. And then, when Mr. Von Steefel left, I thought it was the end of it."

"Do you think he killed her?" asked Plum.

"So you do think she was killed?" asked Saoirse, her hand to her throat.

"No, I have no idea," said Plum quickly. "But you said you were suspicious."

"I don't know what to think." Saoirse sighed. "It seems odd that she would have fallen off the boat. She was experienced. But where's the motive? Lastly, I don't see how Mr. Von Steefel could have done it. He had already left the boat by then. Departed in Villalba."

"That's right," said Plum. "Was it a planned departure?"

"I am not privy to the guests' personal arrangements."

"But?" prompted Plum.

"But I don't think so," Saoirse confessed. "I heard him say he had business, and he left. But I thought he left because of Lysette."

"How did Suki react to his leaving?"

"His wife didn't seem very happy. That said, she's not the nicest anyway, so it's unclear if she's ever happy. You know the sort."

Plum nodded. "I do, unfortunately."

"I heard the Von Steefels having a row at one point, before he left, but I made myself scarce," said Saoirse. "Couldn't make out what they said, and I might not have thought much of it, except he left right after. I did see Mrs. Von Steefel roll her eyes when she told the guests he was off. But she seems to have kept herself busy with Mr. Campbell."

She gave Plum a knowing look. So Plum wasn't the only one who thought Suki was making a play for their host. Was that the reason Suki's husband had left? Or was it Lysette?

"I appreciate you telling me all this," Plum said.

"I'm not normally a blabbermouth, but I feel comfortable telling you," Saoirse confided. "Because she trusted you."

"Who trusted me?"

Saoirse glanced up at her with surprise. "Lysette."

"Why did she trust me? How do you know?"

Saoirse appeared confused. "When you arrived on the boat, she told me that she thought perhaps you were undercover."

"Me?" Plum exclaimed, immediately flustered. "Undercover? What? That's absurd."

She was instantly paranoid. Was Lysette a psychic? Or did Saoirse know she was currently on the yacht under false pretenses—to solve Lysette's murder?

"Well, you talked about solving those crimes," explained Saoirse. "And you were an obvious outsider, not part of this fancy group. More working class like, you know."

Gee, thanks, Plum wanted to say. Was it that obvious she didn't attend fancy boarding schools like India or grow up with a staff like Harris?

"Don't take offense now. It's a good thing," Saoirse said when she saw the look on Plum's face. "I just meant to say Lysette thought she could trust you. She said you were a 'straight arrow.' Those were her words."

They heard movement at the other end of the dark corridor. They both waited, their breaths heavy. Finally, Plum and Saoirse ceased their tête-à-tête and continued walking in silence until they reached an entrance.

"Here we are," said Saoirse. She jerked her head to indicate that Plum should enter. "You can go up there to the helm."

After ascending a sleek staircase in the front of the yacht, Plum found herself at the captain's deck. There were wraparound windows affording a panoramic view of the

Caribbean. The walls were blond wood, the plush chairs a cream leather, and the carpet a dark red.

"Heya, you must be Plum. I'm Captain Dave," said the man at the wheel in a broad Australian accent.

"Nice to meet you," said Plum, sizing up the captain.

He appeared to be in his early sixties, with closely cropped powdery-white hair and a neat white beard. He was fit and in obvious good shape, and his skin was tanned, with a smattering of broken blood vessels covering his nose. He wore aviator sunglasses, a white captain's shirt with the gold lapels, white pants, and white moccasins. A giant platinum watch adorned his wrist, and a thick gold wedding band circled his ring finger.

"Welcome aboard. This here is my first officer, Jomer Gandela," he said, motioning to the man next to him.

Jomer was Filipino with dark hair, large dark eyes, and a slight build. He also wore a white uniform and looked to be in his midthirties. Plum exchanged pleasantries with him before Dave asked him to get something and Jomer took his leave.

"This is very high tech," said Plum, motioning to the elaborate equipment on the dashboard of the boat.

Captain Dave laughed, a booming sound that echoed off the walls. "Yes, this is a big ship we're driving. Not to mention expensive. Need more than just a wheel."

"That looks like a joystick for a video game," said Plum, pointing to the dashboard.

"I suppose it does," agreed Captain Dave. "But it isn't." Then he launched into a mini tour of all the equipment and gadgets and explained their purpose.

Plum listened with interest until the captain wrapped up his explanation. "But you're not here to talk about yachts," he said, his tone now serious. "Captain Diaz informed me that you're here to investigate Lysette's death. I think it's absurd. Sounds like you got a bunch of bored coroners on that island all trying to show they're worth their grain of salt. I don't know how they made the leap to murder. It was an accident."

"But it is strange that she fell overboard. The railings are quite high," said Plum.

"She might have been down by the hot tub. It was her responsibility to clean that area. Make sure the speaker was turned off. Sometimes the stewardesses take down the railing to clean under. She could have done that and slipped and fell."

"Would she really do that in the middle of the night?"

"If she'd forgotten to do it earlier, yes. The crew has to perform many tasks, so she was probably busy that day."

"Do you have cameras?" asked Plum. "Any security?"

He nodded. "Most yachts have some type of security system to enhance safety, security, and vessel operations," he explained. "We don't put them in the guest rooms. It wouldn't go over with the caliber of guests Mr. Campbell has on board."

He walked to the wall next to the staircase and opened a panel. Inside were several screens angled at various parts of the yacht, including the staterooms, kitchen and lower deck hallways, and bunk rooms as well as the outside decks. Plum could see Nachelle suntanning on the front deck while Robert read the newspaper next to her.

The chef was in the kitchen preparing dinner. Harris was in what looked like an office, sitting at a desk and reading a document.

"There is an infrared camera that catches movement between all the floors including the crew quarters and the upper floors, right there," he said, indicating a screen on the right side of the panel. It showed an empty carpeted hallway with a narrow staircase. There was currently activity.

An idea occurred to Plum. "Do you record the footage?" she asked excitedly. "Maybe we can see what Lysette was doing."

He shook his head. "No."

Plum was instantly deflated. "Were you on duty that night? Do you remember seeing anything?"

"No, it was first officer, Jomer. But he told me he didn't see anything."

Plum made a note to question Jomer. "Shouldn't he be watching this all night?"

"He has other responsibilities."

"Is it possible someone—an intruder—could have gotten on the yacht?" asked Plum, changing tack.

"You mean snuck on board?" asked Captain Dave.

"Yes," said Plum.

"I'm sure Jomer would have heard or seen on the monitor if a boat approached. We were docked far out from shore, so that would be the only way someone could approach. Not to mention we turn on the sensor alerts at night for the exterior decks, when we believe the guests have retired for the evening. A small ping is emitted if there's movement."

"So Jomer would have seen Lysette if she was cleaning by the hot tub."

"He might have, but he said he didn't. It's possible Officer Jomer was busy with something else at the time or was in the bathroom and didn't notice. You can become immune to the pings after a while because sometimes it's just a flag flapping in the wind. Also, sometimes we do have to shut off the sensor to give our guests privacy."

He said the last part while wiggling his eyebrows suggestively.

"Oh, you mean, in case there's an amorous couple?"

"Exactly." Captain Dave nodded. "Honestly, we really just do that on the camera aimed at the hot tub. Which is exactly where I think Lysette was."

He pointed toward the screen that illuminated the back deck. Plum leaned forward and, squinting, could see Joel and India were currently looking very cozy in the hot tub. She watched as Joel went over to a speaker and turned up the volume before swimming back to India and nestling in under her arm. Plum inwardly groaned on Ellen's behalf. Ellen's suspicions about their relationship looked more correct every minute.

"I can understand why you don't want to see what's going on there," agreed Plum, her eyes glued to the screen. "You might be subpoenaed to give a deposition in a divorce one day."

"It's happened," said Captain Dave. "And it is very messy."

"I can imagine," said Plum.

Plum slid into a chair and gazed out at the window, where the turquoise sea spread out in front of them and continued as far as the eye could see. It was a bright, shiny day, and glints of sunlight shimmered on the water. Captain Dave sat in the chair next to her.

"If you can speak candidly," said Plum, leaning closer to Captain Dave, "have you felt anything suspicious occurring on the boat?"

He shrugged. "Nothing more suspicious than usual. You'd be surprised at how people can behave on a yacht. It's like there are no rules."

"I believe it," remarked Plum as she conjured up the image of Joel and India in the jacuzzi. "And what about Lysette? What was your relationship with her?"

A strange expression quickly flashed across his face but disappeared just as swiftly. "What do you mean?"

"I mean were you glad you had her on your team? Was she a good worker or a troublemaker? What was your impression of her?"

He shrugged but didn't meet her eye. "She was fine. I barely knew the lass."

"And did you sense she was in any danger, or was there any sort of red flag about her?"

"No, she was all right. There was an issue with her and Mr. Low, but I think his accusation was unjust."

"What accusation?" asked Plum. No one had mentioned this to her.

"He claimed she had intercepted a parcel meant for him. But she said no such parcel had arrived."

Plum made a mental note to talk to Harris. Would a stolen parcel be a motive for murder?

"Did you believe her?"

"I did," he said.

"You felt she was honest?"

He smiled. "Sure. You have to understand, these stew—stewardesses or stewards—live a peripatetic life. The burn-out is high, and there is a lot of turnover. Some realize it's not the life for them. They don't like taking orders from rich people, or they get jealous, or they start to feel like the yacht is their home and people are mistreating it. Like others before her, I didn't see Lysette being someone in it for the long haul."

"And it turns out you were right," murmured Plum.

"But I can tell you one thing," said Captain Dave roughly. "If I did find out someone on this boat had anything to do with Lysette's death, I'd take matters into my own hands."

"And do what?" asked Plum.

He shook his head. "Make sure they paid for it."

CHAPTER

15

PLUM DESCENDED THE STAIRCASE AND was making her way along the hallway to the back deck to interrupt Joel and India's cozy conversation in the hot tub. She had no problem third wheeling it and disturbing whatever "pillow talk" they were engaging in. She owed that to her friend Ellen, who seemed somewhat cowed by her philandering husband. Plum was so engrossed in her mission that she almost didn't hear Harris Low call out to her.

"You look so serious! Come and join me for a cocktail!" he chirped. He was reclining on a lounge on the side deck, sucking on a straw attached to a fruity pink concoction. He wore a purple velour athletic suit, and his tiny, fat feet were stuffed into black velvet slippers embossed with some sort of gold crest. He greeted Plum with a broad smile.

"You must sit down next to me," he said, motioning toward the adjoining chaise. "I am having the most divine time, and you look absolutely glum, if you don't mind my saying. I will consider it my good deed for the day to cheer you up."

Plum realized this was a perfect opportunity to pump Harris about the parcel he claimed Lysette had taken. Plum collapsed into the chaise next to him.

"I suppose I could take a rest," Plum conceded as she stared out at the endless sea of blue that melted into the cloudless sky. The sun was warm and felt good, and she was grateful she had applied a thick coat of sunblock before she left her cabin.

"That's what we're here for," squawked Harris. "And you need a drink."

He lifted a small remote from the side table next to him and pressed the intercom button.

"Yes, sir," warbled a voice through the device.

"Please bring up another dragonfruit daiquiri to the side deck for Miss Lockhart. And make it strong."

"Yes, sir," came the reply.

Harris turned to her with a satisfied grin. "It's always cocktail hour here." He took a big sip of his drink. "You have to remember you need to enjoy yourself. Life is too short."

"Did you finish your work?" asked Plum.

"My work?" asked Harris with confusion. He placed the glass on the side table.

"Yes, weren't you just in an office?" as soon as Plum said it, she realized she shouldn't have opened her big mouth. She couldn't let anyone know she was conferring with Captain Dave and watching people on monitors.

Harris had a strange expression on his face, one of trepidation and suspicion. He paused a beat before laughing facetiously. "What, are you following me? Wow, Big Brother is watching!"

"No, of course, I'm not watching you. I thought I saw you go into what I assumed was an office."

He bristled and then said defensively, "Well if you must know, I did slip into Robert's office. I needed to borrow a pencil. I had to mark up a very important document to send to my estate attorneys, and I didn't have one."

"Who has pencils these days, right?"

"Exactly. Let's keep that between us, though. I don't think he likes anyone in his private chambers."

"Certainly," said Plum.

"We businessmen have to be discreet. I don't let anyone into my offices on my estates, so I can understand why he's touchy."

"What exactly do you do?"

Harris's countenance relaxed. "You probably don't know this, but I am very well known in Asia. I'm one of the hugest landowners."

"Oh?" asked Plum. "I didn't know that."

He nodded solemnly. "I thought I should let you know to save you from later embarrassment."

"Why would I be embarrassed?" Plum inquired.

"If people don't know who they're consorting with, they can get embarrassed. I'm not trying to be boastful, but it has happened that people were commenting on various buildings or resorts that I own and had no idea that I owned them. They were mortified. I just want to give you a heads-up."

Plum wasn't sure what to make of that, so she said, "Thank you."

"You're welcome."

"So that's what you do for work? Manage your properties?"

"I will admit I was born not only with a silver spoon in my mouth but an entire silver tea set. Actually, a gold tea set. I'm very fortunate. I used to be ashamed that I was born into privilege, but that's useless. I'm lucky to be rich. However, I've also made my own money as well. I do cryptocurrency."

"I don't understand cryptocurrency at all."

An excited Harris immediately launched into a detailed and somewhat mundane explanation of what that was. Plum tried to follow, but she was so confounded by the entire industry that she found herself nodding with a blank look on her face. Fortunately, Saoirse came with Plum's drink, and she was able to change the subject.

"What do you make of the death of Lysette?" asked Plum with faux casualness when Saoirse had left them.

"Who?" asked Harris.

"You know, the stewardess who was found dead?"

Harris took a large suck on his straw and dabbed his mouth with a napkin before answering, "I don't think about it at all."

"It is a bit jarring."

He tsk-tsked her. "Oh, darling, please don't fret about such matters. I, for one, can't worry about it," said Harris dismissively. "I employ huge staffs at all my villas and chalets, and I have learned it is imperative not to get involved with their personal lives. In fact, I much prefer how it works among my contemporaries in Asia. We don't even know the names of our employees. We just call them all *you*. Americans become very chummy with their staff, and that is an absolute no-no. Quite tasteless, really. Next thing you know, you are paying for their children's college tuitions, and everyone wants a handout."

"I never had that problem," said Plum, taking a sip of her drink. "I didn't even have a cleaning lady."

A sorrowful look came across Harris's face. "What a pity! Who cleaned your toilets?"

"Me," said Plum.

He bent his head back and roared with laughter until he saw Plum was serious. He froze. "Oh, you're not joking."

"Nope. And it wasn't toilets plural. I only had one."

"Darling, now you're pulling at my heart strings! I have an image of you with a scrub brush bent over a filthy latrine. I don't want to imagine that! It gives me goose bumps!"

"Yes, it was not a very glamorous childhood."

"It's a pity. It's so nice to have staff."

Plum realized they had gotten off track. She had to return the topic to the deceased. "Speaking of staff, do you suspect foul play in Lysette's case?" asked Plum.

"Foul play?" asked a befuddled Harris. "Gosh, no. The silly girl lost her balance and went *ker-plat* off the edge of the yacht. Tragic."

"You think?"

"I would venture she was sneaking a bit of liquor on the side. You know Robert stacks the boat with the best booze available. He even has a Pappy Van Winkle aged twenty-five years. He insisted I take a nip of it last night. It's absolutely irresistible."

Plum shifted her weight in her seat. She decided it was

time to press Harris. "I heard you had a bit of a kerfuffle with Lysette."

Harris paused before rolling his eyes. "Yes, I was expecting a very important package from my attorney. Robert had requested it for our deal to proceed. It was delivered to the yacht and signed for, but Lysette claimed she never laid eyes on it. Even went so far as to accuse my lawyer of lying! Can you imagine the audacity?"

"Maybe another staff member signed for it?" asked Plum.

He shook his head. "No. I asked them all, and that day Lysette was in charge of receiving mail. She managed to give Ms. Brown her package from her pharmacy and Joel some script he sent for, but she misplaced mine. And I know she received it. It was signed for by someone with the initials LN."

Plum frowned. That was a new variable. "Why do you think Lysette would want your legal papers?"

"I've no idea." He shrugged. "She probably wanted to blackmail me. But I'm not that idiotic to have anything important like my bank account passwords sent through the mail. It was all information for the deal I'm doing with Robert."

"What's the project if I may ask?" asked Plum.

"It is a fabulous investment opportunity in my homeland. I'm actually doing Robert a favor, including him in this transaction. I have many, many other friends interested."

"Then why don't you go to them?" asked Plum.

"I wanted to give Robert one last chance," said Harris. "He's a dear friend. But time is ticking. I'll give him until the end of the trip, and then I'll move on. My time is precious.

I can't even tell you how many things are demanding my immediate attention. I've just bought a cottage in the Hamptons, and I need to meet with my decorator and architect, and from there I will head to the city and finalize the deal with my other colleagues."

"Seems like everyone is buying a house in the Hamptons these days," lamented Plum. "Where is yours?"

His eyes brightened. "It's on the ocean, of course. I simply will not accept anything other than oceanfront. And it's in East Hampton. Next to David Gifford's house. It's very modest... I'll be tearing it down actually."

"Oh, really?" asked Plum.

He nodded and took a large sip of his drink, making a slurping noise as he drained it. "I know it seems silly to spend sixty-eight million on a teardown, but *c'est la vie!*" He giggled.

This rang a bell in Plum's head. Hadn't Lucia just read to her from *Chisme* that a Norwegian tycoon had bought the house in East Hampton next to David Gifford? Was Harris lying? Plum opened her mouth to say something but then thought better of it and snapped her jaw shut. She examined him closely. He certainly played the part of an eccentric zillionaire well. But maybe that was just it—he was "playing." And if he was pretending to be rich, what else was he pretending? Or more importantly, what else was he hiding?

"I think I'll head down to the hot tub," said Plum finally.

"You don't want to interrupt that," said Harris, a devilish grin on his face.

"What do you mean?"

"Oh, don't play dumb. You know Joel and India are in there rubbing each other's backs. It's beyond obvious they're fooling around. Poor Ellen. I can't tell if she's oblivious or so downtrodden that she pretends to not care."

"Joel's just a flirt. I'm sure it's nothing," lied Plum.

Harris threw his head back and laughed. "Oh, to be so naive. Of course, it's nothing, if you call having an affair right in front of your wife's face *nothing*. I tell you, that India has her eyes on the prize. She plays the ingenue quite well, but she is a shark."

By the time Plum made it to the hot tub, Joel and India were nowhere to be seen. The speaker was still blaring music, but there was no one around. It had been announced that lunch was at 1:00 p.m., so Plum decided to return to her room and quickly check her emails. She had several from Juan Kevin, who was concerned and asked her to call him.

"It's me," Plum whispered into the phone.

"Everything okay?" he asked, his voice full of apprehension.

"Yes, don't worry, I'm fine," she said.

"I don't want to worry, but you're on a boat with a potential murderer, and I don't want anything to happen to you."

"I'll be fine," she said. She held the phone on her ear and walked into the bathroom to refresh her sunblock and makeup. "Changing topics, I have a question. Do you know Arne Larsen?"

"Yes, he's Norwegian. Nice man," replied Juan Kevin.

"I heard he recently bought a house in East Hampton next to David Gifford. Any chance you can confirm that?"

Plum squeezed some sunblock in the palm of her hand and applied it to her cheeks and nose.

"I can ask... Is this related to Lysette?"

"It could be. Harris Low is claiming he bought the house. I just want to make sure," said Plum.

They talked for a few more minutes. The connection was tenuous, but she was so happy to hear his voice. She reached for her mascara, and as she did, she knocked over her makeup remover. The cap came undone, and the blue liquid began to spill out onto the counter.

"Oh shoot!" she said. "I can't multitask! I should probably go."

"Okay, but I want you to stay in touch. You're on my mind."

"I will," promised Plum. It was nice to be on someone's mind for once.

She hung up and began to wipe up the liquid with the washcloth. It was slowly trickling across the marble counter and snaking into the grouting. Plum slid all the cosmetics in its path to the side and lifted a decorative bird's nest coral that was on an acrylic base. As she did so, she noticed a piece of white paper tucked under it. Plum picked it up and glanced at it. It was a place card. On one side ROBERT was written with a fancy fountain pen in an elaborate script. She flipped it over. On the opposite side, someone had written a message in blue ballpoint pen:

I know about your wife.

Plum blinked with confusion. What did that mean? Robert had a wife? What about Nachelle—wasn't he dating her? Why was this card even here? This wasn't even Robert's room.

Plum flipped the card over again. Something dawned on her. Ellen had said they had all switched rooms. Ellen and Joel had stayed in here, followed by Suki and Gunther. She recalled that Ellen even said Robert slept here one night when he couldn't get into his cabin. Was it that he was unable to get into his cabin, or had there been some sort of fight and he slept in the guest room for the night?

Plum kept twisting the card in her fingers. Did Robert write the card, scribble something, and then hand it to someone? To Gunther? And that's why he left the boat so abruptly? That would make sense. But what did Robert know about Suki?

Whatever it was, it meant there was discord on the yacht. Someone was sending menacing missives. Were they blackmailing anyone? Plum had to find out. She couldn't very well bring the card out and show it to people and find out if they wrote it or if it matched their handwriting. She had to think. She stuffed the card into her cosmetic kit.

Suddenly there was an earsplitting clanging noise so deafening that Plum jumped. It took her a minute to realize it was the grinding and groaning of the anchor. They must be docking for the day. She had heard Nachelle mention she wanted to stop the boat to swim, and Robert must have acquiesced. The sound was so grating, Plum wondered if she would ever become accustomed to it. That said, she didn't expect to spend much time on the yacht, so perhaps she didn't need to.

CHAPTER

16

WHEN PLUM LEFT HER CABIN and made her way along the corridor to the dining room, she heard someone yelling as she passed the staircase leading upstairs. She paused and listened, tilting her head upward and craning her ears. She was quite certain it was Nachelle, and she sounded furious. Plum could hear the R & B artist lay out a string of expletives. Intrigued, Plum quietly took a few steps up the spiral staircase to make out exactly what Nachelle was saying.

"Saoirse, I have been patient, but please, girl. I need you to get it right," bellowed Nachelle. "When you draw my bath, I want one-half hot water, one-half Fiji water, and one-half baby oil, understand?"

"Yes, ma'am," came Saoirse's Irish lilt.

Plum wondered if Nachelle even realized three halves didn't make up a whole, but she figured Saoirse wouldn't dare correct her. Plum quietly slipped back down the staircase and made her way toward lunch.

Nachelle was a temperamental diva. Plum had met

many a celebrity so conceited and arrogant that they treated everyone like garbage. Most of them got their comeuppance at one time or another. Very few performers could sustain the lifelong fame and glory, and most crashed through all their money by the time their popularity was on the wane. Nachelle was talented, but that didn't mean she would be famous and rich forever. Plum hoped she would gain some perspective and learn how to treat people better. She had to have redeeming qualities if Robert was in love with her. He didn't seem like the type to tolerate a bad attitude.

The smell of fresh flowers permeated the dining room, along with the tang of salt air. All the windows had been opened, and the bright sunshine was streaming through, making a pattern on the mahogany table. Harris was already situated, and Plum noticed he had ensconced himself next to the head of the table, where Robert always sat. He was definitely trying to acquire his host's attention, thought Plum. He had a large plate full of food in front of him but absent-mindedly tapped his knife against the edge of the table while he waited for others to join.

Plum greeted Harris and headed over to the sideboard, where a bountiful lunch buffet was laid out. There were trays of sushi and sashimi, platters of fish ceviche, grilled chicken and lamb kebobs, marinated octopus, various green salads, conch fritters, corn bread, and sliced exotic fruit such as mango, papaya, passion fruit, and guava. It was enough food to feed a small country, mused Plum.

"This looks lovely," said Suki, who collected a plate

and cut in front of Plum on the buffet line. "I'm absolutely famished."

Suki wore a long formfitting floral dress that clung to her svelte figure. On her wrist were several carved wooden bangles that clacked up and down as she speared an octopus tentacle. Her perfume was musky and fragrant, which was undoubtedly alluring to most men. She exuded confidence and sexuality, but the more Plum analyzed her, the more she sensed a harshness underneath. She recognized the trait in many women who had worked hard to achieve the position they wanted in life, either professionally or personally. Not unlike herself.

"The food in the Caribbean is delicious," remarked Plum. "And Robert has an excellent chef."

"Only the best for Robert," said Suki, who plucked several pieces of sashimi from the tray. "He acquired a taste for the finer things in life and made sure he was able to get them. You have to admire him."

"Yes," said Plum. She noticed Suki had commented on Robert's ambition and success frequently.

They brought their plates to the table and sat down. Suki made sure to sit as far away from Harris as possible and didn't even acknowledge him. Plum positioned herself halfway between each of them, so as not to profess a favorite.

"Suki, have you heard anything from your husband?" asked Harris. He took the liberty of pouring himself a large glass of rosé.

"Of course, I have."

Harris returned her glance with a sly, condescending

smile. "Oh? How is Gunther? Everything okay with his 'work emergency'?"

He said the last part as if it were in quotes, thought Plum. No doubt needling Suki.

"Obviously, everything is okay with his work emergency," said Suki, taking a sip of her water. "Gunther is a titan of industry. Even if one of the many, many small companies he owned were to have the slightest blip, all would be well in our universe. Can you say the same, my dear?"

Harris's normally jovial face darkened. Before he could respond, India and Joel entered the room together, laughing and sharing an inside joke. To Plum, they looked guilty, and indeed they stopped giggling as soon as they saw the assembled guests, as if they had been up to no good and didn't want to let anyone else in on the joke. India mumbled hello and then straightened the shoulder strap of her bikini under her cover-up.

"How is everybody?" asked Joel, striding up to the buffet table. He smacked his lips greedily. "I tell you I worked up an appetite today all right."

His eyes were locked on India as he spoke, and she turned away quickly before grabbing a plate and diving into the buffet.

"Yes, you were doing a lot of laps in the pool," she said. "That's a lot of exercise."

"Yeah, laps," said Joel, his voice dripping with sarcasm.

"Joel, I've been looking for you," said Ellen frantically. She rushed into the dining room and stopped dead when she saw her husband standing next to India. She eyed them both suspiciously.

Joel turned and shrugged. "What up, babe? I'm not that hard to find. It's a big boat, but it's not a cruise ship."

Ellen looked about to say something but then stopped and laughed nervously. "You're right. I probably didn't look hard enough."

"Obviously," insisted Joel, laden with a sharp undertone.

As soon as Robert and Nachelle entered and selected their food (just guava and french fries for Nachelle), the dining room was filled with the sound of chatter and silverware clattering. Saoirse and the chef's wife, who was now acting as stewardess, had come in and were refilling glasses and clearing plates. Plum slid her eyes across the table and studied all the guests. What secrets were they keeping? Was it just the usual run-of-the-mill secrets that everyone holds? Or was one of them a murderer?

"The chef really outdid himself today," said Harris, waving his knife in the air. "This sashimi is exquisite. I may have to steal him away when my new yacht is up and running."

"New yacht?" asked Suki mischievously. "Are you implying you had an old yacht?"

He sniffed at her. "Of course. It was too small, so I'm building a new yacht."

"What did you do with the old yacht?" asked Plum.

"*Miss Conduct?*" he said as he slid a piece of sushi into his mouth. "She's resting."

As he spoke, Saoirse, who was filling his water glass, dropped it on the ground. They all turned and looked at her. She bent quickly and wiped it up.

"I'm so sorry," she mumbled.

"It's okay, Saoirse, it's only water," Robert announced.

Saoirse rose, gave Plum a tense look, curtsied, and quickly left the dining room.

What did that look mean? Plum wondered. Saoirse was rattled. It was as if when Harris mentioned his yacht's name, it triggered something. Plum had to find out.

"Yummy, right?" asked India, breaking Plum's reverie.

Plum turned to the starlet and blinked. India was scooping passion fruit pulp and seeds into her mouth. She possessed that vitality and freshness of youth that Plum still felt she retained—that is, until she came across people like India. The young starlet's skin was naturally tanned, with a salubrious luster enhanced by the genial sun and Caribbean air, and her eyes sparkled.

"It is delicious," agreed Plum, temporarily pushing thoughts of Saoirse out of her mind. "So, tell me, India, how did you come to be on this trip? Are you friends with Robert?"

India shook her head but didn't look at Plum when she answered, "Joel invited me. He's producing my next movie."

"I see," said Plum. And bringing her here was a typical casting-couch move. "And how did you get into acting in the first place?"

India glanced up and pulled a piece of her flaxen hair behind her ear. She said with excitement, "I've always loved acting, since I was a child. But I was mostly riding and showing my horses. It wasn't until I was at Foxeden that I got the theater bug."

"Foxeden?" asked Plum, perking up. That was the name

of a juvenile detention center in Upstate New York. It was a grim, depressing place situated in the town next door to the one Plum had grown up in.

"Foxcroft," India said swiftly.

"Oh, really? I thought you said…"

"I said Fox*croft*," India corrected somewhat testily. But then, as if she suddenly realized she was rude, she quickly changed her tone. "I apologize. I've been rehearsing my lines all day, and my character is still in my head. Isn't that right, Joel?"

"Yeah, she's doing a great job as the hardened cop," said Joel.

India nodded in agreement. "It's very difficult to turn on and off a role. I really get into character."

"I can imagine," said Plum, who could not.

"I'm sorry if I snapped," said India, now gentle as a lamb. "For creative types, it's difficult to live in the real world."

"Sometimes it's challenging for anyone to live in the real world," mused Joel.

"Anyway, what I was saying," continued India, "is that I starred in a theater production of *A Chorus Line* at Foxcroft, and that's when I knew I was born to be an actress. I just have to perform. And I've been pretty fortunate that my career has taken off…"

"It has?" asked Plum.

"Yes," said India, making her eyes wide. "I mean, obviously I lost out on a few auditions when I was just starting out. But it turns out I was super lucky I didn't get stuff. I was so naive, I actually tried out for a reality show and almost got one. I thought it was going to be so major at the time, and I was so beyond devastated when I lost out to…well, doesn't matter. The show tanked. Like, totally. And the fact is, thank God! Because a really successful producer discovered me and put me in his movie. I'm sure you've seen it—it's called *The Right Address*?"

She gave Plum a knowing look. But Plum shook her head. "No."

"*The Right Address*," repeated India as if Plum hadn't heard.

"Nope," repeated Plum.

"Really?" asked India with surprise. "It did really well in the festivals. Total critical darling. I mean, I only had a small part, but the *New York Times* did call me 'a bright light' in the film."

"Good lighting is important in movies," said Plum, intentionally playing coy.

"It was their chief critic who said that. And the film was nominated for best screenplay. You sure you didn't hear of it? *The Right Address*."

Plum shook her head. "I don't get to the movies a lot."

India bit her lower lip with disappointment. "Oh."

Plum felt bad. "But I'm sure you were amazing. What a wonderful start to your career. Now what?"

India brightened "Well, one thing led to another, and here I am. Joel said it would be great if I came along so we can rehearse my role and I can really immerse myself in my character."

"Your role as a homicide detective?"

India took a bite of her papaya salad before nodding. "Yes."

"How is being on this yacht preparing you for that?" asked Plum. "Unless you thought there was going to be a homicide on board."

India laughed. "No, I didn't. But what a strange coincidence that there was a suspicious death. I mean, Lysette...."

Plum turned and leaned closer to her dining partner. She saw out of the corner of her eye that the others were now talking among themselves; this was her opportunity to solicit information from India. She whispered, "You think that was suspicious?"

India's eyes got wide, and she leaned in conspiratorially. "As an artist, particularly one who studies other people for a living, I keep an open mind and examine all possibilities. And I do think it's weird that Lysette would fall off the boat in the middle of the night and die."

Plum's heart was beating with excitement. Finally, someone was discussing this. She whispered, "Who would want her dead?"

India's eyes skated around the table. Then she said in a low tone, "If I had to bet, I would say Nachelle."

"Nachelle?" asked Plum. "Why do you say that?"

India leaned closer. "Because she's a bad person. She treats everyone horribly and loses her temper all the time. I even heard her getting mad at Lysette right before. Apparently, she sent Lysette to the island for something at the pharmacy, and I don't know what happened, but Nachelle said she messed it up somehow. And she was, like, super mad. Not normal. Then they had to send out the first officer to get it. It was, like, a bad situation."

"But is that cause for murder?"

India shrugged. "People kill for less."

"Do they?" asked Plum.

India returned to her plate of food and pushed arugula around with her fork. "I don't know. You asked me who I thought would do it, and that's who I said. I mean, the only other person who was kind of suspicious was Gunther, but he left."

Plum leaned in eagerly. "Why was he suspicious?"

"He was like, all bottled up. Like, super uptight as if about to explode. And he got really mad for some reason and took off. It was after Lysette cleaned his room, and he freaked out or something. I don't know if it was related, but I thought maybe it was."

"It could be," murmured Plum.

"Okay, now tell me your tips." asked India. "What should I know about portraying a detective? I want to keep it real."

Plum thought for a second about her past experiences solving crime. It had only been out of necessity. "You have to think like a victim."

"Like a victim?" repeated India.

Plum nodded. "Be prepared for danger."

"Oh, you mean like wear a bulletproof vest and carry a gun everywhere you go."

"I don't know if you need to be that extreme, but proceed with caution."

Plum could see India was taking her suggestions seriously. Although Plum knew nothing about being a professional detective, she was flattered by India's obvious reverence.

"Like, look at everyone as a potential killer?" asked India.

"Yes. Don't trust anyone. Check where the exits are everywhere you go. Don't be caught off guard. Have eyes in the back of your head."

It was all information Plum could have garnered from a fortune cookie, but it sounded good to her.

"You've been so helpful. Thank you."

"My pleasure." Plum beamed.

CHAPTER

17

"WHAT WERE YOU AND INDIA all chatty about at lunch?" asked Joel. He had followed Plum down the corridor when she was returning to her room after everyone left the dining room.

"She was telling me about her career. How she almost ended up on a reality show," replied Plum vaguely.

Joel nodded, his shrewd eyes examining Plum's face. "Yeah, she better count her lucky stars that she met me at the right time. I plucked her out of obscurity, and now she's heading for the big leagues. Without me, she'd be doing some obscure Bavarian reality show rip-off of *Downton Abbey*."

"Then she really did dodge a bullet," said Plum. "Now she's undoubtedly headed for fame under your tutelage. Do you think her homicide detective role could garner her an Oscar?"

Joel stared at Plum as if assessing whether she was being sarcastic. She was, but she smiled as if she weren't. Plum had never really cared for Joel. He possessed all the deplorable traits that one read about in Hollywood: arrogance, tacki-ness, unfaithfulness, and deviance.

Finally, Joel laughed. "Maybe she'll get an Oscar, just maybe," said Joel. "Academy Awards don't come easy. You gotta work for them."

"Oh? How's that?" asked Plum.

Joel shrugged. "You need to win a lot of people over."

"I see."

"I mean, I'm not a dollar bill, so not everyone will like me. What do I care? I had no beef with Gunther. Not sure why he was so pissed off."

"Gunther?" asked Plum.

"Yeah, the guy can't take a joke."

"What joke did you make?" asked Plum.

He shrugged. "His wife was being all bitchy, and I said something like, *you want me to take her out, a good wife is a blind, deaf, or dead wife*, and he got all mad. It was a joke."

It was a reprehensible "joke" that made Plum want to slap him across the face. She restrained herself. "I can imagine most people don't share your unique sense of humor."

"Yeah, funny thing is he seemed to hate his wife. They fought like hell. I guess he had some soft spot for her. She's no great prize. Acts all fancy, but she was a coat check girl back in the day. Doing the bidding for rich people who gave her a dollar tip."

A coat check girl, mused Plum. That's where she knew her from! Club Zasmo. Suki was the one who had taken off with Plum's date, Elliot Niederhover. She had changed since then, was definitely more glamorous.

Joel snapped his fingers in Plum's face. "Hello? You listening?"

"Sorry, you jogged my memory. I knew Suki looked familiar," said Plum. "I used to go to Club Zasmo."

"She probably hung up your fur coat."

"I never wore a fur coat."

"Then your parka, whatever you had. You don't wear fur? What are you, an animal lover?"

"Yes."

He rolled his eyes. "So she hung up your hemp coat."

"Did she tell you she was a coat check girl?" asked Plum. "I don't see her as confiding in you."

"Naw, but I remembered the news stories. She tied up some rich guy and extorted him for a bunch of money. She denied it, but it was all over the newspapers. Then she moved to Europe and reinvented herself."

"Suki was the one who tied Elliot up?" she asked with astonishment. Although she experienced a slight flicker of pleasure. He should have never dumped her for Suki—see where it got him. "I knew he had dated her, but I didn't realize it was Suki who actually tied him up."

"You knew Elliot? Yeah, it was her. She blackmailed him. She is one cunning lady."

"Yes," Plum concurred.

"I'm pretty good at spotting crazy, you know. Especially with women."

"Undoubtedly," fibbed Plum. Then feeling bold, she asked. "Was Lysette crazy?"

Joel's eyes became fiery. "Why are you asking me about the maid?"

"I was curious if your crazy radar went off on her."

"I never even talked to her, so how would I know?"

Maybe he didn't talk to her, but he had certainly put his hand on her butt. "I was just trying to get a sense of if there was any other crazy on the yacht."

This seemed to make sense to Joel, and he relaxed. "Everyone else is pretty decent," said Joel. "Harris drives me bananas with all his name-dropping. It's like, buddy, shut up, I know all these people for real. I do business with celebrities day in and day out. Calm down. You're not their friend."

Plum wondered if she could hold up a mirror and tape recorder to Joel so he could hear himself. It was definitely a case of the pot calling the kettle black. Instead, she bit her tongue. "You don't think he's genuinely friends with them?" she asked instead.

Joel chuckled and shook his head. "Naw. You can tell he's a fraud. I mean, maybe he travels in the circles, but he gets all the details wrong, which is a real tell. Told me he bonded with Jeremiah over a few shots of vodka, and I mean, come on. We're talking *Jeremiah*. Booze? No, no, no," clucked Joel.

Plum nodded. She had no idea who Jeremiah was, but she assumed that he was a celebrity who was a renowned tee-totaler. "I suppose some people feel special the closer they are to fame."

It was a jab at Joel, but it went over his head. "Yeah, I see that a lot. It's really pathetic."

"Right," she said neutrally.

"I'm lucky I don't care. With my success, you know, it doesn't matter."

"Are you complimenting yourself again?" asked Robert.

He was making his way toward them in the corridor and heard the tail end of their conversation.

"If I don't, no one else will." Joel laughed.

"No one else needs to," said Robert archly. "You more than make up for it."

"Ouch," said Joel.

"He's going to break his arm patting himself on the back," Robert said with a wink at Plum. "Not sure why I keep him around."

"You like to be among movers and shakers," said Joel smugly.

"Exactly," said Robert. "So I'm not sure why you're here. A *former* mover and shaker."

Joel was about to say something, and his eyes darted to Plum. He looked embarrassed and blurted, "Are you going swimming?"

Robert had changed into a swimsuit and a neatly pressed blue polo shirt with the starched collar pointed upward. Plum remembered the wealthier boys used to wear their collars like that when she was in middle school.

"We've pulled out the Jet Skis. Thought we could take them out," Robert responded.

"I want in on that," said Joel.

"How about you, Plum?" asked Robert.

"I think I'll pass for now. I have some work things to do," she said.

"I admire your work ethic," said Robert. "Come on, Joel, let's go."

They walked down the hall.

Plum wondered what Robert meant when he called Joel a *former* mover and shaker. Was he teasing him? Maybe she should do an internet search on Joel's current work status.

She was turning the knob of her room when a door to a bedroom opened down the hall. She glanced over. Captain Dave was emerging from a bedroom, and he turned and stopped to talk to someone who was inside. Plum wished she could make herself a fly on the wall and disappear so she could see who he was talking to. But it would be no use even trying to flatten herself—he would still see her. Fortunately, he didn't glance down the hall.

"Don't use it all at once, love," said Captain Dave in his broad Australian accent.

"I won't," came the reply.

Plum craned her ears. Was it India? Plum thought that was her cabin. She watched as a feminine hand stretched over the threshold and tucked folded bills into Captain Dave's breast pocket. There was the small turquoise bracelet India always wore. It was her!

"And remember, discretion is the key. You better not say anything to anyone."

"I'm not a moron," said India.

"Good. Wouldn't want to throw you overboard," he said, before taking off in the opposite direction. He whistled his way down the hall, never even having gazed in Plum's direction. She quickly went into her bedroom.

What was India paying Dave for? Drugs? Was he dealing the turtle eggs and India was his customer? It was possible.

Captain Diaz couldn't completely vouch for Dave's character. He had been embroiled in some sort of past scandal involving theft. Perhaps he hadn't redeemed himself. She would have to investigate.

In the meantime, she clicked on her computer and googled Joel's name. There were various articles about his career, mostly charting his ascension to the top of his studio. He had been responsible for numerous blockbuster films that made billions of dollars and garnered many awards. There were the requisite photographs of Joel with his arms around every celebrity known to mankind. (Plum finally figured out who the sober Jeremiah was that Joel had referred to: his name was Jeremiah Sloan, and he was apparently the lead in the new Marvel movie.) All the articles were very industry based and gushing.

Plum was about to click off after scrolling down when she saw one article that caught her eye. It was a mention in the comments section of a well-known movie industry blogger's newsletter. The item that ran was this:

This high-ranking Hollywood executive is desperately working out his exit package, calling in all the favors he can to leave with some money and dignity. The studio has yet to announce his termination, as they are still frantically trying to quell all the sexual harassment lawsuits pending from his illicit behavior. Although he has a great track record for films, people are distancing themselves right and left. Word is he left town hoping it would all blow over, but when he returns from his Caribbean cruise, he's going to find out he no longer has friends or a job. But he will need a lawyer.

It sure sounded like Joel to Plum, but what really confirmed it to her were all the commentators who had mentioned Joel Katz underneath. Some said his name, others were less charitable. But most alarming to Plum was the commenter @metoosurvivor2030, who said, "Joel Katz is the biggest scumbag in the world. He preys on young actresses. His wife, Ellen, is just as complicit and evil. I wrote her a million times to tell her and even went to their house, but she slammed the door on my face. He ruined my life."

"Wow," gasped Plum. This was horrible. She felt a sinking feeling. Plum did not want to be part of this sordid mess. She had to get out now. Just then her phone rang.

"Hello?"

"Senorita Lockhart, at last. I have been attempting to reach you, but the service has been terrible. It has been difficult getting a connection. How are things progressing?" asked Captain Diaz.

Although she did not have a chummy relationship with the policeman, he had caught her in a vulnerable moment. Before she even knew it, she had blurted all her recent discoveries, including her despair about Joel Katz and Ellen.

The officer clucked on the other end of the phone. "Senorita, you must take some deep breaths."

"Deep breaths won't help me," exclaimed Plum. "And it certainly won't help all of the women Joel harasses."

"That is true," agreed the captain. "Let me ask you a

question. Are you surprised by this revelation that your friend's husband is a scoundrel?"

"No," admitted Plum. "But the depths of it surprise me."

"Do you not read about all the insidiousness that goes on in Hollywood every day?"

"Yes. I just hoped my friends weren't a part of it. And it's discouraging that Ellen knew."

"That doesn't make her complicit," warned Captain Diaz. "You would be surprised what women tell themselves to turn a blind eye to their husbands."

Plum remembered Ellen had admitted she knew Joel had "friendships." Maybe she did just think these were women Joel had cast aside. "Okay."

"You must keep your eye on the prize. We need you to find out who killed Lysette."

"I am working on it!" snapped an exasperated Plum. "Probably putting my life in danger."

"A risk we are willing to take."

"Very funny," sneered Plum. "While I do all the work here, what about you? Have you done any investigating? Come up with any leads? Or are you just sitting there twiddling your thumbs?"

"I would enjoy it very much if you would show me how to twiddle my thumbs. But while I understand you're being sarcastic, I can assure you that yes, we have done more than thumb twiddling. We have discovered a member of the yachting party—a female member—went to Laszlo's antique jewelry store when she was on the island."

"I know what Laszlo's is." Plum sniffed.

He ignored her interruption. "And this woman sold a very expensive diamond necklace. She received twenty-thousand dollars in cash."

"Ellen told me her necklace was missing. She thought India had stolen it because she was wearing something similar. But then she found it. But now...who knows? There is definitely a timeline when the necklace was gone. What did this woman look like?"

"The store owner said she wore a burka, so she was impossible to identify."

"A burka? No one on board wears a burka."

"It was evidently a disguise. She did not want to reveal herself."

"But she must have had to present an ID?" asked Plum. "You can't just walk in off the street and sell expensive jewelry, can you? What if it's stolen? I would think Laszlo's has a reputation to uphold."

"She did present the necessary paperwork, including a 2019 purchase receipt from Tiffany & Co. as well as her driver's license."

"And? Who was it?"

"Her name was Suki Von Steefel."

Suki Von Steefel? Why would she steal then sell a necklace? She had tons of money, didn't she? "That makes no sense," said Plum.

"It is up to you, senorita, to make sense of it for us."

CHAPTER

18

PLUM PEEKED HER HEAD OUT of her cabin door. She did not want to run into any guests. It was fortunate they were all participating in the water sports. She could not think of anything less enticing. When she established the coast was clear, she down to the galley kitchen. She wanted to find Saoirse and ascertain why she was so startled when Harris mentioned his yacht.

Saoirse was not in the galley, but the chef, Vadim, and his wife, Brigitte, were there, putting away the lunch. They were surprised to see her.

"Mademoiselle, are you lost?" asked Vadim in his French-accented English. He wore a neat apron and a chef's hat. His name was embroidered in swirling font on his white jacket, with *Jackpot* underneath. He fastidiously wiped his hands on a clean dishrag when he saw her.

Plum took a breath and introduced herself before adding, "I am looking for Saoirse." She glanced around in amazement. "This is a very impressive kitchen."

"*Oui,*" agreed Vadim.

The appliances were all stainless steel, and the eucalyptus wood cabinets were dyed blue with marquetry details and brass accents. The countertops were thick slabs of a natural veined quartz stone. Plum's eyes flitted around the room, and she noted a six-door oven, two pizza ovens, a fancy cappuccino maker like the kind in Italian bistros, a Sub-Zero refrigerator, and a rotisserie spit. Everything was immaculate and shining.

"Yes, we are very lucky to work here," agreed Brigitte as she placed a Tupperware container in the refrigerator. She was also French, and Plum thought her typical of most French women she had met: innately chic, no matter if she were wearing a uniform (which she was) or if she were clad in Chanel. Brigitte was slender, with dark hair that she wore short. Her eyes were gray, the type of eyes that saw everything but revealed nothing. She kept her makeup minimal (maybe even nonexistent) and was attractive. Plum placed her around forty.

"Would you like me to help you find Saoirse?" asked Brigitte.

"No, I can find her," said Plum. She realized she had a very good opportunity to question more staff members about Lysette. "But now that I have you both here, do you mind if I ask you some questions?"

Vadim stopped what he was doing and stood erect, as did his wife. "Of course," they both said.

"I was wondering about Lysette," said Plum.

They both stared at her quietly. Neither of their

expressions changed when Plum said the name of the deceased girl. In fact, they didn't do anything at all, so Plum continued, "You know, Lysette?"

"Yes, we know," nodded Brigitte.

"Well, can you tell me anything about her death?" asked Plum.

"Why do you want to know anything about her death?" asked Vadim, matter-of-factly.

"I..." Plum faltered. Why did she want to know anything about Lysette's death? Damn it, she should have been prepared for this question. She couldn't exactly say, *Because the Paraison police believe she was murdered and have asked me to come here under phony pretenses to investigate*. That would probably not go down well, not at all. "Because I feel guilty," said Plum dramatically.

Brigitte's expression was quizzical. "Guilty? That is so American. Why do you feel that way?"

"Because..." began Plum. She was biding time. Why did she feel guilty? "Because I was with Ellen and Harris and Nachelle one day, and we were shopping, and the paparazzi came, and they left Lysette on the shore. I should have intervened and made sure they included her..."

It was one of the weakest excuses Plum could think of.

"But...perhaps it is my English...I don't understand. Why would that make you feel guilty about her death?" asked Vadim.

"Because..." said Plum, grasping. She suddenly straightened. She just had to appear lucid and confident, and they would have to buy her story. "Because I feel horrible if she was upset about that."

Brigitte and Vadim looked at each other, and Plum could tell they were trying not to smile. Brigitte shook her head. "*Non, non, non,*" she said. "That was not why she was distraught."

"It wasn't?" asked Plum.

"No," replied Brigitte, not offering any further information.

"Then what was it?" asked Plum, feeling a smidge impatient.

Vadim looked down at the platter in front of him and began wrapping the leftovers in tinfoil. Brigitte fluttered her hands in the air, waving them as if that were explanation enough. When Plum wouldn't let her off the hook, she capitulated.

"I do not feel comfortable doing the gossip," said Brigitte. "But you have asked me directly, and I will answer. Lysette became very unhappy with the diva."

"The diva?" asked Plum.

"The singer," offered Vadim.

"Oh, Nachelle?" Plum queried. "Why is that?"

"I believe she felt the woman had accused her of something she did not do. Lysette was embarrassed and angry, but she could not complain. And then this diva sent Lysette out on nonsense errands to punish her," replied Brigitte.

Plum nodded. "I see."

"In our business, you must understand, we manage many personalities. There is an intimacy on the ship between everyone. Not the guests alone but the staff as well. And that is a result of proximity rather than any similarity of taste," explained Brigitte.

"Yes, I can imagine. It is a small space for an eclectic group," concurred Plum.

"And when people are at sea, surrounded only by water with no other humans in sight, it unleashes strange behavior," added Brigitte.

"What sort of behavior?" asked Plum eagerly.

Brigitte glanced at her husband, who shrugged, as if to say, *You brought it up.*

"I am talking in generalizations," explained Brigitte. She removed a tea canister from a shelf and set it on the counter.

"Oh," said Plum, disappointed. "But can you be more specific about this trip? Has anything strange happened. Obviously, besides Lysette dying."

"There were some irregularities…" began Brigitte.

Vadim jerked up his head and quickly said something to Brigitte in French, but although Plum thought herself proficient in that language as well as Spanish, she couldn't understand what he had said. Brigitte responded to him in rapid-fire French, her tone cold. He then shrugged and lifted a giant urn into the sink and turned on the tap to fill it.

"What did he say?" asked Plum.

"Nothing," said Brigitte quickly. "I apologize, my husband was reminding me we must prepare the tea."

She moved over toward the cabinets and withdrew several mugs and a teapot. Plum eyed Vadim suspiciously.

"Listen, if you know something about Lysette's death and are not telling me, you could be putting others in danger. It's important we find out what happened, or else more bad things could happen," said Plum. "So tell me about the irregularities."

Vadim shook his head, but Brigitte sighed and placed her palms on the counter.

"On the night of Lysette's accident, there was a very large dinner. Mr. Campbell had requested an eleven-course tasting menu, reminiscent of the meals they served in the court of *Louis Quatorze*."

"Fancy," remarked Plum.

"It was delicious," insisted Vadim.

"I'm sure," Plum agreed.

Brigitte continued, "It was a very long evening, course after course. Many plates. And the guests went through many bottles of wine. As you know, it was the responsibility of Saoirse and Lysette to clear the table and offer the guests after-dinner drinks when they moved into the den. My head was down washing and scrubbing the dishes as well as helping Vadim plate his food when they came in. I did not notice it was only Saoirse bringing down the dishes. But that said, I did not question as I assumed Lysette was upstairs serving the guests. Ultimately, Saoirse came downstairs and started airing her grievances. She said Lysette was nowhere to be found. She had not appeared since the fourth course was served. Saoirse was angry her colleague had abandoned her."

"Did she go looking for her?" asked Plum.

Brigitte shook her head. "There was no time. She was attempting to do everything herself. I had to come upstairs and help her serve and clear."

"It was unprofessional," said Vadim grimly.

"Did anyone see her after?" asked Plum.

"I did not see her again," said Brigitte. "I was working very hard—as you Americans say—like a dog. We had no time. When everything was cleaned, I had to help prepare breakfast for the morning, and then we retired to bed."

"Did Saoirse see her again?" asked Plum.

"You will need to ask her," said Vadim.

"But it was unprofessional of Lysette. I was irritated with her," said Brigitte.

"She had disrespected us," said her husband.

"But my anger was nothing like Saoirse. I have not seen her like that. We have worked with Saoirse before, and she is usually very easygoing and happy," said Brigitte.

"*Alors*, they did bicker very much," said Vadim.

"*Oui*," agreed Brigitte.

"Who did, Saoirse and Lysette?" asked Plum.

"Yes, Saoirse was dismayed by Lysette's work ethic. That was very evident."

"Really," mused Plum.

"*Oui*. Saoirse said Lysette was unprofessional. And when she did not show up for the final dinner service, Saoirse was furious," said Brigitte.

"Furious," echoed her husband. Then he added cheekily, "Her pale skin was all red and puffy. It was not the Saoirse we know. She could not even speak."

Plum thought about that. Why hadn't Saoirse mentioned that to her when she'd talked to her earlier? That seemed like a big thing to omit. She had also made it seem like everything was okay between her and Lysette. Was there more to the story?

"Was that usual, for Lysette to disappear like that during work?"

"No, but we only worked with her a couple of weeks," said Vadim.

"Didn't you worry? Or check on her?" asked Plum.

"I did not want to investigate when I was tired. Was she a lazy girl? I do not know. I did not believe so at first, but then sometimes first impressions on boats vary wildly from reality. I thought there was the possibility she had not felt well and had gone to the bathroom or to her bed, but I never knew," said Brigitte.

"Or maybe she had already fallen overboard?" asked Plum.

"It is possible," concurred Vadim.

"There was something else," said Brigitte. She leaned closer. "I did not think of it at the time the police questioned me. But when I went up later to do one last survey of the dining room, I could hear arguing. It is my job to be invisible, therefore I did not investigate, but I believe they were female and male. Angry voices. Quarreling. Followed by the sound of someone running along the corridor before a door banged."

"Any idea who it was?" asked Plum.

"*Non*," replied Brigitte. She hesitated. "But I must confess…it has not been my choice, but I have fallen witness to several very bad fights between the guests on this journey. The German man who left was very angry the night before he departed. I heard him shouting on the deck, and the veins in his temple were throbbing."

"Who was he yelling at?" asked Plum.

"I thought it was his wife…" Brigitte faltered.

"It was not possible," grumbled Vadim, who was heaving the urn onto the counter. Plum turned toward him.

"Why not?"

He emitted a deep sigh, one that demonstrated his reluctance to partake in this conversation before he spoke. "Because at the moment my wife saw the German upstairs, I saw his wife in the servants' quarters."

"What was she doing there?" asked Plum.

"I was very startled to see her there, as was she when she saw me, but she informed me she was searching for either Saoirse or Lysette because she was in need of allergy medication. Saoirse came down the steps right after that, and she assisted her," said Vadim.

"So you don't know who Gunther was yelling at," said Plum to Brigitte. "But do you have a suspicion?"

"After I completed my duties cleaning the den, I went out to the deck. Mr. Von Steefel was not there, but the Malaysian man, Mr. Low, was leaning on the balcony smoking a cigar. His demeanor was tense, and as he is usually very jolly, I thought perhaps it was he who quarreled with the German."

Plum nodded. Interesting, she thought to herself. But did this mean anything?

Brigitte continued, "But I was wrong. Mr. Low said good night to me. I picked up the glasses and cleared the ashtrays. And I heard a noise. I glanced up, then saw Mr. Von Steefel. He was standing on the upper deck, his face furious. And then I heard a noise and saw Lysette coming quickly down the side stairs. She did not know I saw her."

"So they were having the argument?" asked Plum.

Brigitte put up her hands. "I do not know. But it does seem as if that were the case."

And if that were the case, thought Plum, she had to figure out what they were arguing about and how Lysette and Gunther Von Steefel were acquainted.

CHAPTER

19

WHEN PLUM EMERGED FROM THE galley and made her way upstairs, she was overwhelmed by the sounds of loud motors. Could they be lifting anchor already? The group had only just started swimming and doing water sports. As Plum moved through the corridors, she peeked out her window and saw that they were surrounded by several speedboats and Jet Skis coming precariously close to the yacht. People shouted and screamed, and the atmosphere was frenzied and chaotic.

Plum rushed to the rear of the boat to where the others had gathered. She found Harris, India, Suki, Joel, and Ellen standing at the railing.

"What's happening?" Plum asked, out of breath.

"It's the paparazzi," trilled Harris gleefully. "They've discovered Nachelle is on the yacht."

"Not just Nachelle," said India, flipping her hair.

Plum scanned the surrounding vessels stuffed with photographers holding long-range zoom lenses tracking all movement on the boat. They were shouting Nachelle's name and saying things in various languages and clicking away.

"Is this even legal?" asked Plum.

"Of course," said Harris.

He waved to the photographers and stepped forward. Plum watched how he shamelessly lowered his head and then raised his eyes, batting his eyelashes at them before putting his hands under his chin and giving them a demure come-hither glance. Plum found it bizarre. Why was he acting like a celebrity? It was strange how people yearned to be famous.

"Harris, I think they're here for me and Nachelle," said India. "Would you mind announcing me?"

Harris looked about to rebuff but then smiled. "Sure, darling. Yoo-hoo, paparazzi! India Collins is in the house! I'm sure you all saw her in the movie *The Right Address*!"

He turned and rolled his eyes at Plum, as if it were all a big joke, but the photographers went wild. When India moved to the edge of the boat and thrust her front leg out, they began furiously snapping and whooping.

"I can't believe they'll take pictures of just anyone." Harris sniffed. "Even a little juvenile delinquent."

"I guess they have a quota," Plum said.

Robert appeared and sternly announced, "I've told the captain to lift anchor. We will try and evade them now."

"So soon?" exclaimed Harris.

"Let's leave them in the dust," sneered Joel. "Those guys are animals."

"They're just doing their jobs," admonished Harris. "You can't blame them."

"They're bloodsuckers," replied Joel, motioning to the paparazzi. "Every single one of them."

"Without the paparazzi, actors and actresses wouldn't be famous, and then your movies would make zero money, Joel, so I would be careful what you say," cautioned Harris.

"I don't have to be careful about anything I do or say," Joel seethed.

Both men stared at each other before Harris returned his attention to the photographers and continued preening. India dropped the wrap tied around her waist so she now stood in front of them in a tiny bikini. She turned left and right, posing.

The photographers looked poised to move away when, all of a sudden, they started hooting and howling and raising their cameras higher. Plum turned around and saw Nachelle had appeared behind her. She had changed out of her prior outfit and was wearing a leopard bikini with a gauzy bright yellow cover-up open to the navel. Numerous long beads of varying colors were draped around her neck, and dangling feather earrings reached down to her shoulders. She'd let her hair down and applied dramatic eye makeup. She looked every inch the diva. Even Plum was impressed.

"Gentlemen, gentlemen, please settle down and you'll get your picture!" cooed Nachelle.

She moved toward the stern of the boat. Robert put his hand out as if to stop her.

"Nachelle, you don't need to do this; just ignore them," he insisted.

Nachelle turned. "Robert, doll. I signed up for this. I have to give them a few pics so they'll back off."

"They'll never back off," he said.

She nodded. "Truth. But I like to please my fans."

"You're on vacation. You don't need to please anyone," he said sternly. "Except me."

"Maybe I like to be famous?" she retorted. "Maybe I like making a very nice living so I don't have to rely on any man. Did you ever think of that?"

Robert paused before retreating and allowing Nachelle to take center stage.

"All right, India, thanks for warming up the crowd. I'm here, and they're ready for a superstar," said Nachelle. She moved in front of the starlet.

India looked as if she was about to protest when she saw all the cameras had turned to Nachelle.

"I was done anyway," India replied. And under her breath, she added, "Be careful, Nachelle. I wouldn't want you to end up flailing on the ground and swallowing your tongue."

Nachelle acted as if she didn't hear India, who backed away with a satisfied look on her face.

They all watched as Nachelle stepped up on a table and assumed various poses as if she were a supermodel at the end of the runway. The paparazzi lapped it up. Robert retreated back into the boat, his face furious. Plum noticed Suki quickly slipped away, pursuing him.

After a moment, Plum decided to follow Robert and Suki. She walked along the corridor until she was about to reach the dining room. She paused outside the door when she heard hushed voices.

"Robert, darling, you seem unhappy. I know how you find this circus repellent. Everywhere we go with Nachelle, it's always crowds and a major scene."

It was Suki's voice. Plum leaned closer against the door to listen.

"I'm absolutely fine, Suki," said Robert.

Plum could hear Suki sigh deeply and dramatically before she continued. "Honestly, Robert, I do not know what you see in her. She is absolutely childish. You're a man of the world. Intelligent, a fabulous businessman. She is a liability."

There was a pause before Robert said sternly, "I would prefer you not to talk about Nachelle like that."

"I'm sorry, darling," purred Suki. "I'm only thinking of you. Looking out for your best interest. We all witnessed her temper the other night. Frankly, I'm surprised the police didn't accuse *her* of killing that maid."

"The maid wasn't killed," Robert quickly corrected. "She fell overboard."

"Yes, she did," said Suki before hesitating. "However, let's just say she didn't fall overboard. Nachelle was irate about her blouse being ruined. We both know she has quite a temper."

"She has a temper, but she is not a murderer," said Robert. "And I would advise you not to insinuate that."

"I didn't mean to overstep, Robert," cooed Suki. "I'm just looking out for you. I have your best interests in mind. We go way back, remember…"

Suki's voice dropped to an indecipherable murmur. Despite Plum's best efforts, she could not understand what they were saying. She was practically plastered against the wall, doing everything to hear, but it was futile. Suddenly, voices and footsteps sounded at the end of the corridor, and Plum leaped back to an upright position and strode into the dining room. She found Suki talking closely with Robert. They both appeared startled, and Suki dropped her hand that had been holding Robert's arm. Her copious bracelets clanked as she did so. Robert appeared relieved that Plum had interrupted them. Suki, on the other hand, glowered.

"Plum, don't concern yourself with the paparazzi. We will be taking off shortly," announced Robert. "Let's adjourn to the deck and have some cocktails."

Without waiting for an answer, Robert strode out of the room. Suki gave Plum a coy look. It was the first time they were alone together since Plum had learned from Captain Diaz that Suki had pawned a necklace in Paraiso. She had to figure out how to broach the topic.

"I'm on to you," Suki said finally.

"Me?" asked Plum, flustered. Could Suki read her mind? "What do you mean?"

Suki cocked her head to the side and then gave Plum a small, ironic smile. Plum wasn't sure if Suki was serious or teasing.

"You have become ubiquitous," said Suki. "Oh, don't be offended. I merely notice you have a habit of inserting yourself into many conversations and situations that have nothing to do with you."

"I didn't mean to," protested Plum weakly. It was not true; she totally meant to. That's why she was here after all.

"I understand, we're in a confined space."

"Yes, although it's a large yacht, we inevitably will run into each other in the public rooms."

"True," conceded Suki. "But you have a particular timing where you seem to be poised to overhear a great many things."

Plum started to protest.

"Don't worry, it doesn't really bother me," Suki replied. She walked over to the sideboard and poured herself a glass of white wine. "I suppose you had to do what you had to do to get ahead in the world. You're not the only one."

"Perhaps," agreed Plum. "I don't mean to eavesdrop, but I have a radar that goes off. It's an occupational hazard, I guess. I was a journalist."

"Yes, I know," said Suki. "It's a pity the industry is shutting down. It must have been very challenging to launch an entirely new career."

Suki plopped herself on the sofa and took a large sip of her wine. Plum walked over and sank into the armchair across from her.

"It's been a learning experience," said Plum diplomatically. "But most people have to switch gears and reinvent themselves. I'm sure you've done the same."

Suki appeared as if she didn't hear the implied question and instead took another sip of her wine.

"In fact," said Plum, emboldened, "I think we met years ago when you were a coat check girl at Club Zasmo."

Suki's eyes widened. "Oh, really? That was so long ago. How can you possibly remember?"

"Because I went on a date with Elliot Neiderhover once, and we met there."

Suki laughed. "You did? You poor thing! He was such a drip."

"I guess," said Plum. "I didn't really get a chance to know because he left with you."

"He did? Oh, I'm sorry. Don't hold it against me. He wasn't worth it anyway."

Plum sat back farther in her chair. "Yes, I heard it didn't end well for you as a couple."

Suki gazed at her as if considering before saying, "Oh, you are referring to that vicious rumor that I tied him up. No truth to it at all. It was salacious gossip," said Suki, staring at her evenly.

"It was? I thought there was a lawsuit," pressed Plum.

Suki gave her a fake smile. "Misunderstanding. I try to stay away from scandals."

Plum paused. Now was the opportunity to bring up the stolen necklace. She wanted to be diplomatic, but instead she blurted, "Speaking of scandals, it's so funny because someone told me you sold a stolen necklace at Laszlo's when you were on Paraiso."

Plum was surprised to see genuine confusion on Suki's face. She cocked her head to the side and shook it. "What are you talking about?"

"Oh, you know, you stole Ellen's necklace and then hocked it at Laszlo's," insisted Plum.

Suki shook her head. "I don't like what you're implying."

"I'm not implying anything. I'm stating. Someone presented your ID to sell the necklace."

Suki was aghast. "You cannot be serious."

"The police know," insisted Plum.

"The police? Are you in contact with the police?"

Dammit, thought Plum. She was blowing her cover. "No. I just assume they know."

Suki was completely silent and simply stared at Plum, who was unnerved. As soon as Plum had made the accusation, it appeared flimsy.

Suki remained very calm. "I have no idea what you are talking about. I stole nothing. And as far as I know, Ellen found her necklace. She was hysterical over nothing. I don't understand why you would concoct this story that I was fencing stolen goods. I don't need the money."

Despite the evidence, Plum believed her. At least for moment. But for now, Plum needed to backtrack and have an exit plan. "I'm just kidding," said Plum, adding a phony laugh.

Suki was confused. "You're joking?"

"Yeah, just a silly April Fools' joke," said Plum weakly.

"It's April Fools'?" asked Suki.

"Well, it was. A few weeks ago. But no matter, just don't listen to me, it's all good," said Plum.

Suki took a deep breath. "You have an odd sense of humor."

"Yes, I know."

CHAPTER

20

PLUM WENT TO HER ROOM to freshen up before dinner. She sent Captain Diaz a quick email, informing him Suki seemed genuinely surprised about the accusation that she had sold her necklace at Laszlo's. He wrote her back that he was working on getting footage from the surrounding store cameras to see if they could figure out who it was. When she finished with him, she checked her phone and saw Juan Kevin had texted her.

> Arne Larsen bought the house in East Hampton next to David Gifford. It was the only one recently sold.

It was confirmation that Harris was lying. She wasn't surprised. But did Robert know this? Did everyone see through him? It was bizarre that they all carried on this facade. She quickly texted Juan Kevin back a thank-you emoji and then, without thinking, added a heart. Before she could regret it, he immediately responded with a heart. She smiled.

She became carried away with fantasies of the two of them together. She imagined them riding horses on the beach, clad all in white, like they were posing for the cover of a romance novel. They would lie on the rocks, entwined and feeding each other grapes. The surf would lap at them, but they would not have a care in the world.

Plum's phone buzzed, interrupting her reverie. She checked it. Big mistake. All the daydreams immediately dissipated when she read the email from Lucia. Even though Lucia had prefaced the email with *Don't Freak Out* in the subject line, the warning was lost on Plum. Apparently, Damián had been successful at persuading Barbara Copeland to list her villa with him. Before she could even think straight, Plum dialed Damián's cell phone. He answered on the first ring, and she spoke before he could even say hello.

"Listen here, you perfidious snake! How dare you steal my client. I worked long and hard to get Barbara Copeland to even consider renting her villa. And then you swoop in and steal her from me. What kind of mongrel are you? You are a lowlife. Totally incapable of doing anything for yourself. But I can tell you, your pathetic greasy charm won't work any longer. I will expose you as what you are! A dog-hating, womanizing, pathetic, useless, incapable loser. That's right!"

There was breathing on the other end of the phone but no response. Finally, a bitter laughter erupted. "Plum, is that you, my old friend and colleague?"

"You know it is," hissed Plum. "But I'm not old."

She knew her response was as pathetic as it sounded, but there was something about Damián that riled her up so intensely that she could not even think before she spoke.

She heard a clucking from Damián, which drove her into a rage. "Plum, Plum, Plum," he said. "It is clear I have upset you. This is so much emotion from one person. I am responsible for so much passion from you. For that I am sorry."

"You don't elicit passion, you moron!" she raged.

"Darling Plum. No one wants to make you unhappy, least of all me," cooed Damián. "You are a friend. No, no, no, don't even try to protest. From the minute you came to my beautiful homeland, I felt nothing but pity for you. It has been so hard for you. You have been plagued by unhappiness and murder. Everyone around you dies, and you are responsible. You came to Paraiso because you failed in New York City, and now you are failing here. I feel so bad for you, my friend. Let me know what I can do to help. You need help, it is clear—"

"I need nothing!"

"See, the first sign of needing help is identifying that you need help," he said in a condescending tone. "It is so, so sad that you are unable to do this. Please, my dear Plum, let me know when you are ready for my assistance."

"I'll never be ready. I don't need you!"

"Sorry, my friend, I must go. I am very busy. Please get some rest and get some help."

He hung up before Plum could scream a response. If she could have, she would have slammed her phone on the receiver, but there were no more receivers, and if she slammed her phone, she would only break it. The bastard.

How was he able to do that to her? He always turned things around in his favor, as if she were the weak and pathetic one and he was some sort of real estate genius. Meanwhile every achievement had been through either manipulating vulnerable women who found him attractive or using other colleagues' contacts and skills to gain business. He was the worst. Plum wanted to vomit, she was so irate.

How vexing it was that Barbara chose to sign with him. Plum had done everything to win her over. There must be revenge. It would take some time for Plum to conceive of the perfect way to retaliate, but she was up to the challenge.

She took a long hot shower, taking her time under the water. It calmed her. Finally, her blood pressure was not off the charts. Damn that stupid Damián. She would not allow him to ruin her day.

When she was done, she lingered in the steamy bathroom, liberally applying cream all over her body to stave off the dry skin that would come with sun exposure. She gingerly applied cosmetics and makeup, and took her time luxuriating in her pampering. She wasn't in the damn army; she had a right to enjoy herself while she was on board a yacht. To hell with Damián.

There was a large puffy bathrobe hanging on the back of the bathroom door and fresh white disposable slippers like in a high-end hotel. Plum took full advantage, indulging and enveloping herself in all the finery. When she retreated from the bathroom, she thrust herself down on her soft, comfortable bed, sinking into it like a fork poking a soufflé. This investigatory work was intense, she thought as she took a moment to close her eyes and regain her strength. She felt as if her Herculean efforts to suss out a killer were on a par with Seal Team Six's efforts to track down Bin Laden. She was a damn martyr. She deserved a break.

Plum did not intend to nap. She told herself she was only taking a quick break, but then she inadvertently fell into a deep slumber. In her dream, Juan Kevin was battling all her enemies on her behalf—using karate moves to decimate everyone from the girl who used to mock her at gymnastics class to Suki. She woke up satisfied.

Plum put on an embroidered purple tunic she had purchased in Egypt over white cigarette pants. She decided to slick her hair back in a tight ponytail, as she was feeling particularly badass this evening. After spritzing herself with a musky fragrance, she set out for dinner.

The evening was warm, and stars sparkled through the ribbons of puffy clouds that skittered across the sky. There was a soft breeze as they moved over the water. Even with the advancing hours, the air was still warm and ripe. The sound of waves lapping against the ship's hull accompanied her as she made her way to the deck for cocktails.

Saoirse was standing by the entrance with a silver tray of assorted drinks.

"Hello, Saoirse," said Plum as she selected a glass of white wine.

"Good evening, ma'am," said Saoirse.

Plum wanted to discreetly ask the stewardess about Lysette's last night. But Saoirse was all business and kept her eyes averted from Plum.

"I'd like to talk with you later," whispered Plum. "Can you please come find me?"

"If I can, ma'am," said Saoirse. "I'm very busy now that it's just me."

"That's what I want to talk to you about," said Plum. "I have some questions about Lysette."

"Plum!" said Ellen from across the deck. "Come sit next to me." She patted the seat next to her. Ellen was wearing a clingy bandage dress in a leopard pattern and had giant sapphire earrings and was looking very glamorous.

Plum hesitated. "Promise me," she whispered to Saoirse.

"Okay, ma'am."

Plum greeted everyone before situating herself next to Ellen on the sofa.

"What sort of tricks do you use?" asked Ellen in a low voice so the others couldn't hear.

"Excuse me?" asked Plum.

Ellen's eyes darted around as if to make sure no one else could hear her before she whispered again, "Tricks. I mean, I know you're single now, but what sort of tricks or devices or, you know, positions do you use in the bedroom to make sure your man is satisfied?"

Plum followed Ellen's gaze and saw Joel and India chatting on a banquette in the corner, having an intimate conversation, oblivious to others. Plum felt bad once again for her friend. Ellen looked tired and, honestly, as if she had perhaps ingested a few too many cocktails. Despite the gourmet food on the yacht, Ellen appeared to be shrinking and malnourished. This would simply not do, thought Plum.

"I don't have any tricks," said Plum. "Maybe that's why I'm single. What you see is what you get. If he doesn't like it, he can take a hike."

She was tempted to say something about Juan Kevin, but she knew she had to keep up the facade that it hadn't worked out with him, even if it meant lying by omission to her oldest friend.

Ellen nodded and took a big sip of her skinny margarita. "I've tried everything. *Kama Sutra*, gadgets from the Pleasure Chest, exotic aphrodisiacs, tantric sex, costumes, role-playing—you name it. It works for a while, but then, well, Joel...Joel is Joel. His interest wanders. He always wants the next thing, so I have to keep up to date."

Something she had said piqued Plum's interest. "What kind of exotic aphrodisiacs?"

"Oh, you know..." said Ellen, her voice trailing off as she took another sip of her drink.

"I don't. Tell me."

Ellen waved her hand in the air. "I have no idea. Joel got them somewhere. He's always on the lookout for new stuff. It always tastes awful, and I am convinced it does nothing, but I don't want to be a party pooper. I don't want him to find someone else who will do what he wants."

Plum wanted to say that it looked like it didn't matter what she did, Joel went and found someone else anyway, but she bit her tongue. No use putting salt in the wound. She tried a different tack. "Have you ever heard of tortoise eggs used as an aphrodisiac?"

"Sure," said Ellen. "I've tried that."

"You have?" exclaimed Plum excitedly. Joel and India glanced up from their conversation across the deck. Plum lowered her voice again. "I mean, when? Where?"

"I don't remember," said Ellen. She took another sip of her drink. "Joel gets all that stuff. He's always on a quest to find the latest sexual fix. He'll stop at no end."

Interesting, thought Plum. "Really?"

"Oh, don't look so demure, Plum. Everyone does things like that. Nachelle was talking all about how she and Robert get their kicks the other day."

"I must have missed that."

"She's also into all that aphrodisiac stuff. I think she and Joel were actually comparing notes."

Plum thought it bizarre that grown people were sitting around talking about their sex lives, but then perhaps she was a prude. Or maybe it was that Hollywood lifestyle, which she had always thought a bit promiscuous for her tastes. In any event, the last thing she would want to do was discuss her intimate relationship with Juan Kevin over cocktails with a group. It was nice to keep things private. Besides, she had often felt those people who overshared had troubled romantic lives and that was why they were casting around for input from others.

"I have a hard time getting a grip on Nachelle. What do you know about her background?" asked Plum finally.

Ellen took a large sip of her margarita. "Nachelle's father was ambassador to the U.S. from the Bahamas. She went to all the fancy finishing schools and went to Wellesley College, a Seven Sister. She's as preppy as they come."

"Really?" asked Plum. "I would not have guessed that. But then, you can never tell where people come from." She gazed out at the endless blue sea and thought how different it was from the gray town she grew up in. Undoubtedly there would still be snow on the ground, despite the fact it was spring. In her memory it was always cold, dreary, and depressing. She was so happy to be as far away as possible.

"That's the wonderful thing about life," said Ellen. "You can reinvent yourself."

"Ellen, if you weren't a studio wife, what would you want to do?"

"Nothing. I only want to be what I am."

"But are you happy?"

"Generally. Yes. Happiness is a range. I can't always achieve perfection."

"But what will you do if say, Joel changes jobs?"

Ellen gave her a look of astonishment. "Why in the world would he do that? He has a fabulous job and an incredible career."

Plum fell silent. Ellen clearly didn't know the rumor that Joel had been fired. Very strange. How could a husband not confide in his wife? What kind of weird marriage did they have?

Plum peered over the edge of the boat. They were cruising now, leaving small foamy waves in their wake. There was no sight of land anywhere, and Plum felt very remote. She wondered what Juan Kevin was doing right this minute. Thank heavens he was so different from Joel. He was honest and straightforward, and she could not fathom him behaving like that cad. She missed him. She hoped he missed her.

"I was only thinking that maybe it would be nice to have a change in your life. Don't you miss New York? Maybe you guys should move back."

Ellen threw her head back and laughed. "Oh, Plum. That's too funny. When you have the life we have, you don't give it up. Even with our challenges, we'll do everything to maintain it."

"Right."

"It's important to marry well, that's what my mother always said," exclaimed Ellen. "She said when you marry well, you can decipher fake jewelry from real jewelry." She laughed.

"Does that make you happy?" asked Plum earnestly.

"Plum," said Ellen, pedantically. "You have to understand, this is a very select group on the boat. No one is unhappy with their life. We have all achieved."

"Speaking of which, let me ask you something about Suki," said Plum. "I can't figure her out. Is she financially secure? Not to be crass."

"I would assume so," remarked Ellen. "They own half of Europe."

"So she wouldn't be selling off assets or anything," asked Plum, thinking of Ellen's necklace.

"Not that I know of. But what are you referring to?" asked Ellen suspiciously.

"Oh, nothing," said Plum, who was not eager to explain. She had already blundered today when she accused Suki of stealing; she couldn't bring it up again. Instead she asked, "What's the deal with her husband?"

"Gunther?" Ellen shrugged. "He left abruptly when we

docked in Villalba. Apparently, they had some big blow-out, and he was pissed off. Joel thinks it's because Suki was making eyes at Robert. Those are his words. Well, not really. He said something a bit cruder. You know Joel…"

"Yes," said Plum. Unfortunately, she did.

"But I don't think that's necessarily why Gunther left."

"Why do you think Gunther left?" asked Plum.

Ellen leaned in conspiratorially. "I have the cabin next to them. And I heard them arguing, but it wasn't about Robert. Gunther was angry at Suki for 'bringing something up.' He kept repeating that, asking her why she was 'bringing it up' and 'reminding him' of something. I wasn't sure. My impression was that Suki was angry at him for taunting her about another woman. But then, that's all through the muffled doors of the cabin. God knows if it was what really happened."

Plum nodded. That was interesting. "God knows," she repeated.

"Let's go in for dinner," said Robert from across the room.

"Everything okay?" Plum asked as she and Ellen rose to follow him.

"Fine," he said tersely.

"Where's Nachelle?" asked Harris. "Planning on making one of her grand entrances?"

"Nachelle will not be joining us this evening," replied Robert. "She's under the weather."

"Oh, that's too bad," said Ellen. "Can we bring her anything?"

"She'll be fine," said Robert.

The dinner was tense for a reason Plum couldn't quite

put her finger on. Although Nachelle was controversial and aggrandizing, her absence made everything feel as if a light was extinguished. The power of charisma, thought Plum.

Whereas Robert was morose and quiet, Ellen drank too much and became garrulous. Joel started making cutting comments and telling everyone to ignore her, while Suki was using Nachelle's absence to ingratiate herself with her host. There was an awkward moment where Harris attempted to tease Robert about the fact he had not yet signed the contract for their deal, and Robert snapped at him.

"Shut up about your contract! You know there's no way this is happening," Robert said. Then he stood and threw his linen napkin on his chair. "If you'll excuse me," he said before he left the room.

Brigitte and Saoirse were bringing out the desserts just as Robert had his outburst. Plum glanced down at the quivering flan seeped in a thick layer of caramel sauce that Saoirse had placed in front of her. Although no one had much of an appetite anymore, they all began to eat in unison, as if that would erase what had just happened.

"Delicious dessert," remarked India.

"Scrumptious," agreed Suki.

"I'm looking forward to docking at Jolly Island tomorrow," said Plum brightly.

"Yes, that will be exciting," Harris said.

"It will be nice to get off this boat for a bit," said Plum. She would actually like to get off the boat permanently.

"Yes, I'm feeling claustrophobic," said Suki. "I need my space."

"I think we all do," agreed Joel.

After they had finished, everyone refused coffee and made their way to their rooms. Plum walked down the corridor, chatting with Harris. Before she reached her room, they heard a scream, and India came running out of her bedroom.

"There's a giant spider on my bed!" she yelped.

"Oh, come on, it can't be that bad," said Harris.

"It is! You look."

Plum refused—she was no fan of spiders—but Harris marched in full of bravado. He quickly exited, looking pale and shaky.

"That is the mother of all spiders," he exclaimed. "How did it get in your room?"

"How would I know?" asked India. "Someone must have planted it."

"Nonsense," said Harris. "But I'll go get a crew member. We'll need assistance."

Harris dashed off.

"I'm either super unlucky, or someone is out to get me," sighed India. "First the hornet's nest in Paraiso, and now this."

"What hornet's nest?" asked Plum, intrigued.

"Oh, I was on my way to Carmen Rijo's ladies' lunch when I sat on a hornet's nest in the tender. I ended up staying in. I was lucky, only got a few stings. But it's weird."

"Yes, it is."

Plum made her way to her bed while India waited for the creature's removal. Plum wondered if someone had indeed put it in India's bed as a warning. Or if she was becoming paranoid and suspecting attempted murders around every corner.

CHAPTER

21

PLUM CHECKED HER PHONE AND saw several missed calls from Gerald, as well as texts demanding she call him ASAP or ELSE. His neediness irritated her, and she was tempted to ignore him, but she knew he was voracious and wouldn't stop hounding her until she called him. She capitulated and dialed his number.

"I don't know why I have to find out through the internet that you're on a yacht with Nachelle and India Collins," he said by way of greeting. "This is one of the most despicable moments of my life. I cannot believe you didn't ask me to come with you. I am deeply, deeply offended. In fact, I might not even talk to you ever again!"

"Okay, well, if that's the way you feel, then goodbye," said Plum, calling his bluff.

"WAIT!" he commanded.

Plum knew he was stewing on the other end of the phone, trying to strategize the best way to achieve his goal. She slipped off her shoes and flung them into the closet. Then she strolled into the bathroom and stared at her reflection in the mirror. Were those wrinkles flanking her eyes? She leaned in closer to examine them and to her horror saw she was developing crow's-feet around her eyes. She would have to remember to apply more sunscreen; that would hopefully help.

"What do you want, Gerald?" she asked.

This time, his tone was more conciliatory, even obsequious. "Plum, darling," he oozed. "You know you're my best friend. And you know I have done *so* many favors for you. I need you to tell me exactly where you are."

"I am somewhere in the Caribbean Sea, Gerald," she replied.

"That's not helpful, sweetie," he said, trying to remain calm, although she could hear impatience creeping into his voice. She loved to torture him.

"We are heading toward an island, ultimately," she replied.

"What island?"

"I don't know," she replied vaguely. This was fun: she could hear Gerald emitting steam on the other end. She leaned into the mirror and started to examine her pores, all the while wishing the lighting were a little worse.

"You don't know? That's impossible. Tell me this instant," he commanded.

"Why should I?"

"Because...okay, well, don't. That's fine," he snapped. "But it won't be my fault if you get murdered. It's your funeral."

Plum froze and stopped staring at her reflection. "What did you say?"

"I said if you end up murdered, it's on you!" he roared.

"Who have you been talking to?" she asked. "Did Juan Kevin say anything to you? Or Captain Diaz?"

"Juan Kevin? Captain Who?" he repeated. "I don't know what they have to do with anything. I'm talking about the scandal involving India Collins and the last film set she was on. I don't care what you read—I know the real deal because of my inside information and top-secret contacts, and I refuse to tell you anything until you tell me what the next port is where you will disembark."

Plum's mind raced. What was he referring to? She decided to bluff. "I know all about India's scandal."

"Oh, really?" he asked. "She probably told you she had nothing to do with it. And she was very lucky that her publicist took charge of the situation earlier and killed the story in the press. But that's not the real story. I have the inside scoop. And if I were you, I'd sleep with a knife under my pillow!"

Plum couldn't keep up the facade any longer. She had to know. "Okay, okay, I'll tell you where we're going. Our next stop is Jolly Island."

"Jolly Island!" squealed Gerald. "So posh! They say it's the best place you can ever visit and the worst."

"Why the worst?" asked Plum.

"It's apparently haunted. It's almost like *Fantasy Island* on acid. Some people go and have all their wishes fulfilled. They find love and romance and all that junk. But others say it's horrible. But I would take it any day of the week. I need a vacation."

"Gerald, you just had one! Maybe you should think about putting your head down and getting to work."

"You hypocrite! You're one to talk, gallivanting around on yachts with rock stars."

"That's work also."

"I don't believe you," he said, and Plum could hear him pouting on the other end of the line.

"You don't have to," Plum insisted. "Now tell me what happened with India Collins."

"Maybe I won't now," he said petulantly.

"Gerald," she said in a warning tone. "We had a deal. You had better or else."

"Fine," he said peevishly. "I'm sure you know—"

"I know nothing. So start at the beginning."

"India makes like she's nice as apple pie. She's trying to be the next Reese or Drew. She's always smiling and friendly. But apparently, she has a real dark side. She was recently filming that movie based on the comic strip, you know the one…"

"They're all based on comics," said Plum with a wince. "It's unfortunate."

"True," agreed Gerald. "This one had all the celebs you know, Chris, Kate, John…the whole gang. Anyway, she had a small part, but it was a good one for an unknown like her. It's not as if she's Scarlett Johansson, for lord's sake. She had a scene with Jennifer, not Aniston, the other one, and in the scene, they struggle and India's character trips Jennifer. Well, as you know from the news—okay, you didn't watch it, but India accidentally slid, and she tripped Jennifer, who ended up falling and breaking her arm. But the truth of the matter is India didn't do it by accident. She hated her costar and purposely tripped her. It was all covered up."

"And you know this how?" asked Plum, skepticism in her voice.

"Rafal did the makeup."

"Who's Rafal?" asked Plum.

"Zeke's boyfriend," replied Gerald in an exasperated tone.

"Who is Zeke?" asked Plum.

"Rafal's boyfriend."

"I'm confused," said Plum.

Gerald emitted a long breath. "I'm losing my patience. It's clear you never listen to me and don't bother to know who my friends are. But whatever. It's not important. Rafal told me that before the scene, India was in the makeup trailer and going off on Jennifer, saying what a bitch she was and how she had no time for India and thought she was so great. She said one day Jennifer would be very sorry she was rude to her."

"Flimsy," replied Plum.

"She said it in a very sinister tone." Gerald sniffed.

"That doesn't tell me anything. Think of the number of times you and I both have ranted about people, and we are hardly homicidal maniacs."

"Well, Rafal said she was very angry and he wouldn't put anything past her. And if you don't believe Rafal, because you don't even bother to remember who he is, you should at least believe all the stuff that came out after."

"What stuff?" asked Plum.

"The press wrote about how India had been fired from a reality show because she destroyed one of the contestants' dresses. Slashed it to bits before the gal was about to wear it. India denied it, of course, but because it was one of those reality shows, they had the footage."

"Now that's interesting," said Plum. "Can I watch this reality show online?"

"It never aired," said Gerald. "They were scooped by that reality show *Below Deck*. They were both about the staff on yachts, so it was redundant."

Plum stood up straight. "India was on a reality show that took place on a yacht?"

"That's what I said."

"Maybe she knew someone from this yacht," said Plum. Her mind was racing. Could this have been a connection? Maybe she knew Captain Dave?

"I don't know, but that's not the point. The point is she's mean and nasty..."

But Plum was no longer listening.

"I've got to go, Gerald. It's been nice chatting with you."

"Okay, you probably have to get back to all those fantastic people. So you'll be at Jolly Island tomorrow?" asked Gerald.

"No, the next day," she lied. She didn't want Gerald tracking her whereabouts. She wouldn't put it past him to alert paparazzi, who would descend on them. As it was only a day trip, they would be long gone from Jolly Island tomorrow night.

Plum had trouble falling asleep, most likely because she had napped and that always destroyed her REM cycle. When she finally did fall asleep, it was fitful, and she found herself tossing and turning. She woke up abruptly and looked at the clock. It was only 12:34 a.m. She glanced around the room, squinting through the darkness. What had woken her up?

She heard a very faint tapping. Someone was knocking at her door. A tide of fear passed over her. She flipped her covers off and walked to the door. Before she opened it, she decided to it would be wise to have some sort of weapon in case it was the murderer. Her eyes skittered around the room. What could she use?

The knocking continued. In desperation and haste, Plum grabbed a small decorative porcelain pineapple on the chest of drawers. She clutched it in her hand and raised her arm, prepared to deliver a fatal blow should a killer be on the other side, and slowly opened the door.

"Who is it?" she asked.

"It's me, Saoirse."

"Saoirse!" Plum exclaimed. Relief flooded her. She dropped her arm and let the young woman in. "You scared me to death."

"I'm sorry, ma'am, but you asked me to come see you. I've only just finished up work."

"Yes, come in."

Plum ushered her into the bedroom. She motioned for the chair, and Saoirse sat. She looked tired and drained, and Plum could tell that the events of the past few days compounded with the increased workload must be taking a toll on the young woman. Plum sat on the edge of the bed across from her.

"First off, I noticed you had a very startled expression when Harris mentioned the name of his yacht. Why was that?"

Saoirse's face went dark before she explained, "The yacht network keeps tabs on one another. We don't know everyone, obviously, but there are message boards and Facebook pages where we exchange information. I had heard about the *Miss Conduct*. In fact, I heard a lot about it. There was an accident there as well. It was about two years ago. A steward from Germany had just started working on board. Apparently, his boss kept making overtures at him—romantic overtures— that he wanted no part of. He complained to the employment company that hired him. Next thing you know, the man was dead."

"How did he die?"

"They said it was an accident, of course. He'd gone out for the night after working three back-to-back shifts, and when he came back, the *Miss Conduct* was locked up for the night. He couldn't get in any of the doors, so he tried the emergency entrance. He slipped and hit his head on the quay and drowned."

"Sounds so similar to Lysette..." gasped Plum.

"Yes. That's why I was so shocked when Harris said it was his boat. First the German lad, then Lysette—who's next?"

"It is suspicious."

"I'll agree, ma'am."

"Saoirse, why didn't you tell me you were angry at Lysette her final night? That she had disappeared?" asked Plum.

Saoirse hesitated, clearly conflicted. Then she said reluctantly, "I didn't want to speak poorly of her. I felt bad speaking ill of the dead."

"Walk me through that last night."

"Lysette helped set the table, and we were preparing for the dinner service. I asked her to get a set of napkins from the linen closet, and she took a very long time returning. I had to set the entire table myself. I was angry."

"Where had she been?"

Saoirse hesitated. "I hadn't wanted to say, ma'am..."

"Will you please not call me *ma'am*?" implored Plum. "We're practically contemporaries. I am sure we were born in the same decade, probably even the same year. You're making me feel old."

"You were born in 2002?"

"*You* were born in 2002?" Plum repeated before nodding. "Close enough. Anyway, go on. I can tell there's part of the story you're holding back, and I would like you to get out with it."

"Fair enough," said Saoirse. She took a very long, deep breath and exhaled. "Lysette was having romantic relations with Captain Dave. And I don't approve of it at all. Mostly because he has a wife back home. And wee ones. But also because it's unprofessional. And it was becoming a problem."

"Captain Dave and Lysette?" mused Plum. "He didn't say anything about it."

"Now why would he?" asked Saoirse. "He's a married man. I think if Mr. Campbell found out, he would have been angry."

"Agreed. How was it affecting their work?"

"Lysette was scattered. She was distracted by something. I think it was Captain Dave, but also she didn't like Mr. and Mrs. Von Steefel or Miss Brown. She was a very opinionated girl. I don't think she would have lasted long here, even if she hadn't met her maker."

"Why didn't she like Miss Brown?" asked Plum. "Besides the obvious?"

"She said she was a drug addict. She made Lysette go to strange places to pick up pills for her. Not pharmacies. It was these shady places that only took cash and no insurance. Drug dealers. Miss Brown said not to tell anyone, especially Mr. Campbell. But Mr. Campbell had told us in the beginning not to get anything for Miss Brown unless it's from a pharmacy. It put us in a bad spot."

"Nachelle is a drug addict?" asked Plum. "What kind of drugs?"

"I only know pills. Not certain what kind."

Wow, thought Plum. *I am traveling with a completely degenerate crew. Killers, drug addicts, blackmailers. What next?*

"Did anyone have a motive to kill Lysette?" asked Plum.

"I think everyone did, ma'am...I mean, Miss Lockhart. The fact is Lysette was taking notes on everyone. She was gathering all the bad stuff, all the sordid information, and planned to do something with it. I'm not sure what. But she wanted to bring people down. And bring others to justice."

CHAPTER

22

WHEN PLUM WALKED OUT OF her cabin to breakfast, she noticed the boat was not moving. The motor was shut off, and they were idling in the middle of the ocean. Plum walked down the corridor and outside and saw Captain Dave and Jomer standing at the stern, conferring with Robert. He looked irate, and they were gesticulating wildly.

"Something's wrong with the motor," said India, who had sidled up behind her.

She wore a bikini top and short jean shorts and had her blond hair in two braids. Plum thought she looked about ten years old.

"What's wrong with it?" asked Plum.

"I have no idea," said India. "I don't know much about how things work."

"Me neither," confessed Plum. "I don't even know how to change a tire."

"That I do know," said India. She took a sip of green smoothie out of a plastic straw.

"Not to be the environmental police, but do you know plastic straws kill endangered turtles?" asked Plum.

"You know, I did hear that but don't understand why it's specifically straws that are a problem."

"I actually read up on this after a friend told me," Plum said, remembering the first time she and Juan Kevin had come across a turtle crossing the road and he had told her how special they are. "There are so many varieties of turtles on Paraiso, and they are something of a national treasure, so I did the deep dive on them."

"And?"

"Well, turtles mistakenly identify plastic straws and eat them. Which is detrimental because plastic doesn't break down and remains in the stomach of the turtle and builds up over time, sending erroneous message to their brains that their stomachs are full and they don't need to eat. They literally starve to death."

"Wow, you really know a lot about turtles."

"Yes, but it doesn't just affect turtles," Plum continued, becoming agitated. "Microplastics get into the food chain when they're consumed by smaller creatures, and then the turtles eat them—it's a vicious cycle of destruction. Furthermore, the straws break down into smaller pieces and get into sheltering seaweed mats. Then their hatchlings eat them, and young turtles get tangled in the seaweed mat and can't breathe. It's really horrible."

"That *is* horrible," said India. She popped the straw out of her smoothie. "Now I don't ever want to eat them again."

"You ate them? Like in soup?"

"Well, actually, I love their eggs. They're a wonderful aphrodisiac."

Plum's heart began racing. "So you're the one!" said Plum in a bogus joking tone. "You're out there digging up all the turtle eggs in the middle of the night."

India shook her head. "Not me."

"Really? You didn't eat them here? Go digging for them just for fun?" Plum coaxed.

India shook her head. "I would never go out digging for turtle eggs in the middle of the night."

"You can tell me," urged Plum.

India looked confused. "Honestly."

Plum remembered India's interaction with Captain Dave. What had he given her? "Was it Captain Dave who sold you the eggs?"

"Captain Dave? Of course not."

"Look, India. The other day, I was minding my own business, but I saw Captain Dave hand something to you outside of your cabin. And you slipped him some money."

India's eyes widened. "Were you spying on me?"

"Not at all," lied Plum. "Just walking by."

India appeared irritated. "Look, not that it's any of your business, but I had asked him for Ambien. I couldn't sleep. And I paid him for his troubles."

"Oh," said Plum, deflated. That made sense. Then a thought occurred to her. "When did you try the turtle eggs?"

"I don't know," mumbled India.

Plum stared at her. "India, stay away from Joel. He's a married man."

"I never said anything about Joel," India responded.

Plum gave her a skeptical look. "Come on."

India sighed. "Okay, listen. It's not what it seems. I really want to break into Hollywood and be a big star. A guy like Joel will make it happen."

"You shouldn't have to sleep with him," pressed Plum.

"No one's forcing me to," admitted India. And then she sighed with deep exasperation. "Look, he's gross, I admit. But he's powerful, has tons of connections, and it's not like I'm getting *nothing* out of it. Lots of nice clothes and expensive jewelry and a good movie role."

Plum looked at her with disgust and disappointment. "India, you're young. But remember he's a married man. And there are other ways to get ahead."

"I know that," India insisted with defiance. She stood up straighter.

"Then you should figure out a way to succeed without sleeping with Joel."

India glanced around the hallway to make sure no one else was listening. She leaned closer. "I actually have a plan. You know there are cameras on the boat? I'm using that to my advantage. But you can't say a thing. Once I have some footage of us, I can tell him to back off or I will release it."

Plum was surprised. She hadn't thought India was that savvy. Or manipulative for that matter. "How are you getting footage of him?"

India gave her a coy look. "Well, I'm tight with Captain Dave now."

Plum shook her head. "So you're going to blackmail Joel?"

"It's not like that. I am going to use him the way he used me. And if he allows me to end it, then I won't have to do anything drastic, and we can all end as friends. Ellen can have him all to herself."

At least until he finds another wannabe actress, thought Plum.

Plum was still en route to breakfast when someone called out.

"Hey, you!"

She glanced toward the end of the hall and saw Nachelle standing in the threshold of the main suite.

"Me?" asked Plum.

"Yeah, who else?" remarked Nachelle. "I don't see anyone else around. Can you come here a minute?"

She wagged a beckoning finger at Plum, curling it to indicate the direction she should proceed.

"Sure," said Plum. She walked toward her de facto hostess, internally grumbling that the diva had not said *please* or *thank you*. Nachelle disappeared into the room without waiting for her.

Plum wasn't sure what to think about Nachelle after the information Saoirse had told her last night. Was the singer really a drug addict? Probably, she supposed. It went with the professional territory. But what did Plum know?

Plum entered the suite and glanced around. The plush cabin was bathed in natural light, with large panoramic windows facing the blue sea. The walls were pearl gray, and there was a king-size bed in the center adorned with different natural hues and flanked by two antique black-lacquered side tables. There was a sitting area in the corner with two comfortable chairs, a sofa, and a small Chinese coffee table with a beautiful flower arrangement on the center.

Nachelle stood in front of a mirrored wardrobe with about a dozen discarded dresses puddling around her feet. She wore a long shimmering gold dress that plunged to her navel and was checking out her reflection.

"Looks like we're stranded," said Plum. "The boat isn't moving."

"Jolly Island will be a bore anyway," replied Nachelle. She turned to Plum. "What do you think?"

"Beautiful," said Plum.

The ethereal hand-beaded dress was truly a work of art. The top was constructed like armor, whereas the tiered skirt was sheer with the most delicate streaks of gold.

"They want me to wear it to the Met Gala next month, but I'm not sure. I think it might be too pedestrian," she said as she began to pull it off.

"I think it's gorgeous. Is it couture?" asked Plum.

"Yeah, worth like two hundred thousand dollars," said Nachelle as she dropped it on the floor and kicked it to the side. She retrieved another gown from the closet, this time a yellow silk caped gown that folded into a rosette-like shapes with a ruffled skirt and a headdress. She slid it on. "I kind of like this one."

"That is also stunning," said Plum. She stood appraising the singer's outfit and nodding her appreciation. Gerald

Hand would be so jealous when she told him she was consulted on Nachelle's outfit. He would literally give an eyeball to witness this.

"Yeah, this is okay." Nachelle shrugged.

"Exquisite," replied Plum.

Nachelle took it off and threw it on the small sofa next to her. Losers got the floor, winner got the sofa, Plum noted. Nachelle threw on a cherry-red brocade tunic dress that looked faintly Uzbekistani and sat on the sofa. Right on top of the yellow gown, Plum noticed with dismay. Nachelle began to try on high heels. Plum was still standing and wished Nachelle would at least ask her to sit down, but her hostess seemed distracted.

"Listen, I obviously didn't pull you in here to ask your fashion advice," Nachelle said, her voice full of amusement. She slid her eyes up and down Plum.

"I worked at fashion magazines," responded Plum haughtily.

"Right," said Nachelle. She slid her foot into a black satin pump. "And I was queen of England."

"No, really," insisted Plum.

Nachelle removed the pump and threw it back in the box. She selected another shoebox and pulled out a strappy gold sandal. She put it on. "I need you to do something for me."

"What's that?" asked Plum. She fervently hoped Nachelle wouldn't enlist her to buy drugs. That would be awkward.

"I want you to tell Robert to clear out all these sycophants and scheming bitches. I'm tired of them."

"Who are you referring to specifically?" asked Plum.

There were several guests on the yacht who fit that description.

Nachelle waved her hand in the air. "Suki, India, Harris. I'm tired of them. Time for them to go. They can catch a plane home from Jolly Island."

"Well, it's not really my place. Why don't you tell Robert?" asked Plum.

"I did tell Robert," snapped Nachelle. "But for some reason, he refuses to. I think he's trying to torture me. But these people are insufferable, and I want them out. I can't relax around them. Even Harris with all his pedantic simpering irritates the hell out of me. Normally I like to have that type of guy around, who clearly adores me, but he's irritating. He's always trying to corner Robert. And Robert is avoiding Harris, so I have no idea why he hasn't booted him."

"And what makes you think I could help?" asked Plum. "I only just met Robert. I only just met all of you. I have no clout."

Nachelle threw the gold shoe into the box and pulled another box closer to her. She extracted ten-inch stilettos with a hyena motif.

"That's why I think he'll listen to you. You're not trying to get something out of him or me like everyone else on this yacht. Robert won't be suspicious of your motives. I want you to make up some reason why they need to get off. You have no ulterior motive, which is useful."

"I can't imagine what I could say that would persuade him," Plum responded.

"You say you saw Harris snooping around Robert's office.

Looking at his computer. That will irritate Robert. In fact, tell him they all were."

"How did you know he was snooping around Robert's office?" asked Plum.

"I caught him doing it the other day. He was pretending to look for a paper clip."

"I caught him doing it the other day, and he said he was looking for a pencil." Plum laughed. She decided to sit in one of the chairs, despite getting no invitation. If this woman was asking her to scheme and lie to her host, Plum felt at the very least she could sit down. "What is he after?"

"Harris is broke. The guy is full of hot air. Has no more money and wants Robert to bail him out. Robert is kind, so he feels bad for Harris. He's known him a long time. But he's not going to hand over millions of dollars because he's a kind guy. He's a shark when it comes to business."

"Robert knows he's a fraud?" asked Plum. "I thought no one knew. He was telling me he just bought a house in East Hampton that someone else bought."

"And I'm sure he told you about his yachts and islands and servants." Nachelle laughed. She threw another shoe across the room. "He is delusional. A pathological liar."

"It's odd because he would be charming if he weren't pretending to be so fabulous," said Plum.

"Maybe." Nachelle sighed deeply and dramatically. "They all annoy me. I want them gone."

Plum felt as if this was an opportunity. She decided to make an audacious move. "I could suggest that...well, that they had something to do with Lysette's death."

"Yes, yes," said Nachelle, her eyes shining. "That's brilliant."

"Do you think Robert would believe me?"

"Well, you would have to have some proof. Or a reasonable explanation," said Nachelle.

"Like what?" asked Plum coyly.

Nachelle smiled slyly. "You could say Lysette was blackmailing them. That she knew something about their past and was threatening to go public with it. That she had dropped hints and had some dirt on all of them, and they decided to pull a *Death on the Nile* and all murder her together."

"That was *Murder on the Orient Express*," Plum corrected.

"Whatever," dismissed Nachelle. "The point is they all wanted her dead. She brought up sensitive issues, and they had to teach her a lesson."

"But do you think Robert will believe that?" asked Plum with faux naivete.

"That girl had an attitude. She wanted everyone to know she had the goods on them. She was not Little Miss Innocent, no, siree. In fact, I caught her snooping around my stuff and threw a fit. I told Robert I didn't want her cleaning our room, made sure Saoirse was the only one who came in here. And I let that girl know I wouldn't put up with her crap. I made her do all the miserable tasks and errands to teach her a lesson."

"Really?" asked Plum. She thought of the drugs. "What do you think she was trying to find out about you?"

Nachelle's face became angry. "Not important. You should focus on what she had on Harris, India, and Suki. I know she got into it with all of them."

"What do you mean?"

"Well, the night she died, she had been preparing Harris's room, you know, turning down his sheets and such. And he said she was looking through his stuff—the same thing she did to me, and I'm sure she did it. She denied it, and then he piped down, but I think she found something because when he was yelling about her, I saw a look she gave him, and he clammed up said he had made a mistake. So, obviously, she got something she wanted."

"Interesting," murmured Plum.

"And Suki didn't like the flowers Lysette put in her room."

"Yes, I remember that," said Plum. "But that's not cause for murder."

Nachelle shrugged. "Suki seems unhinged. And desperate. No wonder her husband took off."

"Why did he take off?" asked Plum.

"I'm sure the dude tries to get away from her as much as possible. Plus, I heard Robert say Gunther has serious money issues right now. He's a count without an account. And Suki won't stick around without the dough. That's why she wants my boyfriend."

"Oh, you noticed that?"

Nachelle smiled. "Anyone with a pulse noticed that. If I were not more secure in my relationship, I would be freaking out. But again, I think it's bad form to be hitting on the host when his girlfriend is there. Another reason for her to be gone."

Plum nodded. She did agree it was good cause for expulsion.

"And India?"

"That girl needs to learn her place. I think Ellen is all right, but Joel's behavior is uncool. He's basically having an affair in front of his wife. And that little up-and-comer will learn the hard way that it's not the way to get ahead. Things like that boomerang."

Plum nodded. "I'll see what I can do, Nachelle, but I really doubt I can get them kicked off the boat. And honestly, I don't feel comfortable doing it. You should just have a talk with Robert. He seems besotted with you. I think he would do what you want."

Her face became stormy. "You would think. There's something holding him back. And I'm losing my patience. If the situation doesn't change on this boat, I'm out of here."

CHAPTER

23

"WHAT WAS THAT ABOUT?"

Plum turned around. She had just exited Nachelle's suite and hadn't even noticed Joel was standing outside his room in the corridor. Almost as if waiting for her.

Plum took a minute to compose herself and gather her thoughts before answering, "Nachelle asked me to look at some of the gowns she's contemplating wearing to the Met Gala. She wanted my advice."

He scoffed. "Oh, really? Nachelle wanted your advice?"

"Is that so ridiculous?" asked Plum. "I did work at a fashion magazine at one point."

He laughed. "It's not crazy that someone normal would want your advice. But we're talking about Nachelle. I don't think she takes anyone's advice."

Plum nodded. "Probably right."

Joel gave her a long glance. "Listen, I want to talk to you. Let's go to the upper deck. Where we can have more privacy."

"I was on my way to breakfast."

"It can wait."

Plum's stomach was rumbling, but she felt as if she had little choice. "Fine."

The sun had risen even higher, and the sunrays felt like warm honey on Plum's skin. It was so bright outside that Plum slipped on her sunglasses and still felt herself squinting. Every ray was reflected off the water and bounced off every surface of the yacht.

Joel stopped. "I think Ellen's been giving you the wrong idea. Don't listen to her. Look, you guys are old friends, but you haven't seen each other in a while, so I'm not sure if you know about all her breakdowns."

"Her breakdowns?" asked Plum.

"Yeah," said Joel. "The fact is your bestie has been in and out of the loony bin for the past decade. She's totally unstable."

Plum was seized by a surge of concern. "What do you mean?"

"Look, I love her, you know I do. We were, like, a golden couple. We still are. Everyone in Hollywood envies us because we've been married over a decade. That's like a world record there. But Ellen, you know, she never should have quit her job. She's a great mother and tried to be a great corporate wife, but you know, she doesn't have enough to do. She got bored, and then the booze and the pills started. And she's totally paranoid. Thinks I'm banging every chick that comes along. Delusional."

"Is she?" Plum asked.

Joel gave her a skeptical look as if she were crazy. "I am the most faithful person I have ever met."

"Are you crossing your fingers behind your back, Joel?"

His expression grew pugnacious. "What are you implying, Plum? You got any proof?"

"No, but what I see is you all over India Collins every second of this trip. It's no wonder your wife is quote unquote 'paranoid.'"

Joel leaned his head back and laughed, but it felt artificial to Plum. "Honey, that's work. India Collins is the next big thing whether I like it or not, and I got to schmooze."

"Schmoozing is one thing, Joel, but egregiously seducing her and making everyone around you believe you're sleeping with someone and committing adultery is a completely different thing."

"I don't like your tone, Plum," he said petulantly.

"And I don't like your behavior, Joel," said Plum, who crossed her arms angrily for effect. "You are humiliating your wife. Everyone on the boat watches you flirt outrageously with an actress young enough to be your daughter. It's pathetic. I hate what you are doing to my friend, and you should remember you're a married man in a position of power and not exploit it."

The left vein on Joel's temple started to throb, and Plum thought it might explode. But that would be too good to be true. She didn't regret what she had said to him, but she also felt a little hesitant about the outcome.

Joel thrust his finger toward her as he made jabbing motions in the air. "You don't know what you're talking about."

"I don't?" she asked, arching an eyebrow. "Are you sure India is on board with your affair?"

"You have no idea what you're saying.," he insisted.

Plum didn't want to betray India's confidence, so she dropped that line of questioning. "What about the fact you were fired? For sexual harassment. Why haven't you told Ellen yet?"

This took him off guard. "You better not say anything to anyone about it."

"I don't have to," she retorted. "It's all over the internet."

He looked stricken but quickly retaliated. "I'm clearing that all up. In the meantime, I'm warning you to keep your mouth shut."

"Or what?"

"Or what?" he repeated. "Or you will regret it."

"Like Lysette did?"

"That bitch deserved death!" he snapped. "She was stirring up trouble, poking around where she should not have been. Just like you! Watch out, Plum. You're next!"

Plum was shocked. "What are you saying?" she asked.

"You know nothing! You're so naive!"

He turned his back and stormed away before she could respond. Plum gasped. She felt as if she had been holding her breath for hours and was only just able to breathe.

Plum decided she needed to hear a friendly voice. She darted back to her room and dialed Juan Kevin.

"It's me," said Plum.

"Hi," said Juan Kevin warmly. As soon as Plum heard his voice, she felt her tension slide away. "How are you? I've been worried."

"All good," lied Plum. "I'm just happy to talk to you…"

The connection was choppy.

"I'm happy to talk to you," came Juan Kevin's broken response.

"I honestly can't wait to get off this boat," said Plum.

Juan Kevin's response was muffled. Then Plum heard what she thought was a woman's voice in the background.

"Who's that?" asked Plum.

Juan Kevin didn't respond, and Plum repeated the question.

"It's Victoria," Juan Kevin replied. "She's here—"

But Plum couldn't hear the rest of his sentence. Victoria? What was she doing with Juan Kevin? And what was she doing with him this early in the morning?

"Why is she there?" asked Plum.

"We're—" said Juan Kevin. She couldn't make out the rest of what he said.

"Hello?" asked Plum.

But the line went dead. Incensed, Plum put down the phone. Why was Victoria there? Was that woman taking advantage of Plum's absence and wiggling her way back into Juan Kevin's life? She wondered if she had made a mistake not telling Juan Kevin that Victoria had threatened her. Was that the type of woman he wanted, one who was vicious?

She was suddenly burning with jealousy. What was going on? He had said he was over his ex. That they were divorcing. Was it a case of out of sight, out of mind now that Plum was away?

She felt drained and disappointed. It made her realize just

how much she cared for Juan Kevin and hoped he felt the same. Didn't he?

The day felt endless and ominous. Although it was initially bright, clouds moved across the sky, creating a thick layer of gray. The crew was working on fixing the engine, but they were currently stranded in the middle of the sea, with no land visible and no other boats around.

Normally this would be a blissful sensation, but they were all querulous and impatient and in dire need of a distraction. Scattered showers deterred them from sunbathing, and everyone rejected Robert's suggestion that they take the Jet Skis out again. They could see lightning in the distance, and a gloom fell upon them.

Rather than the usual group breakfast and lunch, the guests all ate in shifts, and some did not show up at all. Plum didn't see Ellen all day and wondered what her friend was up to. India and Joel were huddled together in the screening room watching a movie, and Plum wanted to stay as far away from them as possible. She agreed to play a few games of backgammon with Harris just to distract herself before she retired to her room and did some work.

She had an endless back-and-forth with Lucia about how they could retaliate against Damián, but she was not left satisfied since they could not come up with a plan. Plum was restless. She knew there was a gym on board and thought about going to work out, but the very thought made her exhausted. She congratulated herself for even thinking of it and instead took a big fat nap. There wasn't much to do on a yacht, she realized.

CHAPTER

24

WHEN SHE WOKE UP, IT was already cocktail hour. Yacht life was going from one meal to the next, with drinks in between. Plum was certain it was not for her. She needed more action. But she still felt gloomy and upset about Juan Kevin. She tried to push him out of her mind, but images of him and Victoria in tight embraces flooded her head. She hopped in the shower and prepared for dinner.

When Plum emerged from her room, she observed a spring thunderstorm had seized the area, and a soft but determined rain was pounding down on the yacht. It was completely dark outside, and with the boat floating in the middle of the sea, there were no external lights illuminating her path. The clouds had converged to cover the stars and sky, and the boat was enshrouded in a filmy and gloomy inkiness.

Plum was no longer used to rain or bad weather, having been spoiled the past four months by relentless sunshine. The arctic frigidness of New York seemed like a distant memory, rendering these current conditions unpleasant.

The yacht rocked with rippling waves that were increasing in size. As she moved along the corridor toward the front deck where cocktails were served, she was snatched by an uncomfortable and unfamiliar sensation, as if warning her this evening would not be agreeable.

Plum had dressed in a long hand-dyed moss-green cotton dress with panels of crocheted lace and mother-of-pearl buttons. It was lightweight, and Plum felt it complemented her red hair and blue eyes. Her espadrilles had a thick sole and made her several inches taller than her usual five-foot-ten-inch frame. She had wanted to look as if she were kicking ass and taking no prisoners tonight. But she felt cool and wished she were wearing something cozier.

Before she reached the deck, she saw the guests had chosen to assemble in the library for hors d'oeuvres, no doubt because of the rain. She stared through the entrance for a moment unnoticed and took everything in. Robert was sitting in an armchair listening to something India and Suki were talking about, but he appeared distracted. Both women were doing their best to engage him. Ellen was in the corner talking to Joel, and she had an uneasy look on her face, while her husband seemed restless. Only Nachelle was missing. Plum felt a twinge of apprehension.

"Well, well, well, looking awfully sassy tonight," Harris purred with approval when she entered the room. He was standing over a side table where crystal goblets overflowed with caviar along with all the fixings—blini, boiled egg yolks and whites (separated), capers, red onions, and sour cream. He was helping himself to a generous portion of the delicacy.

"Thank you," said Plum. "You do too."

"*Merci*," replied Harris. He was attired in a yellow-and-blue checked suit and wore an ascot under his white button-down. Plum noted he clearly had a flair for the theatrical. "I try to bring it every night, unlike some of these people."

Plum glanced around the room. All the women had their hair coiffed perfectly and their faces made up, and were dressed in long, flowing gowns, bedecked with jewelry. Both other men in the room wore long-sleeved shirts, and in Robert's case, a tie and a blazer.

"I don't know what you mean. Everyone looks very nice," responded Plum.

Harris leaned closer to her. "I don't mean what they're wearing! I mean attitude, girl. Everyone is at their wit's end—so much infighting and drama. I feel like I'm on an episode of a reality show!"

"Who's fighting?" whispered Plum as she watched Harris scoop more caviar onto his plate.

"You name it," he said with his mouth full.

Plum was instantly distracted by a figure standing in the shadowy hallway near the door. She squinted. It was... what was his name? Jomer. The first officer. His face looked drawn and pallid, and he gave her a strange gaze. She turned her head quizzically, and he beckoned for her to approach. Something about his expression sent a chill down her spine. She was about to approach him when suddenly there was a large flash of lightning followed by a giant clap of thunder. The noise was so violent that the yacht shook, and the overhead lights fluttered. Both Ellen and India emitted startled shrieks. Plum turned quickly to glance at them.

"This is scary!" said Ellen, clutching her hand to her chest. "Are we safe?"

"Of course," snapped Joel. His wife buried her head into his shoulder, and he reluctantly patted her with his hairy fingers.

"We'll be fine," announced Robert with authority. "I can assure you this boat is made to withstand almost everything. I don't want anyone on board to feel uneasy. In fact, maybe we should put on some music to lighten the mood."

He walked over to the entertainment center and lifted a remote. When he pressed a button, Aretha Franklin's beautiful voice flooded the room.

Plum moved back toward Harris, who was still stationed by the caviar.

"Well, that was something!" boomed Harris. He lifted a champagne glass off the table and drained it.

"Yes," said Plum. Her heart was thumping not only because of the storm but because she knew Jomer had something important to tell her. She began moving toward the door. She took about three steps when out of nowhere Nachelle burst into the room, almost knocking her over.

"I don't like this at all, Robert," Nachelle announced as she stomped across the room to her boyfriend before stopping in front of India, who was seated near him on the sofa. Nachelle glared at India so intently that the young actress slid out of the way, and Nachelle sat down. Her large feathered skirt took up half the seat, flapping into India's lap, prompting the girl to move to an adjoining seat.

"Is the engine fixed yet?" asked Nachelle.

"Almost," said Robert. "The captain promises us it will be tonight. And then we will be on our way to Jolly Island."

"Well, you tell the captain to get us out of this bad weather. I don't want to drown out here," commanded Nachelle.

"Don't be silly," said Robert. "It's fine; the weather system is passing us..."

Plum didn't wait to hear the rest of his explanation. She moved out into the hallway to find Jomer. There was another flash of lightning followed by the roaring boom of thunder. A rush of cool breeze greeted her in the hallway, but that was all. There was no one there. She craned her head to the left and right, but it was empty. Jomer had gone. Undoubtedly, he had probably returned to the captain's deck when the thunder and lightning came so he could help steer them out of this. Isn't this how they came up with the phrase, *All hands on deck*?

Plum heard footsteps. She turned around and found Saoirse behind her.

"You startled me," said Plum.

"I apologize," Saoirse replied. "I've come to call everyone in for dinner."

"Where is Jomer? I think he wanted to tell me something." Plum said.

Saoirse gave her a confused expression. "Jomer?"

"What's going on?"

Plum and Saoirse both jumped before turning around.

Robert was looming in the doorway. His tone was amiable, but his face was dark with anger.

"I was calling you to dinner, sir," said Saoirse with a slight bow.

Robert nodded, his eyes fixed on Plum. "Very well, then. Plum, I would like you to lead the way."

Plum paused a beat before obeying her host. Was there a reason Robert didn't want her talking to his staff? Was he hiding something?

People were on edge due to the weather. Even though it was a state-of-the-art Dutch-built yacht with all the amenities, the boat still rocked back and forth. Plum felt as if she were on a ride at Disneyland. That said, she had never actually been to Disneyland or any amusement park, so she was unfamiliar with the actual sensation and could only conjecture. An ex-boyfriend had once challenged her on this, musing that of course she had been on a ride when she was young. But the truth was her parents were totally indifferent and had never taken her to even a county fair or on a carousel ride when she was a child. It would never have occurred to them to engage in any sort of activity with their only child. She had always been referred to as a burden.

Plum wondered for a brief second what her parents were up to now. Did they still live in the small house she had grown up in? Were they even alive? She had lost contact with them years ago, at first assuming they would try and reach out. But they never did. Plum pushed thoughts of them away as she always did.

She wondered what Juan Kevin would think of her parents.

It was strange because she used to always imagine what her parents would think of any potential suitor. She used to think she would bring home some world-famous businessman or celebrity and they would be dazzled by her choice and her success. Now she didn't care what they thought, and she certainly didn't need someone rich or famous. She wanted someone kind. She did care what Juan Kevin would think of her parents, but it would not bother her at all if he despised them. He was a good man; she would trust his judgment. But if he was good, why was he with Victoria?

"You look lost in reverie," said Suki, who was sitting next to her and holding out the bread basket to be passed along. "Thinking about a man?"

"What? No," Plum responded quickly. Unfortunately, she could tell a red blush was creeping its way across her pale cheeks.

"Thou doth protest too much," said Suki with a sly smile.

"No, really," insisted Plum, feeling foolish.

Suki leaned in conspiratorially as if she were about to say something really supportive. "Plum, if I can give you some advice. I mean this as a friend." She put her hand on Plum's wrist to emphasize the point. "I think you would have a lot more success with men if you were more feminine."

"How do you mean?" asked Plum, indulging her.

"I think you need to flirt more, if you even have that in your arsenal. Men like a soft touch. They like a woman who gazes at them adoringly and tells them how wonderful they are."

"Right," said Plum. "I'll remember that."

"Or wait, perhaps I'm wrong. I apologize. Is it women you're interested in?" Suki's expression was one of mock contrition.

"Thanks, Suki, but I don't need any tips from you on my romantic life."

"I'm just trying to help, please don't take offense."

"Duly noted," said Plum. "But I am curious, where did you meet your husband?"

"Gunther and I traveled in the same circles in Europe," she said vaguely. "We both had starter marriages. Nothing serious. Like most people at this table."

Plum glanced around at the collected guests. "Robert was married before?"

"Of course," said Suki. "As was Nachelle. But then I'm sure we all know *that* story."

"I don't know that story," said Plum, her eyes firmly on Nachelle, who sat across the table and was talking to Joel.

Suki emitted a small laugh. "She killed her ex-husband."

"She did what?" exclaimed Plum, turning to her dinner companion. "How?"

"He was older, a producer, well, not unlike Robert. And he died in the bedroom, you know, when they were intimate. She claimed he always had a heart condition, but everyone knows they were on some sort of drug that enhances those experiences. Of course, I have never needed that…"

"What kind of drug?"

Suki shrugged. "Some sort of aphrodisiac. I have no idea."

Maybe turtle eggs, mused Plum. "And Robert's first wife?" asked Plum. "What happened there?"

"She left him for an Irishwoman. Totally killed his ego. That's why he's been dallying with younger ladies, trying to rebuild his self-esteem," replied Suki. "But I think it's time he put an end to that phase of his life and grew up. He's a successful, attractive man. He doesn't need these pathetic little girls around him. I think he should have someone more mature."

Undoubtedly you, thought Plum. Before she could respond, they were interrupted by Harris, who enfolded them into a rather boring story about a *fabulous* party he'd hosted in Buenos Aires the year prior. Plum allowed herself to zone out and consider what she had just learned. She had thought Nachelle was addicted to prescription drugs, but if it were aphrodisiacs, maybe she was the one stealing the turtle eggs? Or at the very least, perhaps she ordered the staff to procure them. And then maybe Robert was in on it as well? Could it be Lysette had been asked to do this and refused and then ended up dead?

The group imbibed a lot more that evening than they had prior, maybe due to the weather and the creeping anxiety that permeated the atmosphere. After dinner ended, they returned to the library, and Harris suggested they play a game of charades. Plum had been careful with her alcohol intake so that nothing would affect her sleuthing skills, but she noticed everyone was quite drunk. They also appeared reluctant to retire to their cabins, so they agreed to play. Joel and Suki grumbled, as they had become the confirmed naysayers in the party, but India was very enthusiastic to show off her acting chops, and even Nachelle was eager to play.

They had divided into teams based on where they were seated and wrote their clues on pieces of paper, with Harris prompting everyone to not overthink it and just put something down.

"I'll go first," insisted Nachelle, rising and taking a clue out of the basket where they had all deposited them. She unfolded her paper, and her eyes shone brightly. She stood in front of the group. "This is a good one."

"No talking!" whined Harris.

"And no hints," insisted Ellen.

Plum knew her old friend became very competitive in any sort of game. She was practically vicious on the tennis court.

Nachelle pantomimed the motion for an old-fashioned camera, and everyone yelled out, "Movie," practically in unison. Nachelle nodded. She then held up three fingers so they knew that there were three words in the title, and when everyone nodded, she held up her index finger.

"First word!" boomed Harris enthusiastically.

Nachelle indicated agreement then put two fingers together to indicate it was a short word.

"The!" said India.

Nachelle shook her head.

"In!" yelled Joel.

Nachelle shook her head. Then the group started, almost at once, running off a number of short words including *a* and *on* and *to* and *one*.

Nachelle was becoming frustrated and impatient. She motioned for them to keep going with the palm of her hand.

"All?" Plum finally guessed.

Nachelle nodded enthusiastically. "Yes."

"Hey, no talking," Ellen scolded.

Nachelle shot her a dirty look. Then she put up her three fingers.

"Third word," announced Joel.

Nachelle nodded then walked over to India and pulled her out of her chair. The somewhat surprised actress at first looked annoyed but then quickly recovered and put a beatific smile on her face. Nachelle turned India around to face the crowd and pointed to her.

"India?" asked Ellen with confusion.

"*A Passage to India*!" bellowed Harris, who clapped his hands with excitement. "I got it."

"No, you didn't," seethed Suki. "The first word is *all*, you moron."

"And it's only three words," Joel corrected. "*A Passage to India* is four."

"No need to be so hostile," insisted Harris, insult running all over his face. "It's only a game."

"With rules," snapped Suki.

Nachelle clapped her hands to regain their attention. "Come on," she coaxed. "Focus."

"*All of Me*?" asked Plum.

Nachelle shook her head.

"Let's see, India is an actress, maybe it's *All the President's Men*?" asked Harris.

"That makes no sense," said Ellen impatiently. "Once again, that's four words."

"No to mention that India is not a president's man," added Robert with a chuckle.

"I know," said Joel finally. He leaned back in his seat and crossed his arms. "Very funny, Nachelle. Just hilarious," he said sarcastically. "The movie is *All About Eve.*"

"Correct!" yelled out Nachelle with glee.

"*All About Eve*?" asked India, turning to give a quizzical look to Nachelle. "I never saw that movie. What's it about?"

"You'll have to watch it," said Nachelle in a condescending tone. She went to retrieve her cocktail and took a large satisfied sip before flopping down on the sofa.

"I don't remember that movie," said Harris. "Let me look it up."

"You don't need to look it up," said Joel. "It's about a young actress."

Plum had only a vague knowledge of the movie and didn't think she had ever seen it.

"It was a Bette Davis movie," said Ellen quietly. She looked pensive.

Harris had pulled out his phone to google the film and began reading the description aloud. "The film stars Bette Davis as Margo Channing, an aging Broadway star, and Anne Baxter plays Eve Harrington, an ambitious young fan who maneuvers herself into Channing's life and ultimately threatens her career and personal relationship, revealing herself to be a manipulative and cunning villainess."

Harris put down his phone. "Ouch, Nachelle. You have some beef with India?"

India looked hurt. "Yes, Nachelle, I don't understand. Are you accusing me of something?"

"I'm sure she's not," interjected Robert. "She probably just used you as an example because you're an actress."

Nachelle rolled her eyes but didn't answer. She was relishing the tense situation. Plum turned her gaze on Ellen, who appeared anxious and pensive. Was Nachelle trying to signal something to Ellen about Joel? Or was Nachelle sending a warning to India to back off of Robert?

"Genius," said Suki, clapping her hands together. "How clever. Now if I were picking a film to use India as an example, I might pick *Pretty Woman*. That's about the prostitute who by chance lands a rich guy, correct?"

"You bitch," muttered India.

"Or perhaps I'd pick one about a female criminal, although I can't think of any. Maybe India can do a biopic?"

Before things got heated, Robert interjected, "Shall we move on to the next one?"

"I don't think I feel like playing anymore," began India. "I think I'll head to bed."

India made a motion to pick up her shawl and leave, but Nachelle stopped her. "Come on, have a sense of humor, please. It's all fun and games here. As an actress, you'll need thick skin. You know, back in the day, actors and actresses were second-class citizens. The only reason you would have been on this boat would be to entertain us, like a circus performer. So relax."

India hesitated. "You're a pop star, so wouldn't you be included in that second-class citizen group? In fact, maybe you should get up and sing us a song. We could use some entertainment."

The women locked eyes, looks of hostility on their faces. Robert quickly rose. "Ladies, let's move on. In fact, let's forget the game and watch a movie. Joel has brought his latest film that won't even be released for months. Let's pull down the screen and watch it."

Before anyone could respond, the lights were dimmed, the screen was down, and the movie was playing. It was an action movie, one of those vacuous ones with lots of car chases and stupid stunts by the main character, who in real life would have been dead after all the obstacles he had to overcome. Plum snuck surreptitious glances at everyone in the room as the movie progressed and found others doing the same. Something had shifted, and the atmosphere was becoming increasingly sinister. Plum wondered what had happened to Jomer, where he had disappeared to.

In the middle of the night, Plum woke to a loud groaning sound. She bolted upright. It sounded like someone was dragging chains down the hall, and she had a vision of a ghost coming to haunt her. But then she realized it was the anchor being pulled up. The engine must have been fixed. They were on their way again.

She was rattled and her heart was racing. She went to grab a bottle of water but realized she had it all before bed. She threw on the puffy bathrobe and decided to make her way to the den to retrieve one from the minibar.

The hallway was empty and quiet. Everyone was asleep. She padded along the darkened corridor then walked into the den, where everything was still. It felt eerie. She opened the mini fridge. The light came on and buzzed. She selected a bottle of water and closed the fridge. As Plum made her way back to her bedroom, she thought she saw a figure walking quickly down the hall. Was her mind playing tricks on her?

When she walked past India's room, she saw the door was ajar. That was unusual. Plum was about to close it when something occurred to her. She walked into the cabin. India was asleep in her bed. Her flaxen hair lay flat across the pillow like a halo. Plum glanced around the room. Everything seemed normal.

Suddenly India stirred. She opened her eyes and sat bolt upright.

"What are you doing in my room?" she asked Plum. She was disoriented.

"Sorry, your door was open, and I thought someone had been in here," said Plum, continuing to peer around the room.

India's face became worried. She pulled the blanket toward her chest. "Why did you think that?"

"I'm not sure. Does anything look out of place to you?"

India clicked on the light next to her bed, and her eyes flitted around the room, focusing on the dresser, the pile of clothing on the armchair, and the window. "I don't think so, but you're freaking me out."

"Maybe it's nothing. I was just worried."

"My heart is racing," said India, reaching for the glass of water next to her bed.

She was about to press it to her lips when Plum noticed

there was something powdery floating in it. Plum grabbed it before she could ingest it.

"Hey!" protested India.

"Hang on," said Plum. "I don't think you want to drink that." Plum held the murky liquid up to the light. "There's something in here. I think it could be poison."

"Poison?" gasped India. "But why… Oh gosh. You know what? I didn't even have a glass of water next to my bed when I went to sleep. What is happening?"

Plum took the glass, marched into the bathroom, and dumped it in the sink. It made a sizzling sound. She put on the hot water and washed it away, rinsing out the glass thoroughly, before she returned to India.

"I think you want to be careful about what you eat or drink from now on," said Plum. "I think someone is out to get you."

"What can I do?"

"You'll need to be vigilant."

CHAPTER

25

THE MORNING SHONE BRIGHT AND shiny, and there was no hint of the previous evening's severe storms. Wisps of clouds fluttered across the blue sky, and the air was warm and fresh. Plum had slept deeply—a dreamless slumber—and woke later than usual, only to find everyone had already finished breakfast and retreated from the dining room to prepare for the day. Plum quickly poured herself a cup of coffee and grabbed a cheddar scone, then made her way outside to eat it on the deck as she took in the view.

The yacht was gliding into the port of Jolly Island, and Plum could espy the glorious manor hotel tucked into a cove flanked by two rocky promontories that jutted out to sea. The three-story eighteenth-century building was made of brick, and the windows were fringed with sky-blue shutters and window boxes bursting with vibrant red flowers. The ground floor had several French doors opening to a deck where there were assemblages of tables and chairs and hammocks. Two stone staircases running on parallel sides of the hotel led down to the white-sand beach that was dotted with blue-and-white umbrellas. A small anchored motorboat bobbed in the water. The beach was absolutely silent with no visible signs of human activity.

"Gorgeous, isn't it?" asked Robert, who had quietly crept up behind her.

Plum quickly turned around. "You startled me," she said.

"Sorry," said Robert, before motioning to the island. "It was built by a pirate back in the day. He stored his ammunition, alcohol, and women here. A toxic combination if you ask me."

"Sounds like he was courting trouble," agreed Plum. She took a sip of her coffee and examined Robert. He wore a white linen shirt and pants that complemented his ebony skin, and he appeared relaxed this morning. She was glad of it. Last night had been stressful.

"There is definitely a nefarious vibe to the island. Not sure why they call it *Jolly*," said Robert.

"I'm looking forward to seeing it. What exactly is the plan?" asked Plum.

"We'll have lunch at the hotel and meet our hostess. She's a real piece of work. So uptight British that she makes Prince Charles sound like a peasant. Then we'll have a tour of the island. The terrain is rugged, so it gets a little bumpy. The island is still very uncultivated, and there are only dirt roads. Although, of course, there's a landing strip also. It doesn't matter how hard it is to secure an invitation to a place, people want to get in and out quickly," he said with a smile.

"Yes, but I only hear of people wanting to get in," said Plum. "This is such a hard reservation to land."

"It's sort of a scam if you ask me," confessed Robert, leaning on the railing of the boat. "I think some famous person was turned down at one point and then the place garnered the reputation as being exclusive. Then, of course, everyone wanted to come. Once a member of the jet set arrives, they pretend to love it, even though I don't believe they do. The amenities are slight—there's basically only swimming and snorkeling. I don't think they have tennis, even. Backgammon is the only competitive sport. And from what I hear, the rooms are in dire need of updating. Someone told me the bed was so uncomfortable that they felt as if they were sleeping on a pile of firewood."

"Ouch," said Plum. "That's very funny because when I was editing the travel magazine, this was the hottest ticket around. I only ever heard rave reviews."

Robert smiled. "That's because people are so swayed by influencers and fashionistas, and no one dares to venture their own opinion that something is perhaps all hype."

"You're probably right," agreed Plum. She stared at him curiously before deciding this might be the perfect opportunity to glean any information out of him that could help solve what happened to Lysette. "Last night was pretty stressful. Everyone was on edge. I feel as if I'm missing a lot of the backstory."

She could see Robert's shoulders tense, and his entire demeanor changed; it was as if a shield came down over him, and he was instantly guarded. "I think we've been on the boat too long. Time for a break. It's cabin fever."

Plum nodded. "Is that why Gunther left?"

"Gunther?" asked Robert, momentarily confused. "Suki's husband? No, he had business to attend to."

"Wasn't the timing odd, considering that then Lysette died?" pressed Plum.

Robert's face darkened. "Not at all. Why do you ask about Lysette? It's not the first time I've heard you're asking a lot of questions and fishing around. What about that tragedy has your interest so piqued?"

"Nothing," Plum replied quickly. "I just think it's sad."

Robert stared at her, a frown on his face as if he were considering something. Then his hard expression dissolved, and he smiled and changed the subject. "We're here. Best to get ready."

The owner, Claire Smith-Brown, a British woman in her late fifties, was allegedly a minor aristocrat whose great-grandmother was a distant relation to the queen of England. She was a tall, slender woman with short curled auburn hair and very large protruding blue eyes that blinked furiously. Her accent was so posh that Plum had trouble discerning what she said and thought that perhaps that was the reason people believed Jolly Island to be so grand. Her regal hostess might have been reciting her grocery list for all Plum knew, but it sounded so elegant and fancy that one just went with it.

"This manor is fabulous!" swooned Suki as they strode through the octagonal carnation-pink lobby. "So tasteful and understated."

The group trudged across the room, their shoes clacking on the marble floor. Harris's head was bobbing around, and he lifted his cell phone to photograph every angle. The ceiling was tented in bold swaths of blush and cream fabrics, fraying slightly in the humidity. A giant woven chandelier featuring a rather realistic monkey clinging to a palm tree hung in the center. On the walls there were baroque metal-framed mirrors, pale watercolors depicting beach scenes, and oily landscapes enclosed in delicate gold frames. Several seating groups were scattered around, with faded pink and green chintz sofas, lumpy cane chairs with azure-and-white striped fabric that was torn in several spots, and mountains of fringed throw pillows. The side tables were in the shape of elephants, the coffee tables were cluttered with knickknacks and books with peeling spines, and the ferns that were mounted on white plaster urns needed watering. The smell of mildew permeated Plum's nostrils.

"This place is something," whispered Ellen to Plum. "I don't really know what to say."

Plum knew her friend was susceptible to popular opinion and, even if she thought the hotel was horrible, would never put that out there.

"I don't know. This place is a dump if you ask me," remarked Joel, not even trying to lower his voice out of respect to his hostess.

"I agree," concurred Nachelle. "It's no Four Seasons."

If Claire Smith-Brown had heard them, she was too gracious to let on and instead plunged forward, continuing to guide them on their tour.

"Out here is the veranda," she said, leading them out through the french doors. They stepped onto the brick patio and gazed out at the view. Even though the hotel might need some upgrading, the view was sensational.

"Beautiful," mused Plum. She stared at the Caribbean Sea flanked by the green island and was grateful for another day in paradise.

"This is the cove where the notorious pirate Redbeard was captured in the 1600s," said Claire. "I'm sure you've all heard the story."

"I haven't," said India, her eyes wide. "Please tell us."

"Well," said Claire, pausing dramatically. Plum could tell she was quite used to telling this story and preferred to be cajoled into regaling it. "Redbeard was one of the most brutal and violent pirates in the history of mankind. We all hear about Blackbeard, but Redbeard was far more dangerous. He was a huge participant in the slave trade—even selling his own illegitimate children to the highest bidder—and he was known to have a dreadful temper. His wife once served him a dinner that he found repellent, and he took out his sword and hacked her to death."

"Awful!" gasped India.

Suki turned and gave her a look. "You clearly have never been married."

Claire cleared her throat, and they returned their attention to her. She spoke in a dramatic voice. "After killing hundreds of people, plundering their villages, and raiding ships, this rapacious, perfidious madman left the entire Caribbean devastated. Hope was dissipating. Something needed to be done." She paused, her eyes gliding across her rapt guests as if challenging them to disagree. "Ultimately, the king of Spain had heard enough about Redbeard. He had stolen too much. Killed too many. He needed to be annihilated. The king dispatched a band of expert military men from Seville, the finest mercenaries in the world. Acting on a tip, they came to Jolly Island and sequestered themselves here to await Redbeard's arrival. They apparently had to wait several weeks before his pirate ship arrived because he had been marauding Squall Island, stealing piles of gold and silver. Then he made it into this very cove below us."

She pointed downward, and everyone craned their necks, as if Redbeard would be sauntering into port at this very moment. All they saw were gulls flitting from rock to rock.

"Then what happened?" asked Joel before turning to Robert. "You know, this could be a good movie. Pirates, islands, got all the making."

"Yeah, that's why they called it *Pirates of the Caribbean*." Nachelle laughed.

Claire bristled. Plum could tell she didn't enjoy being interrupted. "What happened next is they surrounded Redbeard from all sides and seized his boat. They arrested him and dragged him into the cave below—you can't quite see it from here, but we will visit it following lunch. He was chained there and tortured for days before they killed him."

"Horrible," murmured India.

"Gruesome." Harris giggled.

The group began chattering until Claire's voice boomed above them. "They never did find his treasures."

Everyone stopped talking. "What happened to them?" asked Ellen.

Claire gave everyone a supercilious look. "They believe he buried them before he arrived in this cove. And there is a very valid argument that he buried them on the other side of the island. Yes, right here on Jolly Island."

The guests whispered excitedly before Claire spoke in an even louder voice. "That is why, since my family purchased this island one hundred years ago, we have been quite discerning as to whom we allow on our island. We are guarding our treasure. No one is allowed to search for it. No one."

Plum was certain every member of their party was suddenly thinking about how they could get their hands on that treasure.

"I heard something about a guy recently dying here," said Joel. "Was he looking for the treasure?"

Claire's face froze. "That was a rumor."

"Yeah, but what happened...?" Joel pushed.

Claire waved her hand to silence him. "There are people who push forward the theory that the island is cursed. They are at the same time trying to purchase the island out from under me. I will not speak further about it."

They were served a lunch of conch fritters, a mixed green salad with avocado and tomatoes, and sweet-glazed jerk chicken with coconut rice and french fries. Dessert was pineapple sponge cake with whipped cream. Most of the guests ate very little, Plum noticed as she glanced around at the plates. The truth was they had become spoiled by the gourmet fare the chefs whipped up on Robert's yacht, and a meal without lobster, oysters, or caviar was quite mundane. That said, the dishes served at the manor were subpar: the fritters were greasy; the rock-hard tomatoes were drowning in olive oil on a bed of wilted lettuce; the sponge cake was an egregiously yellow color with a cloyingly sweet taste buried in so much whipped cream that it was a fishing expedition trying to extricate the cake from the mounds. Plum had been served better food at two-star airport hotels when she had layovers.

Plum made a mental checklist in her mind. The manor house at Jolly Island was tired and worn down. The food was inedible. Claire was prickly. What was it that attracted people to this island? The so-called treasure? Most people wouldn't believe it existed. So, what was it? She had little patience for people lulled into thinking a destination was fabulous just by word of mouth (she forgot that she used to be such a person and was even guilty of promoting places like this in her magazine).

"I am sure you enjoyed your meal," said Claire, once lunch had ended. "We farmed for the conch just this morning. It was fresh as can be. You can only find conch in the morning."

Everyone murmured their praise and compliments, which Plum knew to be merely a courtesy. If conch was best in the morning, she wondered what it was like in the afternoon or night. It could not have been slimier.

"I will not accompany you on your island tour, I am sorry to say," Claire said with mock sorrow. "But you will have a pleasant time."

"I'm going with you, Robert," announced Suki when they

exited the manor and walked out to the circular driveway where several old Jeeps idled. Suki linked arms with her host and began pulling him to a car.

"I don't think so," snapped Nachelle, who began pulling Robert toward her.

Everyone watched with shock and amusement as the two women literally played tug-of-war with the music producer.

"Ladies, ladies, I think there is room for three," insisted Robert. "We can all go together."

"She's not going," growled Nachelle, giving Suki a withering look. "She can ride with the others. Ellen, you come with us."

Suki put her hands up as if to signal surrender. Ellen brightened, obviously gratified that she had been selected to accompany her hosts. Plum conjectured that Ellen was the least threatening of all the guests to Nachelle and that was why she chose her.

"Sorry, I was hoping to go with you," said Ellen to Plum.

"No worries," said Plum. "Duty calls."

Once they had all settled into the Jeeps, they set off to survey the island. Plum was seated between Suki and Harris, who had both snorted with derision when they were assigned the same automobile. Plum felt like a martyr for taking the middle seat, while Joel inserted himself in the front passenger seat without consulting the others. Their driver, Conrad, was an old, wizened man with stooped shoulders and a face slashed with so many wrinkles that Plum thought his skin looked like an accordion. Initially the group peppered him with questions, but his monosyllabic answers and reticent manner indicated he was less than eager to play the role of tour guide and they would be forced to glean information about the island based on experience rather than anecdotes.

The air was warm and sticky, and Plum felt the humidity curling her hair. She hoped she had applied enough sunblock but could already see blotchy red marks forming in an uneven pattern on her alabaster skin. Ah, the joys of being a pale redhead.

"Look down there," said Harris eagerly, when the Jeep bumped up to a rugged hill that provided a sweeping vista of the sea below. "So pretty."

"If you've seen one Caribbean island, you've seen them all." Suki sniffed. She was clearly miffed that she had been relegated to riding with them. She leaned forward and addressed the chauffeur. "Listen, sir, we would really like to know more about this buried treasure. You obviously know where people think it is, so drive us there, and it will be our little secret."

The driver said nothing. Joel turned back to Suki, then raised his eyebrows and shrugged. "I guess what happens on the island, stays on the island, right, Conrad?"

Conrad didn't even deign to respond. In fact, he acted as if he didn't hear them and kept his eyes glued on the road. Plum admired his tenacity. She was certain he had been bribed, cajoled, and threatened by previous guests of the island determined to discover the hidden bounty. Best to remain silent. That's what she would do anyway.

"I read up on this place," said Harris. "It's the most

underdeveloped island in the Caribbean. There are literally swathes of land that are a natural habitat for the local wildlife."

"Isn't there a volcano?" asked Plum, remembering a travel article she had read years prior.

Harris nodded. "Yes, but don't worry. It hasn't erupted in decades."

They drove farther north up the dirt track that cut through the craggy hillside and curved inward so they were surrounded by thick vegetation. It was suddenly dark, the sunlight being blotted out by the tall trees. Plum felt as if she were in a jungle.

"Do we have any idea where we're headed?" asked Plum, shifting in her seat. There was a giant metal bar under the ripped leather cushion that dug into her thighs.

"I think they said something about a temple," said Joel. "I don't even know what."

"That's right." Harris nodded. "When the island was discovered, they found the ruins of an ancient temple on the very top. It's called *Kinich*, and it is so chic apparently. No one is quite sure about where it came from. But it was probably the home of some fabulous ancient aristocrat everyone worshipped."

"Or it could be the abandoned set of a movie or TV show." Joel laughed. "Maybe they filmed their version of *LOST* here."

"Oh, come on, you only think in terms of Hollywood and pretend things," chided Harris. "This is real."

"How do we know that?" asked Joel. "I'm telling you, maybe Orson Welles got here first."

"Kinich is Mayan ruins, you ding-dong," Suki reproached Harris, her lips pursed with distaste.

"You're the ding-dong," insisted Harris.

"What year was it discovered?" interjected Plum, attempting to avert the impending argument.

"In the forties," said Harris.

"Well, I guess we won't know until we get there," said Plum.

They continued their ascent. Plum felt as if they were going higher and deeper into the thick frondescence. A musty smell permeated her nostrils. They were completely enveloped in shadows, with only cracks of light penetrating the foliage. At a certain point, as they bumped along, they stopped talking, and Plum felt that the eerie silence was foreboding. When a giant hawk flitted across, flying from one tree to the next, they all almost jumped out of their skins.

"Where are the others?" whispered Plum.

"What others?" asked Suki.

"You know, Robert, Nachelle, India, Ellen? The rest of our group. Where's their car?" asked Plum, who shivered despite herself.

"Aren't they following us?" asked Harris. He craned his neck behind, but there was no other sign of human life.

"I thought they were in front of us," said Joel.

"Could be," murmured Plum.

They all stared in front, but they couldn't see any sign of a car. In fact, it was hard to see more than ten yards in front of them through the dense leaves.

Finally, Plum couldn't take the feeling of dread, and she

leaned forward and tapped Conrad on the shoulder. "Can you humor me a bit and just tell me how much longer?"

He didn't avert his gaze but finally responded, "Not long."

There was a large clap of thunder followed by lightning. Rain started teeming down, sopping the group. The car jolted to an abrupt stop. They all glanced around.

"Where are we?" asked Suki.

Plum strained her eyes to see through the rain. Conrad jumped out of the car and slammed his door.

"Are we here?" asked Joel.

Conrad went to the back of the Jeep and pulled out a large metal pole. Plum was suddenly seized with fear. Had he brought them here to kill them? Before she realized how absurd the thought was, Conrad had used the pole to hoist up the Jeep's roof and click it together, securing it in place. He yanked down the plastic layer on the sides that provided some reprieve from the rain, although made it even harder to see out of.

Suki shivered next to Plum. "I'm ready to turn around now."

"We're almost there," said Conrad.

"I'm ready to turn around and forget this temple," insisted Suki. "This is not my idea of fun, getting drenched in a jungle."

"I agree," lamented Harris. "I'm looking forward to getting back to the yacht and taking a hot bath."

The group grumbled as the Jeep continued bumping along the muddy road, barreling over rocks and sweeping through dirty puddles. Eventually the rain dissipated, and they ended up approaching a large clearing, where the sky became visible. As with most Caribbean storms, this one passed within minutes, and the sun was already peeking through the wispy clouds.

Conrad stopped the car and raised his arm. He pointed in front of him. "Behold Kinich!"

And they all looked in amazement.

CHAPTER

26

PLUM WAS NOT SURE WHAT she had been expecting but certainly not the dramatic and historic wonder she was confronted with. Kinich was a series of edifices arranged in a square around a plaza. The main stone building, which appeared to be a temple, was a truncated pyramid rising about four stories high, with stone stairways leading up to the top. Flanked by two slightly smaller structures, it loomed over an expansive green field completely devoid of any trees or bushes. To the right of the temple was a long, flat thirty-foot building subdivided by rectangular pillars and broad stairways. To the left was a huge partially excavated mound with a flat summit. On the far end, opposite the temple, were several pillars, statues, and unidentifiable ruins.

"This is astonishing!" gasped Harris. He lifted his phone and began to take photographs.

"Why have we never seen pictures of this?" exclaimed Suki, who was finally impressed by something. She also took her phone out and snapped some shots. "It's fabulous."

"Those are Mayan ruins, no doubt," insisted Harris.

They all got out of the Jeep and started to click away. Even Plum couldn't resist taking some photos, although she rarely did so. She could see Harris was about to click on the Instagram button and send his pictures into the social media world when Conrad's fingers curled around Harris's palms. They all glanced up at their guide.

In a very soft voice, Conrad spoke. "The reason this is the most exclusive place in the world is because no one has seen a picture of Kinich. Only the select few who have visited have witnessed this wonder of the world. It is the best-kept secret, and we would like it to remain so."

It was the most they had heard Conrad say, and they all paused. Plum could see Harris was carrying on an internal debate as to whether it was worth it to tell the world he was here or if being part of an incredible secret was more prestigious. For now, he decided to stop posting on Instagram and swiped away from the app. Plum knew he might reconsider later.

"No photos exist in the cyber world?" asked Suki, intrigued.

Conrad nodded. "It's our little secret."

The group had a visible surge of excitement.

"Can we go look?" asked Joel.

Conrad waved his arm as if to allow them to proceed.

They all took off toward the temple.

"Where do you think the others are?" asked Plum, looking behind her.

"Who cares?" Suki shrugged. She strode quickly in front

of Plum as if there were a prize for getting there first. *Let her win*, thought Plum.

"Hey, I care," said Joel. "It's my wife we're talking about."

"I didn't mean anything against Ellen," said Suki, linking arms with Joel. "I only meant we need to live in the moment and enjoy this magnificent place."

That seemed to placate him. "I agree. This place is insane," remarked Joel. "I thought I'd seen everything."

Joel and Suki entered the enormous doorway that led into the center of the main temple. Harris wandered off to look at the statues on the far end, filming his route as he went. Plum decided to venture up the stairs to see the view from the top of the pyramid. It was completely quiet, even though they were outdoors. If it was supposed to have a serene effect on her, it produced decidedly the opposite. Plum felt as if it were the type of silence that implied something was impending. And she wasn't certain that what was to come was a good thing.

She was more out of shape than she remembered as she huffed and puffed her way up the steps, which were much steeper than they had appeared at the bottom. She was glad she had worn sneakers, even though they were designer sneakers as opposed to sporty sneakers, but at least they had rubber soles. It was tricky maneuvering up the stone steps, which were uneven, wobbly, and chipped in places. Plum looked down to make sure she didn't trip, but that also made her worry she would lose her balance due to lack of a railing. She proceeded cautiously.

When she reached the top of the temple, she was out of

breath. The terrain was uneven, but the vista was incredible. She had 360-degree views of the water around her and felt on top of the world. The dazzling views highlighted the crystal blue of the sky as it melted into the even bluer Caribbean. She tentatively walked to the edge, carefully stepping over the rutted ground and not getting too close that she might slip. She glanced below on one side and saw the precipitous slope of the hillside, flush with trees and vegetation, which ended in a rocky cliff that plunged into the sea.

On the other side of the temple, a small boat was coming around the bend and slipping its way into the cove below. Plum squinted. There was something familiar about the boat, but it was too far below to see closely. It pulled itself into shore and stopped. Plum could see two figures, but again, they were so far away that she could not tell for sure, but it looked like a man and a woman. She wondered if there were many locals on Jolly Island.

A strong gust of wind came out of nowhere, and Plum stepped back from the edge, her heart quickening. She'd never experienced vertigo before, but she felt nervous being this high on a precarious roof. A small plane buzzed by and made its way to the other side of the island. She wondered if it was going to nearby Mustique or if it was a new guest arriving here. She moved toward the staircase to make her descent. As she glanced down, she saw another Jeep had appeared, and the rest of her group was making their way into the courtyard. She took her time descending, watching her feet the entire way and making sure to steady herself.

When she reached the bottom, the others had all scattered.

Plum walked into the dark temple. It took a minute for her eyes to adjust. The top of the temple had been so bright, and now she had descended into darkness. The inside was windowless and dank. She held up her phone and turned on the flashlight to illuminate her surroundings. There were all sorts of renderings along the walls that extended throughout the temple, a mixture of very rudimentary drawings; perhaps they were Mayan as Suki had suggested, as well as some more contemporary graffiti. She walked along the musty pebbled path. Several cavernous rooms led into smaller airless rooms. She could hear voices in a distance, but every time she turned a corner expecting to see someone on her crew, she found an empty room.

Her mind raced. Had this been where the man recently died? If he had been alone, it might have been days before they discovered him. There was something reminiscent of a tomb or a coffin. The walls were so thick and impenetrable, not allowing any air or noise to enter.

A wave of panic washed over her. The temple was like a maze she didn't know how to escape. It was stifling, and there was a treacly scent of faded incense and something else unidentifiable that didn't appeal to Plum. She felt claustrophobic, and an ominous sensation pulsed in her chest. Plum turned around and began to retrace her footsteps but found herself in another room she was certain she had not been in before. There were the remains of an altar along the wall, and someone had desecrated the wall with a large X. It was creepy.

Plum began to turn around when suddenly she heard a

piercing scream. Chills ran down her spine. She was about to yell, but then she snapped her jaw shut. Maybe it was best if she didn't let people know where she was. But she knew she had to get out as quickly as possible. She started moving hurriedly, darting from room to room. She had a bad feeling and fervently wished she had more than a tiny pinhole flashlight to guide her. She thought she heard footsteps behind her, but she couldn't see anything, and instead of waiting to find out, she quickly turned a corner. She stopped abruptly. There was someone right in front of her. Plum squinted.

"Robert," said Plum. She was out of breath, and her heart felt as if it would leap out of her chest. "You scared me."

"I'm sorry," he said, concern on his face. "Do we know who screamed? What happened?"

"I don't know," said Plum. She was so grateful to see him, the terror started slipping out of her. "I kind of freaked myself out. I really want to leave. Do you know the way?"

He gazed at her and then nodded. "Yes, follow me."

Plum was engulfed with relief as she followed him. Unlike her, he had no problem leading the way back to the entrance. Once they turned a corner, the bright sunshine streamed through the front door. Plum's nostrils twitched with the fresh wind scented with jasmine that accompanied it. It was as if she had been drowning and finally came up for air.

"Here you are," said Robert. "I should probably go and see what that scream was about."

"Thank you," said Plum. She wanted to fling herself into his arms, but he wasn't really the demonstrative type. Nor was she, for that matter. Instead she gave him what ended up being a fist bump but was meant to be a sort of half embrace. When he was about to walk away, a flash of light flitted across her line of vision. She turned to Robert's receding figure and saw something glistening in his pants' pocket that had reflected the sun. Plum gulped. It looked like a knife.

"Robert…" Plum called.

He turned and stared. She was about to speak but stared at the knife in his pocket and stopped. "Thank you," she said again.

He followed her gaze and looked at his pocket before he tucked the knife inside deeper so it was out of view. "Don't worry about it."

Just then, Joel and Suki came toward the entrance. Joel had an amused look on his face, but Suki's face was contorted in anger. Robert stopped.

"Did you hear her?" asked Joel. "A bat took a dive bomb near her, and she shrieked her lungs out."

"That's what that was," sighed Plum with relief. "I heard the scream. Thought someone had been hurt."

She didn't look at Robert as she said that.

"Talk about an overreaction," said Joel.

Suki scowled and folded her arms. "Those creatures have rabies. Do you know what the cure is for rabies? There is no cure. I am not risking it."

"It's all good now," said Robert, ushering Suki outside. "I think it's time for us to wrap this up and return to the yacht."

Robert whistled loudly, and everyone emerged from the various structures and slid into the Jeeps. This time Plum was riding with Nachelle, Robert, and Suki. She wasn't sure how the groups had decided to mix it up, but it appeared to have been a first-come, first-serve situation.

"Let's get out of here," said Nachelle impatiently. "I want a massage before dinner."

"Is everyone here?" asked Plum.

"They'll be fine, I'm sure their guide will take them back," said Nachelle. She leaned over to their driver, who was younger and heavier than Conrad. "Can you please get us out of here?"

During the entire ride back to the port, Nachelle discussed her new music video and how she thought Kinich would be an amazing location to film it. As she droned on about how some famous designer was doing the wardrobe and some famous director was directing it, Plum wondered about the knife she had seen in Robert's pocket. Why did he have it? Or did he always carry it? He was sitting in the front seat next to the driver, so she was unable to stare at his pants. Had she imagined it? She didn't think so. She would look again when they got to the port.

Claire Smith-Brown was waiting for them on the dock, a furious expression on her face. As soon as Robert, Nachelle, Suki, and Plum disembarked from the car and made their way over to her, she bristled.

"An insufferable man has wedged his way onto the island," she announced.

"What do you mean?" asked Robert.

"I mean that when you asked if you could visit Jolly Island, you provided me with a list of your guests, and I approved them. I did not approve any other additions.

Moreover, you told me you would all be arriving by boat, and yet this afternoon a small aircraft landed on my island, and a grubby homunculus descended into my paradise full of assumptions, including a request for lunch," she said the last part as if the man had requested she donate her kidney to him. "He told me he is an expected member of your party. Then he had the audacity to ask for help with his luggage. He packed as if he were embarking on a world tour on the *Queen Mary*. I told him he must wait on your boat until you returned. He is all yours."

She motioned toward the yacht, and Robert, Nachelle, Suki, and Plum all turned. There, sitting on the deck, his legs up on the coffee table and a large strawberry daiquiri in his hand, was none other than Gerald Hand. He gave them a jaunty wave and raised his glass.

"I don't know that man," insisted Robert.

"Who is he?" asked Nachelle.

Plum felt her anger bubbling up inside her. "I'm afraid he's your number one fan."

They all turned and gave her a quizzical look.

"What are you doing here?" whispered Plum. When she had boarded the yacht, she'd grabbed Gerald and dragged him into the powder room in the hall before Robert and Nachelle had a chance to react.

"Ouch, you're hurting me!" he whined, shimmying away from her in the small confined space.

Plum furrowed her brow. "You have some nerve coming here."

Gerald gave her a defiant stare. "And you have some nerve fraternizing with celebrities and not inviting me. Also, how dare you ruin my moment? I had been planning how I would meet Nachelle for weeks, and you embarrassed me! It's all about first impressions, and yet you treat me like a common criminal." He wagged a finger at her. "I will retaliate. What goes around comes around."

"Gerald, you are crashing this party. You were not invited."

He dismissed her with a shrug. "This is what the rich and famous do. They always show up unannounced, and no one cares a bit. It's all about yacht hopping."

"That's not what it is here," said Plum. "I'm a guest. And I am here on an undercover mission. You could blow it."

"What undercover mission?"

"Never mind," she said quickly, regretting that she had mentioned it. Gerald was a master at getting under her skin.

Gerald gave her a knowing smile. "Another murder."

Plum stood resolute and didn't respond.

"Come on, I know you too well, Plum. Out with it."

"I can't say anything," she said.

"Okay, then I'll just go and tell everyone..." He made a motion to open the door.

"Stop," said Plum.

The reality was that she could use a friend and ally. As irritating as Gerald was, he was loyal and smart. And perhaps if she had someone to talk her theories out with, it would be helpful. Especially since she didn't have any theories currently. She was no better off than before she had boarded the boat.

"Okay, there is something seriously weird going on here," she began. "And I was called in to find out about what happened to Lysette, a young woman who was working on this yacht and was found dead...."

Plum filled Gerald in, and he listened intently but not without plying her with endless questions and adding his own commentary about celebrities and how if she had consulted him earlier, the crime would have been solved. They agreed that she would ask Robert if Gerald could stay on the boat, and he would do some of his own sleuthing to discover any clues.

Although Plum could tell that Robert was disconcerted by the arrival of her friend, he was a gentleman and graciously allowed Gerald to remain on board. After Saoirse showed Gerald to his cabin, he quickly returned and made a beeline for Nachelle, who had ensconced herself in the deck.

Gerald folded his hands as if he were praying and approached the pop star. "You are my goddess," he whispered dramatically.

Plum could see Nachelle assess her friend. Gerald was wearing a French blue-and-white striped formfitting T-shirt, white Bermuda shorts, a white sailor's cap, and a short red scarf tied around his neck. Plum thought he looked like a caricature of a rich person on a yacht. But his eager demeanor somehow pleased the frosty Nachelle, and she gave him a welcoming smile.

"Come sit next to me and tell me why you love me so much," she commanded.

Gerald purred like a kitten, clapped his hands together, and leaped onto the settee next to her.

The rest of the guests arrived in the other Jeep, and there was a flurry of activity. Robert was still appeasing Claire, who was indignant that Gerald had arrived without the appropriate protocol, and he was bombarding her with compliments about her island.

"Ellen's carsick," exclaimed Joel as he helped his wife onto the boat. Ellen did look quite pale to Plum and was leaning on her husband for support.

"All those bumps..." she said. "Oh no, I think I'm going to be sick."

Ellen took off toward the bedrooms.

Harris rolled his eyes. "We had to pull over three times so she could throw up," he told the remaining group.

"Poor thing, I hope she's okay," said Plum.

"She'll be fine," said Joel.

"Maybe you should go check on her," said Plum sternly.

He shrugged but did actually go after his wife.

Everyone was distracted, tired, and impatient. Once Robert placated Claire, he bid her adieu and commanded Captain Dave to set sail. They all clearly felt as if they couldn't get away fast enough. Robert told them they would forgo cocktails and dinner would be early since they were all starving from their less-than-mediocre meal on Jolly Island.

"I need to go clean myself off," said Suki bitterly. She held up her skirt. "Ellen's vomit splattered my dress when she got out of the car. I wish I had something to wash it out. Plum, did you bring Wine Away? That would work on this."

"I actually did," said Plum. She felt irrationally thrilled that she had been so prepared.

"Can I come get it?" asked Suki.

"Sure."

They entered Plum's room, which had been serviced since she was last there. She had fresh towels in the bathroom and new slippers, and even though Plum had made the bed, it had been remade in a more professional manner. Suki sat right down on the edge of the bed, causing the fluffy comforter to deflate. While Suki complained about Ellen and the vomit and lamented about how anticlimactic Jolly Island had been, Plum went into her bathroom and pulled her stain remover out of her cosmetic kit. She walked back into the room with it.

"Do you have any eye makeup remover also?" trilled Suki from the next room. "I've run out."

Plum handed her the Wine Away, sighed, then returned to the bathroom and grabbed her cosmetic bag. She carried it out with her and rummaged through it. As she pulled out the makeup remover to hand it to Suki, a piece of paper came fluttering out. Suki bent to pick it up and froze. She stared at the note and then up at Plum.

"Where did you get this?" asked Suki, her voice strained.

It was the note that said *I know about your wife.*

"It was in my bathroom," confessed Plum. "I'm assuming, based on your reaction, that you've seen it before."

Suki took the note and crumpled it up. "Yes, it was left by someone who wanted to cause problems with me and my husband. All nonsense."

"Was it enough to cause your husband to leave the boat?" asked Plum, emboldened.

Suki rose and took the Wine Away and makeup remover from Plum. "Thank you for loaning me these. The note is irrelevant now. Don't think too much about it," said Suki. "See you at dinner."

Plum took it as confirmation that Lysette had sent the note to Gunther. She definitely was a pot stirrer. Plum wondered what Lysette had known.

When Suki had left, Plum's phone buzzed. Juan Kevin was calling her.

Plum hesitated. Should she take the call? Was he about to tell her he was returning to Victoria? She wasn't sure she could take that right now. But better to address the inevitable.

"Hello?" she said cautiously.

"How are you?" he said, his tone full of concern. "I've been worried. I thought you would stay in touch more frequently."

"I'm fine," said Plum.

"Are you sure?" asked Juan Kevin.

"I'm sure."

There was a pause. Plum waited. She felt as if she could hear her own heartbeat.

"Listen, I know we had a bad connection before. I wanted to tell you about Victoria—"

"It's okay," said Plum. "You don't have to explain."

"I *do* have to explain," insisted Juan Kevin. "And furthermore, I *want* to explain."

"Okay."

"As I mentioned, Victoria is in a bad place. She is trying to hang on to our marriage, and I am trying to end it."

Plum thought about Victoria's phone call to her, warning her. The woman could not let go. "Okay, well, what's the plan?"

"It's over, Plum," said Juan Kevin. "I want to be with you. I promise you I'm doing everything I can to do that."

Plum smiled with relief. "Okay."

"Let's not talk more about her. Please tell me what you've been doing."

"It's been busy. We stopped at Jolly Island, and then Gerald arrived."

Plum began to fill him in, but the conversation was filled with many pauses due to another choppy connection. She managed to tell him about her suspicions after several aborted starts. Finally she sighed.

"I don't know, I feel like my killer radar is off," said Plum. "I'm suspicious of everyone and no one. I think maybe Lysette really did fall overboard one minute, and the next I have a room full of suspects."

"Please take care of yourself."

"I'll keep poking around," said Plum. She stretched out on her bed and sank deep into the luxurious sheets. "But I might not be able to solve this one."

"And that's okay," insisted Juan Kevin.

"What?" asked Plum. "You cut off."

"I said that's okay," he repeated. "You are not a professional detective. And I don't want you to stay away too long," he said. "I miss you."

"I miss you too," she said, a big smile on her face.

There was a large grumbling sound, and the boat vibrated. "What's that?" asked Juan Kevin.

"We're pulling up the anchor," said Plum. "Time to set sail."

"Coming closer to me," said Juan Kevin.

"Soon."

Gerald had already stationed himself next to Nachelle at the dinner table by the time Plum arrived and barely gave her a glance. He looked like a lovesick puppy, gazing at Nachelle and hanging on her every word. To Plum's surprise, Nachelle seemed to find him amusing and witty. That irritated Plum to no end. Gerald's ego would inflate to the size of the room and would become unbearable if encouraged. All the guests made their way into the dining room and took a seat.

Harris was wearing another remarkable outfit—this time it was a purple velour suit with seafoam-green piping—and he glared at Gerald as he sat down. "Who is this interloper?" he asked rudely.

"This is my friend Gerald Hand," said Plum. "He's joining us."

"Are you part of the Palm Beach Hands?" asked Harris haughtily.

Gerald smiled. "I'm part of the Wakatee Trailer Park Hands," he replied.

Nachelle laughed. "You are hilarious!"

This response irritated Harris, who dramatically whipped open his cloth napkin and placed it on his lap.

"Are you feeling better?" Robert asked Ellen, who tentatively slid into her seat next to him.

She nodded. "Thank you, I am."

"I asked the chef to make you some soup. That may soothe your stomach," said Robert.

"That's very thoughtful."

Saoirse began distributing bowls of soup around the table while Brigitte offered bread to each guest. There was a plethora to choose from: parker rolls, olive rolls, rosemary focaccia, pecan-raisin toast, and sourdough baguettes. Harris took a very long time selecting his.

They all commenced eating, fully ravenous as if they had been on a desert island and starving for days. Saoirse poured the wine, giving everyone a hefty serving, which the guests eagerly drank up. Something felt off to Plum, and she glanced up. She noticed an empty chair. Her eyes slid around the table, and she took note of the assembled guests.

"Where is India?" asked Plum.

Robert paused, his spoon in midair. "I'm not sure," he said. He turned to Saoirse. "Can you please go knock on Miss Collins's door and let her know dinner is served?"

"Certainly, sir," complied Saoirse with a slight bow.

They continued eating, mostly in silence as they slurped down their delicious creamy chicken soup. Most people slathered butter on their rolls and stuffed them in their mouths—even Ellen and Suki who normally ate very little.

Gerald eagerly drained his glass of wine and poured himself another. Saoirse returned.

"She's not in her room, sir," said Saoirse.

"You know, I haven't seen her since we were at Kinich," said Plum.

"That's ridiculous," said Harris, his mouth full. "She was in your Jeep."

"No, she wasn't," insisted Plum. Dread was nestling in her breast. "She went with your group."

Joel shook his head and took a swig of his wine. "She wasn't in our Jeep. I thought she went with you."

"No, she didn't," said Robert.

Everyone stopped what they were doing and stared at one another. Finally, Robert rose. "I'll ask the captain to call Jolly Island," he said. "We must have left her behind."

Robert disappeared down the hall. There was tension permeating the room. But hunger surpassed that feeling, and the guests recommenced eating.

"She probably wandered off," said Harris.

"Good riddance, I say," Nachelle snapped. "It's no loss to our party."

"Oh, girl, you are terrible." Gerald giggled.

"I can't say I'll miss her," confessed Ellen, who was swirling her soup with her spoon.

"Ellen, that's harsh," said Joel angrily.

Ellen shrugged. "She didn't add much."

Robert appeared in the doorway. He stood there wordlessly, his face ashen.

"What is it?" asked Plum.

"We've just had word that India was found…dead at Kinich," he announced. He glanced around at everyone in the room. "Someone here must have killed her."

CHAPTER

27

THERE WAS A STUNNED SILENCE. Everyone stared at one another, and no one spoke. Finally, Gerald broke the ice.

"Don't look at me; I just got here," he said with a chuckle. His effort to defuse the tension fell flat.

"I don't believe this," said Joel, standing abruptly and throwing his napkin on his chair. "How can India be dead? Who would do that?"

"The captain received word from Claire Smith-Brown that a body was found by one of the locals," said Robert. "Miss Smith-Brown identified it as being a young woman in our party. I asked if it was possible she had fallen, but they said no, she had been stabbed."

"Stabbed?" repeated Joel incredulously. "It can't be."

"Who would kill India?" asked Ellen, glancing around the table.

Plum was stunned and despondent. She had warned India to be careful. She should have alerted the police. The girl had walked into danger. She would forever feel guilty. She turned and stared at Robert intently. She remembered the knife she had seen in his pocket. He was now distraught, but she wondered if it was an act. Had he killed India? But why? His face betrayed nothing but sorrow, but Plum recalled this was a man who had completely reinvented himself. What else was he concealing?

"I need to call Los Angeles," said Joel. "I need to handle this story before it becomes a big deal. What's the plan? Are we going back to Jolly Island?"

Robert shook his head. "They want us to remain here until a police unit from Saint Wile comes to us. That's the closest island with a legitimate police force."

"We once again drop anchor?" asked Suki.

"Yes," said Robert.

Plum thought of them all stranded on the yacht in the middle of the sea and shuddered. And if the murderer was among them? Poor India.

"How do we know it was one of us?" asked Harris. "It might have been some local who tried to rob India."

"Good point," said Joel. "She was wearing some nice jewelry. Maybe one of those drivers tried to steal it."

"Also, isn't the island haunted?" asked Plum.

"I told you that," said Gerald in a territorial tone. "However, maybe that's a cover and they have some deranged serial killer on the loose."

"I can't believe India was murdered. It doesn't make sense. Who would do it? And to think any of us could have been killed!" gasped Ellen.

They all began murmuring their assent and putting forth their theories.

"The fact is we don't know. All we can do is wait for the police," said Robert.

"He's absolutely right," said Gerald. "I'm sure India would want us to finish our dinner."

Joel gave Gerald a look of disgust. "You didn't even know her."

Gerald returned his look with a supercilious gaze. "I'm from New York. I know everyone. Now let's get the next course going."

Before Joel could leap across the table and strangle Gerald, Nachelle chimed in. "He's right. We need to eat. It's going to be a long night."

Joel was visibly upset. He excused himself and went off to make calls. Ellen watched him go, her eyes sad and disappointed. Robert disappeared to talk to the captain and make arrangements. Everyone else ate in silence, with the exception of Gerald, who continued prattling to Nachelle. Ellen slid over next to Plum and spoke softly.

"Do you think Joel had something to do with this?" she whispered.

"Joel?" asked Plum, her ears pricking. "Why would he?"

"I don't know..." said Ellen. "I probably shouldn't say anything."

Plum turned to her friend, who appeared pale and shaken. "Why would you say that?"

"He was so fixated on her... I don't know. I'm still wobbly from the Jeep ride, just ignore me. Forget I said anything. That poor girl. I mean, I didn't like her, but I feel bad."

"Ellen, if there's something you know, you should come clean. It will always come out," ordered Plum.

Ellen squirmed and shrank deeper into her chair. "I don't know…I don't know…" she said. "I don't want to think about it. I'll tell you later." Her eyes darted around the table. "Now is not the time. I wish I had something to take the edge off. I've gone through all my pills. I need a Valium."

"I might have some," said Plum. She never thought she would actually use the Valium Juan Kevin had given her, but what better use than to give it to her friend?

"Really? I don't think of you as the type who likes to relax," said Ellen.

"Well, it's handy to have," said Plum.

"I would appreciate it."

Plum felt a buzzing in her pocket and realized she had left her phone on. She surreptitiously looked at it and saw she had a text from Captain Diaz. It said CALL ME ASAP.

"I have to take this call. I'll be back in a minute," she said, rising.

Ellen gave her a plaintive look. "Please hurry back. I'm scared."

"I will," promised Plum.

She hastened to her room and called the captain.

"Hello?" came Captain Diaz's garbled voice. The connection was bad.

"It's me, Plum Lockhart."

"I can't hear you, who is this?"

This went back and forth. Plum held her cell phone high and low, walking all over her cabin in an effort to attain a good connection until they had a patchy line. Finally, he understood it was Plum calling.

"I heard about India Collins," he said. "It's all over the Caribbean police wire. What do you know?"

"I don't really know anything," admitted Plum as she sank into the sofa in her room. "I didn't even know she was missing. But one thing was weird. I did see Robert, the owner of the boat, with a knife in his pocket. And there was a scream. What do you know about Robert? Does he have a violent past?"

"Hello?" asked Captain Diaz.

"I'm still here," said Plum, with exasperation. Was it really so hard in this day and age to achieve good cell service?

"I can't hear you very well."

"I asked about Robert."

"I'll look into him," said Captain Diaz. "In the meantime, be on your guard. India Collins had told her agent she was concerned for her life, and he in turn contacted someone in my department. I only just found out now. The yacht had already left town, and it was out of our jurisdiction, so he didn't think to report it. Don't worry, he'll be on desk duty for the rest of his life."

"Did she say why she was worried for her life?" asked Plum.

"Unclear," said the captain. "She told her agent she was—"

The line went dead. Captain Diaz immediately called her back.

"If the line goes dead, I will ring you. What I was saying is Senorita Collins told her agent she was flying home when she landed at the next port with an international airport. And now it's too late."

"Yes," murmured Plum.

"Find out everything you can," he barked. "No more deaths."

"What?"

"No more deaths!"

"You say it as if I'm responsible," said Plum defensively.

"*Tranquila*, Senorita Lockhart. No one says that."

"Humph."

"I have some news about—"

The line went dead again. Plum tried to call him back, but it was futile. She waited, but he did not call her. The connection must have been decimated. There was a knock on the door. Plum went over and opened it. It was Joel.

"Ellen is in dire need of a Valium. She needs help calming down. She thought you had one? Do you think you could give it to me?"

Plum's phone rang again. She held up her finger to Joel indicating for him to wait and then answered the phone.

"Give me one second," she told Captain Diaz.

Plum walked into her bathroom, took out a pill, walked back, and handed it to Joel. He thanked her and left.

"Sorry, Captain Diaz, please continue."

He cleared his throat. "The person in the burka who sold the jewelry at Laszlo's. We were able to procure footage from Sun Beaches, the boutique around the corner in the alley. The burka was discarded, and we have a picture of who was wearing it."

"Who was it?" she asked, but he was speaking at the same time. "What?" she repeated.

"I hope you can identify—"

The line went dead.

She wanted to scream. This was so frustrating. Plum waited for him to call again, but he didn't. Her phone was no longer showing any service bars. She glanced down hopefully at her messages and prayed something would pop up. She was awaiting Captain Diaz's footage, but nothing was coming through. Now was not the time for technology to fail her.

Plum stretched her head back and from side to side. She experienced a wave of sadness coupled with fatigue. It was tragic that yet another young woman's life was expunged prematurely and so violently. What were the links? Why did someone want Lysette and now India dead? And who was the killer?

Plum left her room and was making her way down the corridor toward the dining room. Suddenly the hall lights flickered off, and it was completely dark. Plum froze, waiting for the lights to turn on again, but nothing happened. She put out her arms to help guide her along to the end of the hall. She could make out a doorway, which she rationalized must be Harris's room since he was next to her. She kept walking, her feet slowly padding along the carpeted floor. A door swung open, and she was pulled inside. Plum gasped and was about to shriek, but she was so disoriented that she didn't know what to do. She blinked and realized she was in the back stairway that led down to the kitchen. And she was face-to-face with Jomer, the first officer.

"Don't scream," he said. He put his hands up to show he had come in peace. "I needed to talk to you."

"You scared me half to death, Jomer," she said. Plum's heart was beating so fast, she thought they could hear it all the way in the dining room.

"I'm sorry. I needed to talk to you in private so no one saw us," he said.

Jomer looked pale and shaken, and his obvious distress caused Plum to calm and comprehend he was not out to kill her. "What's going on?" she asked.

"There's a lot of bad business on this boat," said Jomer. He glanced around to make sure no one could hear them. The corridor was quiet, and there didn't appear to be anyone on the staircase, but it had that echo effect, so they had to whisper.

"Gee, you mean like people dying?" asked Plum.

He nodded. "I cannot believe everything is a coincidence."

"What do you mean?" asked Plum.

He sighed. "I've worked in the yacht world for a long time. Several years ago, I was approached to participate in a reality show that was to take part on a yacht."

"I heard about this. Didn't Lysette audition for that?"

He nodded. "Correct. But she was not hired. I had not auditioned, but I had accompanied my friend who wanted to be on it. I was able to watch the casting. The producers were very excited at the time because the studio head was visiting that day. And it was Joel Katz, that very man who is here now."

Plum leaned back against the wall. "Wow."

"He decided who made it based on looks. My friend was not cute enough. Lysette made the first round, but when I saw her again, she said she had refused to sleep with the studio head and therefore did not get the role on the show."

"Doesn't surprise me. He's a dog."

There was a door squeak. It sounded like it was coming from the staircase above them. They both froze and waited. There was no other sound. Jomer motioned for Plum to follow him down the stairs. They quietly walked down, taking every step carefully to avoid making a noise. When they had ascertained they could hear no one else, Jomer continued.

"Lysette was a strong personality. A vengeful personality. I think she arranged to be on this yacht when she found out he would be a guest. She was prepared to come to blows with Mr. Katz. And she waited for him to refer to it. But then she realized he had no idea who she was. She was just one of many girls he tried that with. That made her even madder."

Plum nodded. "I can imagine."

"But like I said about coincidences, there are too many," continued Jomer. "One of the girls who did make the reality show—who took Lysette's spot—was India Collins. This made Lysette irate."

"But I thought India didn't do the reality show."

Jomer shrugged. "Perhaps once she and Mr. Katz became intimate, he had greater plans for her."

"Do you think Lysette was going to do something about it?"

He nodded. "That's why I brought you this."

Plum hadn't noticed he held a small notebook in his hand. He pressed it into Plum's. "What is it?"

"It's Lysette's diary. I know I should have mentioned before, but I didn't know who to trust. We were friends, so she asked if I could keep it in my room. She knew I would be discreet and not read it. I thought at the time that she was silly, that no one would want to read her diary, but it was untrue. Mrs. Von Steefel came down and was rifling through Lysette's things one day. And I even caught Mr. Katz in her room after she died. I felt he was searching for it as well. I kept it safe, but now that things have happened, and well, Miss Collins is dead, I decided to read it. I think I should turn it over to you, and you can decide what to do with it."

"Thank you for trusting me with it," Plum said, clasping the book against her chest. "I'll try and do right by Lysette."

CHAPTER

28

PLUM RETURNED TO HER ROOM and plopped down onto her bed to read Lysette's diary. She had just cracked it open when there was yet another knock on her door.

"Let me in," hissed Gerald from the other side.

"It's open," Plum replied. She quickly stuffed the diary under her pillow.

Gerald entered and hastened toward her. "So who did it?"

"I'm not sure yet," confessed Plum.

"What?" shrieked Gerald. Plum shot him a look and shushed him.

"Keep your voice down!"

Gerald began pacing the room. "Plum, I thought you had a bead on this situation. I'm acting all goofy trying to play court jester, thinking I'm wingmanning it for you while you're busy sleuthing around, and now I hear you don't have a clue?"

"I didn't say I don't have a clue," said Plum, sitting up straighter on her bed. "I just said I'm not sure."

Gerald stopped. "Okay, so who do you think it is?"

"I don't want to commit yet."

"Why not?" he shrieked again.

"Be quiet, people will hear," she admonished.

"I sure as hell hope so. In case someone tries to kill me later and I need to scream my lungs out. And my blood will be on your hands because you wouldn't tell me who you think it is."

"Don't worry, you're not in danger."

"Gee, thanks. I'll sleep like a baby tonight."

"Listen, just give me a little time. I know I'm close. But I need until tomorrow."

He sighed dramatically. Plum knew he was scared, but he was amping it up into Academy Award–performance category.

"Okay, well, let's go back and see the others," he said. "I think it's better to be in a large group than just the two of us. I don't know if I could save you, even if I wanted to."

Plum thought longingly of the diary under her pillow. But she knew it was a good idea to have one more interaction with the group. She had many theories bouncing around her head that she needed to clarify.

She sighed and stood. "Fine."

"What happened to your finger?" asked Gerald when they were walking down the hall back to the library.

Plum glanced down at her right index finger. A small drizzle of blood had trickled out of a slice.

"Must be a paper cut," she said. She had felt it prickle when she had rushed to shove the diary under her pillow.

They walked past the door that opened to the staircase down to the galley and stopped abruptly.

"Did you hear that?" asked Plum.

Gerald nodded.

There was the sound of huffing and puffing, as if someone were struggling, emanating from the stairwell. This was followed by a bang, as if something knocked into a wall.

Plum and Gerald glanced at each other with anxiety.

"We should go look," whispered Plum.

"We should run and save ourselves," whispered Gerald.

Plum pushed open the doorway as Gerald crouched behind her. She was a human shield for him while he cowered. Plum could see the shadows of two people on the steps below, and once again heard effort being exerted. Was it a struggle?

"Everything okay down there?" Plum said. She felt very brave for even asking, although her wobbly voice betrayed her.

The shadows froze. There was silence. Gerald tugged on the back of Plum's shirt, attempting to pull her back. But she wouldn't recede. Instead she stepped into the staircase boldly.

"I see your shadows," she said. She took a few steps down so she could see the tops of heads.

"It is only us," said Chef Vadim, who stared up at her. His wife, Brigitte, was next to him. They were carrying a large covered tray.

"*Oui*, madame," said Brigitte.

"What have you got there?" asked Plum, staring at the tray.

"This?" asked Brigitte. She turned and glanced at her husband.

He turned and glanced up at Plum. "We have been out fishing for conch. We were bringing it down to prepare for lunch tomorrow."

"I see," said Plum. "Sorry to bother you."

"It is no bother, madame."

When Plum exited the staircase, Gerald practically collapsed on her. "See, it was just the chefs. And conch. We're psyching ourselves out."

"It wasn't conch," replied Plum, whose blood was boiling. She finally had the answer to one of the mysteries.

"How do you know?"

"We just learned today that you only fish for conch in the morning. Not the middle of the night."

"Then why would they lie?"

"They were off getting turtle eggs. I saw them on a rowboat today, scanning the area."

Gerald wrinkled his nose. "Yuck, I don't want turtle eggs for lunch."

"That's not what they're for. But don't worry, I'll fill you in later."

When Plum and Gerald entered the library, they found Ellen sitting on the sofa looking almost catatonic next to Joel, who was tapping on his cell phone. Harris and Suki were seated across from them in the armchairs, and both were nursing martinis.

"Can I get you something to drink?" asked Saoirse, appearing out of nowhere.

"Vodka," said Gerald. "In a Big Gulp size."

"I'll have a glass of Pinot Grigio, please," said Plum.

"Of course—oh, what happened to your finger?" asked Saoirse.

Plum glanced down. It was still bleeding. "Paper cut."

"Let me get you something for that," said Saoirse.

"It'll be fine."

"Don't be silly, you don't want it to get on your dress."

Plum followed Saoirse into a pantry off the library. There was a wet bar there with all the alcohol and glasses neatly arranged. Saoirse opened a drawer where there was a little emergency medical kit. She pulled it out and retrieved a Band-Aid.

"I think paper cuts are the most painful," said Saoirse.

"I guess, although I didn't really notice this one," said Plum.

Saoirse opened the Band-Aid and put it on Plum's finger. "There you are."

"Thank you," said Plum.

Saoirse opened the drawer again to replace the box, and Plum noticed a book. It was titled *The Number One Handbook on Becoming a Reality Star* by Paris Marriott.

"Was that Lysette's book?" asked Plum.

Saoirse glanced down and quickly closed the drawer. "Um, no, I mean yes."

Plum gave her a quizzical glance. "Yes or no?"

"It's mine," said Saoirse guiltily. "I was just perusing it."

"You want to be a reality star too?" asked Plum.

Saoirse turned beet red. "I was only reading about it."

Plum's mind was racing. "Did you try out for the same yacht show that Lysette did?"

"That was long ago. It was for a laugh. Nothing came of it," Saoirse said quickly. "Now I'll make your drinks and bring them to you in the library."

Plum hesitated but then returned to the other guests. She sat next to Ellen, who looked dazed.

"Did you bring me a Valium?" asked Ellen.

Plum frowned. "Joel came in to get it. Didn't he give it to you?"

"Did he?" wondered Ellen.

She turned to her husband, who was now on a call. He held the receiver away from his mouth. "What?"

"Did you give her the pill?" asked Plum.

"I gave it to her," he replied. "That's why she's so out of it."

"I guess he did," murmured Ellen.

Just then Nachelle came bursting through the door with Robert hot on her tail. She appeared frenzied. Her eye shadow had smeared, and she had mascara streaks melting down to her cheeks.

"Robert's trying to kill me!" she announced to the room.

Ellen shrieked. Gerald ran and hid behind his armchair.

"Nachelle, come back!" yelled Robert.

He tried to grab Nachelle as she ran toward the group. Joel jumped up.

"What's going on?" Joel boomed.

"He wants me dead!" screamed Nachelle.

"I knew it!" yelled Plum. She pointed at Robert. "He carries a knife!"

Robert was moving toward them when suddenly the pantry door opened and smacked Robert right in the head. Saoirse, who was holding a tray of cocktails, immediately dropped them, and they smashed to the floor with a bang.

"No!" yelped Saoirse. "I'm sorry, sir!"

"Sorry? You just saved us from a killer," squeaked Gerald.

Robert was out cold. Plum bent to check his vitals. "Someone get me a pillow," she commanded.

Suki brought her a pillow, which Plum placed under Robert's head. They all gathered around him. He was breathing, but his eyes were closed.

"We need a doctor," said Harris.

"I think we need the police," said Plum assuredly. "And some handcuffs. We should tie him up and all take turns watching over him, like they did with the shoe bomber on the airplane."

"Why do you think he's a killer?" asked Joel. He bent down and looked closely at Robert.

"I saw him in the temple with a knife right before India was killed," said Plum confidently. "Now we all know. He did it."

Ellen gasped, and even Suki's eyes widened in shock. They were all so focused on Robert that no one noticed Nachelle in the corner. Until suddenly the noises emanating from her caused them all to turn around.

"Oh no," gasped Saoirse, who rushed over to her.

Nachelle had collapsed to the ground. Her eyes were

open, and she had a dazed look on her face. Her entire body was jerking and spasming.

"She looks like she's having a seizure," said Joel.

They all rushed over to Nachelle.

"Don't touch her," commanded Harris. "I heard that's the worst thing to do."

"Oh no! Oh no," wailed Ellen.

Plum's pulse was racing. "What should we do? Go get Captain Dave, Gerald."

Gerald raced out of the room. Nachelle continued to flail, and they were all so focused on her that they didn't observe Robert had woken up. He moaned.

They all whipped their heads in his direction. "In my pocket," he mumbled.

Joel went over to him. "What's in your pocket?"

"Watch out—it's a gun," said Ellen.

This time Harris yelled, "How do you know?"

"What else would it be?" asked Ellen.

"It's a knife. Be careful, Joel," warned Plum.

Joel extracted something from Robert's pocket. Plum braced herself. She knew for certain it was the murder weapon. The knife that had killed India. She held her breath…and then emitted a long exhale.

"It's an autoinjector pen," Robert whispered. "For epilepsy. Go administer it to Nachelle."

"A what?" asked Plum with astonishment. "It's not a knife?"

Joel went and did as he was told. Nachelle's body stopped jerking, and her eyes closed. It appeared as if she had fallen into a deep sleep. Captain Dave came rushing in assisted by Jomer. They held a portable IV rack, which they hooked up to Nachelle.

"Everyone, please give us space," commanded the captain. Ellen, Joel, and Suki backed out of the room, followed by Harris.

Plum was frozen in stunned silence. She turned to Robert. "She has epilepsy?"

He nodded, still grimacing in pain. "Yes."

"But I thought…" began Plum. She was so wrong. How could she have been so wrong?

"She refuses to treat herself for it. She'll only use controversial off-market drugs available in the Caribbean, and none of them help her," he said. "I do everything I can to prevent it. I pleaded with the staff not to provide them for her. I'm certain they're laced with all sorts of illicit and horrible things. But she refuses to listen to me."

"Why does she think you were trying to kill her?" asked Plum.

"Because she thinks the pharmaceutical companies are evil and all these mainstream prescription drugs are just going to kill her. That's why she refuses to get treatment."

"She'd rather have these attacks than take a prescription drug?" asked Gerald. "Doesn't make sense."

"I agree," said Robert. "But I can only do so much. And unfortunately, high-anxiety situations like this are triggers for her."

Robert began to sit up. He rubbed his head. Saoirse placed an ice pack on his head.

"I had no idea," said Plum. She was still rattled from what she thought was about to be a murder, but she was also flooded with sorrow for both Robert and Nachelle. What a traumatic and difficult situation they were in.

"It's our little secret," said Robert. "I would do anything to protect her."

PLUM FELT FOOLISH. HOW COULD she have thought that Robert was the killer? It made no sense. What would his motive be for by killing Lysette and India? That was the question Plum needed to examine. When she went to her room, she sat at her computer and started writing a list of everyone on board and all their possible motives. She put it in three columns: name, why they would kill Lysette, and why they would kill India.

She didn't get very far. It seemed as if there were very little correlation between the murders. Not to mention the motivation was slight. She sighed. She went to her bed and pulled Lysette's diary from under her pillow. She sat in the armchair and flipped it open.

There was a knock at her door. She put down the diary on the coffee table and opened the door. Captain Dave and Jomer stood on the threshold with grim expressions on their faces.

"Everything okay?" asked Plum.

"I'm sorry Plum, but we need to search your room," said Captain Dave.

"My room? All right, but why?" asked Plum, opening the door wider and allowing them entrance.

"We've received an anonymous tip that you're the killer. And that the weapon is in your room. We must take a look," said Captain Dave.

Jomer gave her an apologetic look.

"Me? That's absurd," began Plum. "You know why I'm here, Captain."

She emphasized the last part, while her eyes flitted between the captain and Jomer.

He shrugged. "I have orders from Robert."

"From Robert? He suspects me?"

Suddenly all her admiration for Robert evaporated. Why would he suspect her? Maybe he was the killer after all. Why had she been so quick to dismiss him?

Captain Dave continued. "I have to listen to my boss. Plus, I know that Lysette had your business card in her pocket. Maybe she was trying to tell us something, that you were the killer."

"That's ridiculous," said Plum.

Plum could see Jomer glance at Lysette's diary on the table. He didn't acknowledge it, and Plum could tell he didn't believe that she had anything to do with this mess. He wasn't going to tell the captain that it was Lysette's diary she had in her possession.

Captain Dave began opening and closing drawers. He

went over the closet and riffled around. Jomer discreetly shook his head at Plum behind the captain's back.

"Sir, I think this is a big misunderstanding," Plum protested. "You know who I am. Why are you doing this?"

"I have orders," said the burly captain.

"Maybe you're the murderer and trying to cover your tracks," insisted Plum.

He ignored her. He walked over to Plum's bed and ripped off the comforter. Then he slid his hand under her pillows.

"Ow!" he said, recoiling. He held his hand gingerly and sucked on his fingers. Then he leaned down and lifted the pillow. Underneath was a bloody knife.

"Obviously, that's not mine," insisted Plum.

Captain Dave pulled a rubber glove out from his pocket, snapped it on, and lifted the knife. "Looks like a murder weapon to me."

"Someone planted that," barked Plum. "Undoubtedly the person who gave you the anonymous tip."

"We'll have to see if we find your fingerprints on it," said Captain Dave gravely.

Plum glanced down at the cut on her finger. She had evidently poked the knife when she'd put the diary there. Her fingerprint was possibly now on it. Great.

"I am here working with the Paraison police. I'm not here as a murderer," Plum responded.

"You are under my jurisdiction now. And I will ask you to remain in your room until the proper authorities are here. Jomer will be guarding outside."

"This is a joke!" wailed Plum. "You can't imprison me!"

"I can and I will," said Captain Dave.

Something occurred to Plum. "Tell me about this anonymous tip. Did they call? Because it's very hard to get cell service right now, I know for a fact," said Plum.

Captain Dave shrugged. "There was a note in Robert's room."

"Huh," said Plum. "And you believe that?"

"Now that we found the murder weapon, yes," said Captain Dave as he marched out the door.

Both men left, with Jomer giving her a long look as he did. She heard the loud click of her door locking from the outside.

Plum was furious. She tried to dial on her phone, but there was no service. Her email and texts weren't working. This was horrible. She moaned and groaned before calming down.

She thought Gerald might come to assist her, but even her little buddy didn't come to her aid. What a truly ungrateful friend, she lamented. He would pay.

Soon her fury turned to fear. She was alone, locked in a room, with a killer roaming the boat. If everyone thought she was guilty, no one would help her. She had never felt more vulnerable.

Plum had to find the killer. She opened Lysette's diary and began reading. It was definitely true that Lysette despised her job and felt she was born for greater things. There were long lists of grievances delineated on page after page. However, there were several passages Plum found interesting, like the following:

Vadim and Brigitte have a little side biz going on where they dig for turtle eggs in the night and sell it to the guests claiming it helps their sex lives. They think I have no idea but I have filed away the information until I can use it for my benefit.

Aha! Plum felt victorious and wanted to pat herself on the back. She was right that it was Vadim and Brigitte. Vindication.

A few pages later, another entry confirmed what she had sensed.

Fat old Harris accused me of taking his important legal papers but the joke is, they never sent them. I've heard Robert asking for them and saw him pretend to make a call that he would get them. He was so bugged I heard that he claimed I signed for them. They never came. He'll get his comeuppance.

But the most important passage was about Suki and Gunther Von Steefel. Lysette reserved the most venom for them. Apparently, Suki had stolen Gunther from his first wife, Anita. Lysette had been a maid in their house, and Anita had been kind to her. When Gunther left her, she ended up killing herself. Lysette blamed Suki and Gunther. She wrote:

As soon as I saw those two on the boat, I wanted to throw up.

There were more entries about what she wanted to do to them. Plum wondered, if Lysette hadn't been killed, would she have killed someone?

She turned off the light and tried to sleep. But she tossed and turned for hours. She kept thinking she heard someone at her door. At one point she crept to her door and listened, convinced someone was on the other side. But the loud waves outside drowned out any noise from inside the boat. She glanced around, looking for what she could find to assist her in case someone tried to attack her. She grabbed a shoe from her closet, wishing it were a stiletto.

Plum didn't even remember falling asleep, but she woke when she heard her door unlocking.

"Who is it?" roared Plum, sitting straight up in bed. "I have a gun!" she lied.

"It's only me. Can I come in?" asked Jomer. He held a breakfast tray for her.

Plum sighed with relief. "Yes, thank you. Jomer, you know this is a terrible error, right?"

"Yes, and I'm sorry. I have no choice. I've never seen the captain like this. He is enraged that this is all happening under his watch and wants it solved. You're the perfect scapegoat. I think he'd rather it's you than one of the rich and powerful people on the boat."

"I know who it is," said Plum. She took the coffee Jomer offered her and drank a large gulp.

"You do?" asked Jomer with astonishment.

She nodded. "I stayed up late reading Lysette's diary. I was able to piece together some things. I just need to get out of here. I need everyone gathered in the library. That includes staff as well. I will confront the killer."

"I'll try and help you," said Jomer.

"Make up some pretext, just make sure they're all there," pressed Plum.

"Just give me some time," he said. "I'll come get you when we're ready."

When he left, Plum drank all her coffee and ate some of the toast and eggs he had brought her to fortify herself. She rose and glanced out the window. It was another bright, beautiful, and sunny day in paradise. But now it was time to expel the snake from the garden. Before the snake would expel her.

CHAPTER

30

"SHE'S SUPPOSED TO BE UNDER guard," yelled Joel when Plum walked into the library with Jomer. "What the hell, Robert?"

Robert stood. "Miss Lockhart, you need to remain in your room until you can be taken into custody."

Captain Dave moved toward her in a menacing manner. "Time to go back to your cabin. This is no place for murderers."

Plum glanced at everyone. Someone on this yacht was a killer. And she was the only one preparing to take this on; therefore that made her the number one target. She had no choice but to hold her ground before she might be killed. "You don't really believe I killed India, do you?"

"I don't," said Gerald from the back of the room where he sat with Nachelle. "I vouch for you!"

"Gee, thanks, Gerald. It's the least you can do. Thanks for visiting me last night," said Plum.

"Sorry," he whined. "They told me I couldn't!"

Plum ignored him and instead addressed the room. "If you allow me a few moments of your time, I will tell you who the killer is."

They all began talking at once, until one voice rang louder than the others.

"Let the woman talk!" said Nachelle.

And they all quieted and listened to her. Plum gave her a grateful smile.

"I would like you to know first and foremost that I came here under false pretenses," she began. "I'm not who I said I was."

"Oh, come on, Plum, I've known you forever," said Ellen. She was nestled cozily next to Joel.

"Yeah, you go way back with my wife," added Joel.

"Yes, I know that," said Plum. "But that's not what I meant. I was sent here by the Paraison police department to assist in solving the murder of Lysette Nilsson. I have been working undercover in conjunction with them."

"What?" gasped Ellen. "You can't be serious. Why didn't you tell me?"

Suki and Harris shifted uncomfortably in their chairs. Plum could see anxiety on Saoirse's face. Joel appeared angry. Robert was surprised. Brigitte and Vadim, who were standing against the wall, seemed amused.

"I'll explain," she began. "Let's start with the murder of Lysette. And yes, it was a murder. She was hit in the back of the head before she was pushed into the sea in the dead of night. Who had a motive for her murder? Well, it seems lots of people did."

Plum walked over to Brigitte and Vadim. "Let's start with you."

"*Moi?*" asked Brigitte. "*Mais...*"

She glanced at her husband, who returned her quizzical look.

"Everyone is a suspect," said Plum. "You both worked with Lysette. You shared staff quarters with her. The accommodations were very tight downstairs. It's hard to hide anything from one another. Lysette knew you and your husband were illegally harvesting turtle eggs and selling them as aphrodisiacs. Selling them in the open but also to people on this boat. I'm looking at you, Joel."

Joel glared at her before shrugging. "I didn't know they were illegal."

"Right," said Plum sarcastically. "But everyone else did, especially Brigitte and Vadim. Do you realize what havoc you are wreaking on nature? How horrible this is for the ecosystem and the environment? Have you no shame?"

Brigitte hung her head, while Vadim protested, "We needed the money. We make very little on this boat."

"That's not true," interjected Robert.

"You make enough," said Plum. "You're just greedy. And Lysette knew it. Did she blackmail you? Want a cut of it?"

"She was extorting them, so they killed her?" asked Gerald.

Plum looked at him. "No. They didn't."

She walked over to Harris. He gazed up at her. "Me?" he asked.

"You are also guilty of misrepresenting yourself. You pretend to be a very wealthy crypto businessman who also has inherited wealth, and yet it is all a lie. You are on the verge of bankruptcy. You did not just purchase an oceanfront house in the Hamptons. You referenced your yacht, the *Miss Conduct*, was in need of service, so you retired it. But the *Miss Conduct* was retired from service because there was a suspicious death of a crew member there. Many people believe he was murdered!"

"I didn't kill him!" exclaimed Harris.

"The owner of the boat is under suspicion," insisted Plum.

"Okay, okay, I don't own it," he admitted, looking utterly deflated. "I read about it in a magazine. I pretended."

"It wasn't all you pretended," said Plum. "You were so desperate to do a deal with Robert that you pretended your lawyer had sent you the necessary paperwork that he demanded. You even went so far as to accuse Lysette of intercepting it."

Harris began to weep dramatic tears. "I'm sorry. I'm a charlatan."

"I knew it," seethed Suki.

"But I'm not a killer!" Harris whined.

"I could see right through that man," boasted Suki.

Plum turned to her. "And Lysette could see right through you."

Suki's face darkened. "I'm not worried about what a low-class working girl thought of me."

"Ah, but you were once a low-class working girl just like her," said Plum.

"We all know I did the coat check at Club Zasmo back in the day. I'm not embarrassed by that. It was the hottest club in New York City, and I had a front row seat."

"I'm not referring to that," said Plum. "I'm referring to your job in Europe. After you blackmailed Elliot Neiderhover, you moved to Germany. You took a job as a personal secretary to

Anita Von Steefel, the first wife of Gunther Von Steefel, your current husband. You started an affair with Gunther and ultimately broke up his marriage. His first wife was despondent. She took her own life. His first wife, by all accounts, was a gentle and lovely woman, who was very kind to her staff. Including her young housemaid Lysette Nilsson."

"Now this is getting interesting," said Nachelle. She nudged Gerald. "I wish we had some popcorn."

"It wasn't my fault she killed herself," protested Suki. "She was unstable. I had nothing to do with it."

"Perhaps," conceded Plum. "But Lysette felt you did. In fact, she was astonished when she saw you and Gunther on the boat. She was furious. And she took her revenge in cunning ways. Anita's favorite flower was the peony. She always had vases in every room of her mansion. So Lysette scoured the shore and made certain to acquire some for your cabin here. To remind you. To remind him. She even sent him a note that she knew about Anita's suicide, that she believed you and Gunther had been the cause of it. That's why you kept moving cabins. That's why you fought. And that's why Gunther left. He abandoned ship, as they say. Lysette dredged up painful memories. The guilt was too much."

"I'll get him back," said Suki defiantly. "There's too much money at stake."

"Exactly," said Plum. "Money is a great motive."

Suki rolled her eyes. "Okay, then why did I kill India? What was my beef with her?"

"I'm still working on your motive," admitted Plum.

"Lysette, it makes sense. India, perhaps because she knew you killed Lysette?"

"Which I did not," said Suki firmly.

"But you were in close contact with India's murder weapon, if indeed the one found in my room is her murder weapon," said Plum.

"How's that?"

Plum began pacing. "I found it fishy that you wanted to come to my room to borrow the stain remover. You claimed you had vomit on your dress, and yet I did not see any. And besides, why wouldn't you have just had the maid clean it? Why? Because it gave you ample opportunity to hide India's murder weapon under my pillow while I went to retrieve the remover in my bathroom."

Captain Dave glanced at Suki and spoke gruffly. "You were in her room?"

"Means nothing," said Suki. "Anyone could have gone in there."

"Sure, but it gives you opportunity," Captain Dave suggested. "That's a big part of killing someone. Motive and opportunity."

"Of which you had both, Captain," said Plum.

"Me now? Come on. Why would I kill either girl?"

"Well, let's start with Lysette," said Plum, turning her attention toward the captain. "You were having an affair with Lysette, despite the fact you are married."

"Is this true?" asked Robert.

Captain Dave held up his hands. "I'm not an angel. Sorry."

"That's cause for termination," said Robert.

"It was consensual," insisted the captain.

"But it made your staff uncomfortable. Saoirse was very unhappy with the relationship," said Plum. "It bothered her. It was creating a toxic environment."

"I beg to differ," said the captain. He held up his hands in protest.

"Lysette was a loose cannon. You knew she became obsessed with avenging Anita Von Steefel's death. What if she became so infatuated with you that she told your wife? It was a risk you couldn't take."

"I wasn't worried about that," said the captain.

"You were concerned enough to erase the footage on the night she died," said Plum. "And to not monitor the cabins. Those cameras should have been on day and night, but for some reason, you didn't want them."

"That's not exactly true…" he protested.

"At least, you didn't want it unless it would benefit you. India Collins was not only paying you for Ambien but for footage of her and Joel being intimate on the boat. She was planning on using it to blackmail Joel to advance her career."

"What?" roared Joel. He stood, the vein on his neck throbbing. "This is just garbage."

"Joel?" said Ellen desperately. "Is this true? There's footage?"

"There is footage," said Plum. "Everyone on this boat knew they were having an affair."

"India was after him," insisted Ellen. "She was relentless. She had some hold on Joel."

"She has footage?" Joel repeated in amazement. He put his head in his hands.

"You've been so distracted," said Ellen. "Nothing is your fault, sweetie."

"It's because he's been fired from his studio. He's out of work," said Plum.

"You were fired?" Ellen asked Joel. "When were you going to tell me?"

"It's not a done deal," he insisted.

"Yes, it is," said Plum. "And Ellen, women are lining up to be deposed by attorneys about his flagrant sexual harassment. Women like Lysette, who was denied a job because she wouldn't sleep with him. She was all set to be witness number eighteen before her life was extinguished."

"I wouldn't kill her for that!" said Joel. "I have the best lawyers."

"Maybe you wouldn't, but your wife might," said Plum.

"Me?" asked Ellen. "I love my husband, but murder? Come on, Plum. You've known me forever. Do you really think I would do that?"

"No, I would not like to think you would do that, but you love your lifestyle—you told me yourself," said Plum.

"I do, but there have been other women who have claimed…so many women," Ellen said, putting her hands over her eyes and collapsing into tears. Her shoulders shook with her sobs. She glanced up, her eyes damp. "I know. I've played the idiot. I looked the other way. I thought it was all consensual. I'm sorry. Joel, you need help."

He nodded. "You're right. I'll go to sexual addiction therapy. There's one in Arizona. I'll go for a few weeks, and we'll get this all cleared up."

"I don't think it'll be that easy," said Robert. He turned to Plum. "Okay, my turn, let me have it. Why am I the killer?"

Plum nodded. "You, Robert, love Nachelle desperately. Your first wife left you, and you are determined not to lose Nachelle. But her health is an issue, and you try to keep her alive. You had motive because Lysette was disobeying your orders and going behind your back to obtain the fake seizure medicine Nachelle insisted worked for her. You knew it did nothing, and Nachelle would not listen to you, so you forbade your staff from doing her bidding. But Lysette defied you."

"So I killed her?" asked Robert, an amused look on his face. "Flimsy."

"Agreed," said Plum before turning to Nachelle. "Especially since she didn't defy you—she defied Nachelle. That's right, Lysette brought her the *real* medicine, but substituted it for the fake. She was a double agent. When you found out, Nachelle, you were furious."

"Homicidal?" asked Nachelle with a laugh.

"Perhaps," said Plum.

"Oh, don't be silly, Nachelle would *never* kill anyone!" shrilled Gerald. "She's just too fabulous!"

"Okay, we all have motives, varying in importance, for killing Lysette," said Robert. "But what about India? Why did we kill her?"

CHAPTER

31

PLUM WALKED OVER AND POURED herself a glass of water from a pitcher sweating on the sideboard. She took a long sip before turning to readdress the assembled group.

"India Collins was not the sweet little ingenue she pretended to be. I think we all know this," said Plum.

There was general agreement among the crowd.

"I first noticed something amiss when she slipped and said she had attended Foxeden when she meant to say *Foxcroft*. Foxcroft is a fancy finishing school. Foxeden is a juvenile detention center where India spent her teenage years after assaulting her stepfather."

"I told you she was no good," said Gerald. "Zeke and Rafal told me all about her on the set of—"

"Another time," interrupted Plum. She had no interest in Gerald playing the six-degrees-of-separation game. "Suki knew of India's past and taunted her about it during charades. Even implying she had been a prostitute when she mentioned *Pretty Woman*."

"I don't deny it," said Suki. "She was trash."

"Harris also referenced India's delinquency," said Plum.

"I also don't deny it," he said. "I didn't wish her death for it, but I was not a fan."

"India was savvy enough to have everyone's number on this boat. Just as Joel was using her for sex, she was using Joel to advance her career," said Plum.

"I don't know about that," said Joel. "Some people just like me."

"Possibly," said Plum. "But she was tired of it. She wanted to end it with you, and you refused. You were dangling a successful career in front of her. And you had motive as well as opportunity to kill India."

"What do you mean?" asked Joel.

"You came to my bedroom to get a Valium for Ellen. You could have easily slipped the knife under my pillow when I was retrieving it."

"Come on, what? That's nuts," fumed Joel.

"If you caught wind that India was going to blackmail you with the footage, you might have become enraged. Angry enough to kill her."

Joel seethed. "So you were serious before. She was going to blackmail me? What are you talking about?"

"India made lots of people angry," said Plum. "I didn't realize what India was referring to when she snapped at Nachelle. She said, 'I wouldn't want you to end up flailing on the ground and swallowing your tongue.' She knew of Nachelle's epilepsy, and mentioning it in such close proximity to the paparazzi was a threat."

"Whatevs," said Nachelle.

"Yeah, whatevs," chanted Gerald. "My girl would not kill."

Gerald and Nachelle fist-pumped.

There was a loud noise outside. Saoirse quickly left the room and returned. "The police are arriving on a boat."

"Just in time," said Plum.

"In time for what?" asked Suki. "We are no further along than we were before. You made a nice little case against everyone here, accusing us all of being the killer."

"This has been entertaining, but tell us: Who killed Lysette and India?"

Plum smiled. She could hear the boat pull up alongside the yacht. Just in time.

"I will tell you all who killed Lysette and India," she said, enjoying the moment despite the gruesome circumstances.

"Stop toying with us!" yelled Harris. "I don't care about the maid, but tell us who killed India."

"She can't say it because India Collins is not dead," boomed a male voice.

There were gasps, and all eyes turned to the entrance. Captain Diaz had entered the room, followed by India Collins and Juan Kevin.

"India?" Plum gasped, her jaw dropping. "You're alive?"

India nodded. Joel went over and hugged her, but she shook him off.

Although utterly confused, Plum felt a surge of joy, relief, and happiness, and rushed to embrace Juan Kevin.

"You're okay?" he said.

"Yes, thank you for coming," she said, staring into his dark eyes. She was so thrilled to see him. He kissed her forehead.

"I missed you," he said.

Plum hugged him harder. "Me too, but I'm totally mystified right now."

"Can someone tell us what's going on?" asked Nachelle.

"What is happening?" Harris mused.

"Once again, I wish I had popcorn," said Gerald.

"Yes, I also want to know what's going on," said Plum.

"I'm alive." India beamed. She was wearing different clothes than she had worn on Jolly Island, but she was healthy.

"We can see that," said Suki.

Plum reluctantly broke away from Juan Kevin and went over to give India a hug. "I'm glad you're okay. And not dead. Alive. Gosh, I don't know what I'm even saying."

"I'm glad also," said India.

Everyone began talking at once.

Captain Diaz put his fingers to his mouth and whistled.

"Explain!" commanded Nachelle.

"I will allow Miss Collins to do the honors," said Captain Diaz.

India faced everyone. She was relishing the moment. "I started to think someone was after me on the yacht. First I found a spider in my bed, then someone put poison in a water glass. Plum also thought my life was in danger."

There were murmurs of disbelief, and India waited for them to quiet before she continued.

"I had asked Plum how to portray a detective. She told me to think like a victim. To be on my guard. Make sure I knew where the exits were. Look behind me. So I did. Just before we went to Kichin, I knew the temple would be the perfect place to kill me. As you know I'm a method actress. I had been wearing a bulletproof vest to prepare for my role. I wore it to the temple, and thank God! It saved me."

"You're completely unharmed?" asked Plum.

"I have some minor scratches, and yes, a few stitches, but nothing other authentic actresses don't get on set," admitted India.

"So you just…pretended to be dead?" asked Suki.

India nodded with pride. "Yes. Like I said, I'm a method actress. I lay there frozen until everyone had left. It was one of the hardest roles I have ever played. And finally one of the locals found me. Thank God I had the vest, or else I would have been stabbed to death."

"Who stabbed you?" gasped Harris.

"I didn't see who it was, but I've heard from the police that it was the same person who killed Lysette, so I'll let Plum do the honors," said India.

They all swiveled their heads to Plum. She took a deep breath. The realization of who the perpetrator was saddened her deeply. "I'm so upset to say…I wish it weren't true. But the killer was Ellen. One of my oldest friends."

"Me?" exclaimed Ellen. Her face was awash with shock. "That's nonsense."

Plum shook her head. "I'm afraid it's not. You killed Lysette, and you tried to kill India."

"Why would I do that?" asked Ellen. "I told you I was used to Joel having affairs."

"Yes, but you were getting tired of it. That's why you were framing him for these murders."

Ellen opened and closed her mouth. She looked from face to face, but no one said anything. "It's not possible."

"It was very well planned," said Plum. "You let everyone know you were so upset with Joel's philandering so everyone was watching Joel. You provided multiple people with motives but all the while laying crumbs that Joel was unhinged and behaving recklessly. I was fooled as well. You were infuriated when Joel lent India your necklace. And as revenge, you went to Paraiso and sold it at Lazlo's. That's why you didn't want me to go there with you. And the reason you got rid of it was because Joel had lent it to India for a night and you no longer wanted it."

"That's absurd," protested Ellen.

"We have the security camera tapes, senora," said Captain Diaz. "You took off your burka in the alley around the corner."

"But I have my necklace," insisted Ellen.

"It's a fake," said Plum. "Costume jewelry. A replica. You told me if I married well, I could decipher fake jewelry from real jewelry. I don't need to marry well to do that."

"I gave you that necklace," said Joel. "It's worth a lot of money."

"A lot of money Ellen needs to stash away for a rainy day," said Plum.

Ellen sat up straighter. "I couldn't have planted the knife. I wasn't even in your room. I was so sick after that car ride."

"Yes, that's right, you *said* you were sick," said Plum. "But you contradicted yourself. You told me earlier in this journey about your pleasure in riding with NASCAR drivers. You said you had the 'constitution' for driving fast. This was a small trip on a slightly bumpy road on an island. It would produce way less motion sickness than racing. You had it all planned. When you arrived back at the boat, you claimed you were ill and rushed off. I was distracted by Gerald's arrival, and besides, why would I think twice about it? But you were faking. You ran into my room and planted the knife under my pillow."

"No proof," Ellen contradicted.

Plum continued, "Then you purposely sent Joel to my room, placing him at the location where the murder weapon was found. You covered all the bases. It could've been me who went down for the murder of India, or it could've been Joel. And I think once I explained how he was in my room alone while I retrieved the pills, he would be the suspect."

"This is all conjecture," insisted Ellen. "You have nothing linking me to the murders."

"Nothing except the footage on the boat," said Plum with a flourish. "The cameras show your meeting with Lysette. You are seen arguing. She pulls out my business card and waves it at you before stuffing it in her pocket. I think she was going to reach out to me. To tell me how unhinged you were."

"How'd you get the camera to...?" began Captain Dave. Plum turned to him and gave him the most withering look she could muster. He clamped his jaw shut. She did not want him to expose her bluff. She hoped it would be enough to convince Ellen to confess.

Joel stood and stared at his wife. "Is this true, Ellen? Have you gone mad?"

Ellen's eyes became wild, and she lurched for her husband. "You did this to me! You've made me a monster!"

"I did this?" asked a stunned Joel. "You knew I played around."

"But you were getting more flagrant. Flashing all these women in front of me. Taunting me. Telling me I looked old. Asking me to do better in the bedroom. I was never good enough. How dare you cheat on me and humiliate me!"

"So you wanted to frame your friend for murder?" he asked.

"No, I wanted to frame you! I thought they would believe it was you who put the knife under her pillow. I had taken it after dinner one night, with your fingerprints on it, and then was very careful to wear gloves. Once they ran the prints, Plum would be exonerated. And I would say you were in her room, and Plum would confirm."

"Why would you do this to the father of your children?" he asked incredulously.

"I am tired of you making a fool of me. Lysette told me everything, that you ruined her acting career because she wouldn't sleep with you."

"Is that why you murdered her?" asked Plum.

"I wasn't thinking. She was taunting me. There was a speaker next to the hot tub, which I grabbed. And I hit her, and then she fell overboard. I couldn't believe it happened, so I called Plum. I didn't mean to kill her, but once I did, I realized that if it was ever exposed, I would blame Joel. I would figure out a way."

"And India?" asked Captain Diaz.

"Once I realized how easy it is to get away with murder, I decided to get rid of India. Only this one I would make sure Joel took the fall for. Kill two evil birds with one stone."

Ellen turned and stared frantically at her husband. "I love you, Joel. I love you so much. But I hate you. I want you to go away. I hope you go to jail forever for your abuse of those women."

"Honey, you're going to jail too," said Nachelle.

The police captain and his deputy seized Ellen and hand-cuffed her. She stared at Plum. "I'm sorry I dragged you into this, Plum. I had to take a risk, but I'm glad you didn't take the blame."

The police dragged her off the boat.

"Well done," said Juan Kevin.

"I don't feel good about this," sighed Plum. "Ellen was my friend."

"She also almost framed you for murder, so maybe feel a little good," said Juan Kevin.

Plum felt weary to her bones. "Take me home," she begged. "Please."

CHAPTER

32

"YOU ARE SO LUCKY YOU have me," clucked Lucia when she entered the town house.

It was another hot and sunny day. Plum was at her desk, making up for all the work she had missed. Since she had returned to Paraiso forty-eight hours before, it had been a whirlwind. She'd had to give her statement to the police and then bury herself in catching up on all her villa rentals. She was already so grateful to Lucia for not only holding down the fort while she was gone but also for making everything better.

"I know how lucky I am," said Plum. "What did you do this time?"

Lucia came in toward her. She had a tray of cream cheese and guava puffs in one hand and a bag with all her papers in another.

"Yum! Thank you for making these," said Plum. She took one of Lucia's delicious pastries and popped it in her mouth. "You know, even though I was on a yacht with a five-star chef, albeit a criminal chef, I really prefer your cooking."

"I know, I'm the best," said Lucia. She placed the tray on the counter and unloaded her bag. "But that's not why you're so lucky."

"What did you do?" asked Plum.

"I planted a blind item in *Chisme*. It was about a certain renowned luxury real estate agent…"

Plum blushed. "Aw, thank you."

"Hang on a minute," admonished Lucia. "It's not you."

"Oh," said Plum, chastened.

"It was about a real estate agent who claims to love animals but has been known to kick them."

"Damián!"

"*Sí*," said Lucia. "I was lucky he went to a villa where my friend is the maid. He pretended to be an animal lover, but my friend was suspicious. She waited and spied him kicking the dog. She confronted him, but he denied it. Fortunately, a closed-circuit camera caught him kicking the dog out of the way."

"I'm so glad the camera was actually on!" said Plum. "I pretended I had footage of Ellen pushing Lysette, but I was totally bluffing. Thank God she confessed before I had to provide it."

"Yes, and *un momento*," said Lucia. "Turns out Barbara Copeland's maid is a big reader of *Chisme*, naturally. It's our Bible. She showed it to her boss, and now Barbara wants us to rent out her villa, not Damián."

Plum stood and hugged Lucia. As Plum was not a tactile person, it came as a surprise and was somewhat awkward, but Lucia hugged back.

"You're the best," said Plum.

"I know," said Lucia. "Give me a raise."

Later that evening, Plum filled Juan Kevin in on Lucia's achievement as they strolled down the beach at sunset. It was a glorious night, and a spectacular sunset comprised of pinks and blues and a flaming orange shone brightly in the sky. The air was warm, and the sand was soft and powdery under their bare feet.

"I'm so glad it worked out for you," said Juan Kevin.

He held Plum's hand tightly. His dark wavy hair was combed back, and he looked as handsome as ever.

"I'm glad as well."

Plum glanced out at the ocean. In the distance she could see a yacht. She smiled. It was probably Robert, Nachelle, and Gerald. He was third wheeling it with them for the rest of the journey. Nachelle had managed to dispel the rest of the group and had her own private sycophant. It was strange that everyone's lives would go back to normal. Suki was returning to be reunited with her husband. Harris was leaving empty-handed, without a deal with Robert. He no doubt had a contingency plan and some other person to try and eke money out of. And as for India, she pledged to stay in touch, but Plum was certain the next time she saw her would be on the silver screen. She was a pretty good actress after all.

"I have some good news also," he said. He stopped and looked at her seriously. "Victoria has agreed to the divorce.

I'm almost a single man. That is, legally. In my heart, I'm no longer single."

Plum gazed at him, and her heart was full. "Does that mean I'm officially your lady?"

"You are," he said.

And Plum was happy.

Looking for another tropical mystery to sink into?
Check out an excerpt from the
Trouble in Paradise! mysteries:

SOMETHING'S GUAVA GIVE

CHAPTER

1

PLUM LOCKHART STEPPED THROUGH THE narrow door and felt heavy, gray cobwebs wrap around her shoulders. As she squirmed to brush them off, she inhaled a strong stench of mildew. The air was stifling, heavy with heat and ripe with neglect. She squinted through the darkness, afraid someone might be lurking in the corners, but could see only murky shadows. Her heartbeat quickened.

She spun around, unable to see the person behind her.

"Hello?" Plum asked, her voice echoing around her. "Anyone there?"

"Yes," came the whispered response.

"What godforsaken place have you taken me to?" Plum demanded of her colleague Lucia, who had accompanied her into the dilapidated villa. "I can't see a thing, and if I hadn't known you were following me, I would have assumed I was being hunted down by a serial killer."

"*Cálmese*," retorted Lucia, who flicked on the light switch. "There. Better?"

Plum blinked and glanced around the foyer, which had a grimy, linoleum floor and mushroom-colored walls that might have originally been a cool white. The light fixture above them was coated with a dense layer of dust, and a cracked mirror hung over a small console table with a broken leg.

Plum shook her head at Lucia, who was giving her an assured look from behind the thick lenses of her glasses.

"Decidedly not better," said Plum. "This place is horrible."

Lucia clucked and broke into a wide grin. "We both know that if anyone can improve and renovate this villa, it's you. And besides, you always love a challenge."

Plum didn't disagree. She was incredibly competent. But she had always considered this a secret strength, like a superpower. Yet this small, sixty-year-old grandmother had discovered it after they had only been acquainted for four months. Perhaps Plum was more transparent than she had realized.

Plum sighed. "All right, show me around."

Lucia smiled mischievously. "I thought you would never ask."

As the tall, redheaded American followed the short, gray-haired Paraison through the unkempt villa, Plum marveled at how much her life had changed. At this time last year, she had been editor-in-chief at the glamorous *Travel and Respite Magazine*, based in New York City and jet-setting around the globe on fabulous trips to five-star hotels. When that all came crashing down, she made what she assumed would be a temporary move to the small, Caribbean island of Paraiso, taking a job at Jonathan Mayhew's eponymous travel agency

at Las Frutas Resort. But life wouldn't stop throwing cur-
veballs, so the previous month, she had ultimately (and
impulsively) launched her own villa broker agency: Plum
Lockhart Luxury Retreats.

"This place is a dump, Lucia," marveled Plum, peering
out a filmy window that overlooked an overgrown courtyard. The shaggy ground was littered with rotten guava
that bore deep, brown spots. The neglected gum tree's bark
sported a creeping fungus, and the drooping leaves were
curled anemically.

Lucia shrugged. "We need inventory. It's April, one of the
busiest months here. We have three new clients very eager to
find a place for Easter break."

A splashy article in the *Market Street Journal* by Plum's
former coworker and on-and-off friend, Gerald Hand, had
generated hundreds of queries, and she was now furiously
working to secure more properties to manage, hence the
visit to the squalid house, marketed as Villa Tomate.

"I suppose it is a good problem to have," said Plum, taking
in the fractured surfaces and peeling paint.

"It is," insisted Lucia. She pulled out a notebook and
began jotting down a to-do list.

"The name is kind of pathetic," said Plum. "All of the
villas have fruit names, and this one has tomato?"

"Tomato is a fruit."

"Technically. But most people consider it a vegetable."

"I consider myself a twenty-five-year-old blond with an
hourglass figure, but that doesn't make it true," replied Lucia.

Plum smiled. When she started her agency last month,

she had been thrilled that Lucia agreed to join her (especially since it riled their former unappreciative employer, Jonathan Mayhew, and his deputy, Damián Rodriguez, who was Plum's nemesis). Plum had even offered to make her a full partner, but Lucia had owned a hardware store for years and had no interest in incurring the headaches that came along with running a business. Instead, she accepted a role as "director" (Plum was big on titles) and would work for a salary with commission. The arrangement suited both of them perfectly, as Plum did enjoy the glory of being the boss. But she also fervently admired her colleague's clarity of thought, decisiveness, and clear outlook.

"We're going to need to send in those people who clean up crime scenes in order to get this place ready," said Plum.

"Don't be dramatic."

"Never dramatic, always practical."

"Hurry up and tell me what you think you will need. We have a three o'clock meeting with Giorgio Lombardi back at the office."

"What?" yelped Plum. "Why is that at the office? We've only just moved in, the place has boxes everywhere, it's like we are living out of it..."

"You *are* living out of it."

"I know that, but it's about images and perception," explained Plum. "We need Giorgio Lombardi to support our agency, and if he thinks we're some Podunk, low-rent operation run out of a town house, he will be dissuaded."

"We *are* a low-rent operation run out of a town house," said Lucia. "But don't worry. He knows it is temporary, that you lost your housing when you left your previous employment and that this was all we could find for both office and residence at such short notice."

"Why couldn't we meet him at a restaurant?" moaned Plum. She folded her arms.

"Because we don't have the budget for all these fancy meals right now," Lucia admonished.

"That's what people do in New York."

"We're not in New York."

"No, we are certainly not," lamented Plum. "And the town house is a disgrace."

"Don't worry, he's a man. He won't even notice the decor."

When the handsome and suave Giorgio, sporting an expensively tailored, lightweight suit, entered her office and glanced around the room, Plum could swear she saw his nostrils flare in disgust. It was fleeting, though, and when he greeted her, he oozed charm.

"Plum Lockhart," he said in a suave Italian accent. He was in his sixties, with graying dark hair slicked back like a movie star, and smooth, tanned skin. A strong odor of masculine cologne oozed from his pores. He clasped her hand between both of his and squeezed. "It is so nice to meet you. They were not wrong when they said you were the image of a movie star."

Plum's pale skin flushed a deep crimson, but she remained businesslike. "You are too kind, Giorgio," she responded crisply. "I must apologize for our temporary quarters. We were inundated with work as soon as I announced the formation of my company, so I had no time to search for appropriate offices."

"It is no problem," Giorgio replied warmly, although his wary eyes darted toward the garish pieces of framed art that adorned the walls. Plum made an immediate note to throw them in storage.

After they settled into chairs, and Lucia had brought them coffee and some of her tasty *coconetes* cookies, Plum ended the perfunctory niceties and got down to business.

"Giorgio, I know that you control a vast number of villas at Las Frutas, and I would love the opportunity to represent them. My firm has the most discreet and well-heeled clientele on the island, and they are ideal renters for even the most discriminating landlord."

The last part was complete rubbish; Plum had no idea who her clients were, as she had just opened her firm, but power was perception, she knew from the vast number of marketing classes she had watched on YouTube.

Giorgio smiled, revealing unnaturally white teeth. "You must know that we have a relationship with Jonathan Mayhew, your previous employer."

"I do know that," said Plum. "But his *star* employees—myself and Lucia—have departed his agency, and I venture to say it is in a precarious state."

"Perhaps," said Giorgio. "But as you know, I am merely the president of the Fruit Corporation. The residences are the property of Alexandra Rijo, the owner of Las Frutas Resort."

"I did know that," said Plum. "I have yet to meet her, but I hear wonderful things."

"I'm sad to say she has not heard wonderful things about you," he said.

"What do you mean?" asked Plum defensively. She sat upright in her faded-yellow armchair.

"Mrs. Rijo knows everything that happens on the island of Paraiso, and especially in her resort. And she has heard that you are friends with Carmen Rijo, the villainess who stole Alexandra's beloved husband, Emilio, out from under her, who wrecked her family and thieved part of her inheritance, and who is therefore her sworn enemy."

Giorgio took a sip of his tea, keeping his eyes locked on Plum's as he did so.

Plum bit her tongue. She had to tread delicately. She would not consider herself *friends* with Carmen Rijo, but through some deception and scheming, she had been able to establish a working relationship with Carmen after exorcising the woman's enormous mansion of "evil spirits." The grateful Carmen had allowed Plum Lockhart Luxury Retreats to represent a few modest villas as a reward. Plum could not afford to alienate Carmen (especially since she was one day hoping to lease Carmen's mansion, which was the marquee house on the island), but she knew that Alexandra's rental properties were far superior, and she was itching to control them.

"I absolutely understand Alexandra's concerns," began Plum diplomatically. "But I customize my agreements with all of my homeowners, and I can assure you I would endow Alexandra with the most generous contract that I have ever made."

Giorgio nodded. "I understand the implication. And

Alexandra will be very interested to know that she is getting a better deal than the second wife..."

"I didn't say that," insisted Plum.

"But you implied it. And that is very good. I will bring her this information."

Suddenly Plum was alarmed. If it got back to Carmen that she had given Alexandra a better deal, things could get dicey for Plum. "I hope you will use your discretion."

Giorgio rose and smiled smugly. "I always do."

Plum felt disconcerted when he left, and she walked over to Lucia's makeshift desk, which was really a card table set up in the corner of the room. Her own card-table desk was across from it.

"I think that went well, don't you?"

Lucia released a deep sigh. "You better hope that Alexandra doesn't go crowing to Carmen that she's getting more money out of you. It will be one more arrow in their vicious battle."

"She wouldn't do that, would she?" asked Plum with alarm.

"There is no love lost between them, so yes, I think she would."

Plum tried to shrug it off. "I'm not worried."

"Suit yourself."

Before they could continue, Plum's cell phone rang, and she quickly answered. It was Gerald Hand, calling from New York.

"You need to do me a favor," demanded Gerald, without even offering a greeting.

"Well, hello to you too," said Plum.

"This is important. My assistant, Arielle Waldron, is staying down there at the hotel with a friend. She's having an issue, and I need you to go troubleshoot."

"Me? Why me?"

"Ah, you're too fancy now?" he sneered. "Don't forget who wrote that glowing article on you and got you all that business."

Plum bit her tongue in an effort to control her terse retort. It was true, she did owe him. His article about her agency in the *Market Street Journal* had put her on the map.

"Why do you even care what happens to your assistant on vacation anyway?"

"Normally I wouldn't give a rat's ass," Gerald confessed. "But the brat's father is the owner of the publishing company I work for, and I've got to kiss her butt until she gets bored and quits or gets married to some poor sucker."

"I see."

"Yeah," he said. "And she is trouble. But you can handle difficult people—I mean, you worked with me, right?" he teased.

"True," she said.

"So, quick like a bunny, please go sort this out."

He hung up without waiting for a response.

CHAPTER

2

PLUM MANEUVERED HER GOLF CART under the canopy of palm trees and down the floral-scented road that cut through the center of Las Frutas Resort. The former sugar plantation's five thousand acres accommodated a hotel, twenty-five golf villas, two hundred houses of varying shapes and sizes, twelve tennis courts, a shooting range, a polo field, several dining options, and two spectacular golf courses. All of this was perched on the edge of the glistening turquoise Caribbean Sea.

Plum slowly traversed speed bumps and carefully avoided flocks of bikers heading to the beach and mused about how much her pace had slowed since she had moved to Paraiso. She had been impatient in the past and now considered herself completely relaxed and easygoing, although Lucia still accused her of being high-strung. She congratulated herself on adapting to a quiet life of seclusion in the tropics. In the past, a small-country life would have been an abhorrent concept to her; today, she embraced the opportunity to start anew. Ahead, Plum saw a dark patch in the road and screeched her golf cart to a complete stop. This caused the large sedan that had been tailgating her to also lurch to a halt.

Plum alighted from the vehicle and made her way over to the dark patch, which was a turtle crossing the road. Turtles were a source of pride on the island, and every local—as Plum now considered herself despite her brief tenure on Paraiso—knew their preservation was imperative.

"Stop blocking the road!" yelled the man in the sedan, who had a sweaty face and a cigar hanging out of the side of his mouth.

"I need to make sure this little guy makes it to safety."

"And I've got a life to lead," he sneered and pressed on his horn.

Plum gave him her most withering look and stretched out her arms so no one could pass and waited until the turtle traversed the street. The odious man in the sedan treated her to a litany of profanity as she did so, but she held firm. When the coast was clear, he whipped by her, narrowly missing her with his car, and raced toward the hotel. Plum shook her head. Tourists were the worst. And he was probably from New York, she thought, noting that they were the rudest of all vacationers, while conveniently forgetting that she herself was a New Yorker who had only lived on the island briefly.

Driving a golf cart that went at a snail's pace had initially bothered Plum, but she had learned there were advantages too. It afforded a certain agility, for one thing. When she pulled into the hotel parking lot, she saw the sedan with its blinker on, waiting to turn into a spot that was currently obstructed by a delivery van. Carefully steering her cart along the path and into the grass, she tucked into the unclaimed space.

"Hey!" rumbled the man who had cursed her out at the turtle crossing. "I was waiting for that spot!"

"Sorry!" said Plum, breezing past him into the hotel. "I've got a life to lead!"

The sliding doors opened at the grand entrance of the hotel, and Plum stepped into the air-conditioned lobby, relieved to have respite from the heavy heat outdoors. Although she was becoming accustomed to the balmy weather, her blood ran almost 100 percent Nordic and Scottish according to ancestry.com, and the humidity did not suit her fair complexion. (Not to mention that it made her red hair coil into ringlets that rivaled Little Orphan Annie's.)

The high-ceilinged lobby had a cool, black stone floor and several seating areas, where laid-back guests relaxed on wicker chairs and sofas. Caribbean music drifted out of the speakers, and the smell of coconut permeated the air. Everyone appeared to be in vacation mode, lulled by the tropical atmosphere. After making brief inquiries at reception, Plum was directed to a back office occupied by management. She looked through the glass partition and saw a pretty, young woman, with glossy, long, blond hair that hung below her breasts and darting small eyes, sitting across from Juan Kevin Muñoz, the director of security.

"Knock, knock," said Plum, opening the door.

Juan Kevin glanced up at Plum with surprise. "Miss

Lockhart, can I help you?" he asked, with a formality that took Plum off guard.

She had worked closely with the good-looking Paraison the previous month to solve a murder and had developed an intimacy that Plum had thought might lead to romance. But when she had spotted Juan Kevin at a restaurant with a gorgeous woman, she had distanced herself from him, convinced that she had misread the sexual tension between them and unwilling to make herself vulnerable. He had tried to reach out to her, but they had both been busy with work and now the time that had elapsed made things somewhat awkward.

She had convinced herself that she was not at all attracted to him, but now that she was finally face-to-face with him, she realized that was untrue. Plum still experienced the crackling of sparks when she looked into his chocolate-brown, long-lashed eyes.

"My friend Gerald Hand asked me to check on Arielle. He is her employer. He said there was some sort of misunderstanding?" queried Plum, her voice faltering.

"Definitely," interjected Arielle, nodding furiously and speaking in a nasal twang. "It's a huge misunderstanding, but they won't listen to me."

Juan Kevin sighed deeply, and Plum knew him enough to grasp that he was trying to remain patient. He folded his arms on the table, and a flash of the overhead light made his cufflinks glint.

"Miss Waldron was found with several items in her possession that didn't belong to her," began Juan Kevin.

"Someone planted them," snapped Arielle. She shook her head impatiently.

"Now why would they do that?" asked Juan Kevin. He was clad in his requisite blue blazer and khakis, and his wavy, dark hair had recently been cut, Plum noticed.

A ping from a cell phone squawked, and before she answered Juan Kevin, Arielle fiddled in the pocket of her white jersey dress. She pulled out a phone with a purple case and read a message. Plum watched in amazement as the girl tapped a response. Arielle clearly was not at all flustered by the situation. She glanced up.

"What did you ask?"

"I asked why someone would plant something on you," Juan Kevin said, his voice thick with impatience.

Arielle shrugged. "I have no idea. People are weird."

Juan Kevin nodded. "People are weird," he repeated.

"You can ask my friend Jessica. She was with me the entire time and will tell you this is all a pile of crap."

A look of assurance came across Juan Kevin's face. "I did speak to Miss Morse."

"And what did she say?" sneered Arielle.

"She did not witness you taking anything…"

"There! See?" interjected Arielle.

"But security footage shows that your friend Jessica spent most of her time in the room of another hotel guest and was not always with you," said Juan Kevin, keeping his eyes locked on Arielle's.

"Proves nothing," said Arielle, nibbling at her cuticle. "She can vouch for me."

"May I ask what, exactly, you found in Arielle's possession?" asked Plum, moving farther into the room and glancing from Juan Kevin to Arielle.

When the latter didn't respond, Juan Kevin did. "Several of the guests in the pool area have reported things missing from their chaises over the past few days. Jewelry and sunglasses that they removed when they went swimming. A laptop even."

"*They* put it in my bag," said Arielle, rolling her eyes.

"Yet when we looked through the security footage, we saw *you* putting them in your bag," corrected Juan Kevin.

Arielle became suddenly enraged. "Then it was an accident! I obviously thought it was mine. Do you really think I would steal? I have more money than anyone! My God, why would I take their crap? An old computer? Junky jewelry? Do you see these bracelets and rings?" she said, holding up her wrist, where several bejeweled gold bangles hung. "They're Cartier. Worth a fortune."

Plum wasn't sure what to do. Gerald expected her to aid and abet a thief? A flattering newspaper article that was no doubt lining a soiled litter box by now was not worth staking her entire reputation on. She would leave and tell him to sort it out himself. Just as she was about to flee, she stopped. She did have to consider the future of her company and the ongoing need for publicity. It wouldn't hurt to have the owner of a publishing company be in your debt because you helped out his daughter.

"Juan Kevin, is there anything we can do to remedy this?" asked Plum diplomatically. "I assume everyone's belongings were returned."

"True. But I'm not yet sure if they want to press charges…" he began.

"That's ridiculous!" Arielle exploded.

Plum wished Arielle would shut up and allow her to handle it, but the woman was too hell-bent on making a scene and professing her innocence. Plum ignored Arielle's ranting and stared at Juan Kevin. They exchanged a look as if to say this girl was too much, and Juan Kevin acquiesced.

"As long as she leaves the hotel, we will not press charges," he relented.

"Of course, I'm leaving this sketchy hotel! I'm going to stay with a friend of my parents' who owns a massive villa at the resort and who will be very unhappy to learn how you treated me," Arielle said, rising.

"Good luck to you and to them," said Juan Kevin, standing up. "I hope when you leave them, they don't find anything missing."

"I should sue you for slander," Arielle said, wagging her finger at him. "But you're not worth it."

Juan Kevin gave her a beatific smile but didn't respond.

"Can I have my bag now, please?" she fumed.

He picked up a large, Chanel pocketbook, the kind Plum knew sold for several thousand dollars, and handed it to her.

"I removed all of the items that belonged to other people," he said.

She sneered at him. "If I were dumb enough to ever carry cash, I'd be sure to count it. You're probably just on the take, and that's what this is all about."

"I think the opposite is true," Juan Kevin responded, nonplussed.

Frustrated, Arielle stomped out.

Plum and Juan Kevin stared at each other. It had taken an effort to keep him at arm's length, and now that she was a few feet away from him, she wondered why she had been so determined to do so. She didn't really know if he had been on a date with that woman she saw. He had told her he was having dinner with "a friend." That was harmless enough, right?

ACKNOWLEDGMENTS

Thank you so much to the fantastic Sourcebooks team, Anna Michels, Jenna Jankowski, and Mandy Chahal, and copy editor, Manu Velasco. I also would like to extend gratitude to my amazing literary agent, Christina Hogrebe, and my excellent film and TV agent, Debbie Deuble Hill. I appreciate Carol Fitzgerald's continuous support and cheerleading! And once again, this book could not have been written without my sister, Liz Carey, who is my sounding board, editor, and confessor. Love always to Vas, James, Peter, Nadia, Mopsy, Dick, and Laura.

ABOUT THE AUTHOR

Photo by Tanya Malott

Carrie Doyle is the bestselling author of multiple novels and screenplays that span many genres, from cozy mysteries to chick lit to comedies to YA.

A born and bred New Yorker, Carrie has spent most of her life in Manhattan, with the exception of a six-year stint in Europe (Russia, France, England) and five years in Los Angeles. A former editor in chief of the Russian edition of *Marie Claire*, Carrie has written dozens of articles for various magazines, including countless celebrity profiles. She currently splits her time between New York and Long Island with her husband and two teenage sons.